THE MENDEL PARADOX

THE MENDEL PARADOX

NICK THACKER

The Mendel Paradox: Harvey Bennett Thrillers, Book #10

Published by Conundrum Publishing

WANT FREE BOOKS?

HEAD OVER TO NICKTHACKER.COM/FREE-BOOKS to download three full-length thriller novels!

CHAPTER 1
PROLOGUE

ONE WEEK AGO

Grindelwald, Switzerland

The wind whipped up and caused Alina to pull her scarf higher, covering the lower portion of her face. It was cold, colder here than she'd imagined it would be. It had been years since she'd been back, years since she had left for university in faraway Geneva.

While her parents and grandparents still lived in the small mountain town, Alina had worked hard to get out and "see the world." That world had now expanded by only a bit over 100 miles, and she still had yet to leave her country of birth. Switzerland was beautiful, no doubt, but she wanted more.

She wanted to run along the white sand beaches of the Caribbean islands, to run with the bulls in Spain, and to run down the streets of bustling New York City.

She had chosen the career path that she believed would best allow her dreams and life to collide: international affairs. It was intriguing; she had always been interested in politics and the maneuvering of multinational corporations, and she was enjoying the myriad types of people she worked and studied with in Geneva.

Alina pulled her hat down next, finding that the scarf was barely holding back the oppressive cold. In this area of the country, winter hit hard and stayed long, and if it weren't for the necessity of spending most of their working lives outside, the inhabitants of Grindelwald would no doubt hibernate for the winter.

She picked up her pace, not an easy task during the uphill slog back to her parents' inn. Her family owned a large, multi-bedroom chalet that they used as a rental property for income. It had been in the family for generations. If Alina hadn't decided to run away and do something so brash as getting an education, she would have ended up running the inn and becoming a professional bed and breakfast owner.

They'd even named the place after her — *Alina's* — when she was born.

Her family didn't despise her choice of career, nor did they wish for her to fail. But she knew it had stung her father when she'd told them about her plans to attend the University of Geneva. He had expected his entire crop — three boys and a single girl — to follow in the family's footsteps, to become innkeepers and local business owners. To keep the quaint, tourist-driven economy of Grindelwald alive.

She smiled to herself. It was a good dream, but it was an unrealistic one for children who had grown up with the latest video games, gadgets, and internet access. There was an entire world out there, one that she desperately wanted to see, and she was about to have the ability to do just that.

To her right, just off the small trail behind the first stand of pine trees, she heard a noise.

She stopped, cocked her head to the right.

The snow was deep, more than three feet already, and it dampened the sounds of the forest and nearby town. But it also quieted the air, stilled the early night, and allowed any fresh, close noises to be heard clearly.

She eyed the tree line. This was Gorber's land, and she had played games and pranks in these woods with her brothers. She knew the area well, but at night the entire place had a different feel, a heavier feel. The light, airy openness of the Bernese Alps seemed to be replaced by a deep, intense seriousness when night fell upon the valley.

Perhaps it was because of the cold or the darkness caused by trees fighting for space for their own shadows. Or both.

The noise came again—a small, slight scratching sound.

It was coming from a space beyond a boulder, and it was directly toward the location she believed old Gorber's house sat. To get to the old plumber's house, another trail barely wide enough for a car to fit on it, wound around this stand of trees to the north, then doubled back down and ended up on the porch of his cabin.

But she couldn't be sure. It was dark and getting darker. Surely old Gorber wouldn't be out messing around in the woods at this hour.

She called into the woods. "Hello?"

She tried again in German.

No response came, and she turned back to the path after another moment. Her steps crunched through the compressed snow on the trail, and she was now acutely aware of her own noises.

Breath, hot and fast, a bit ragged.

Footsteps, slow and plodding, obvious and exact.

And the thousand quirks and strains in her clothing and jacket, rubbing and stretching as she moved.

About fifteen feet ahead, she heard the noise again. Her right ear picked it up first, and she flicked her head sideways but kept moving. This time the noise was louder.

Closer.

"H — Hello?"

The scratch came again, and then again, faster. The noise sounded like someone scraping pinecones against tree trunks, dragging them along the bark as they passed.

As they came closer to her.

Alina broke into a jog, then a run.

The sound turned from a gentle scraping to a pounding rhythm.

Or was that the sound of her own heart?

She ran faster, pushing and urging her legs to cooperate, to fight against the tight pants she'd thrown on at her parents' house before leaving for the inn. Why had she decided to wear something with so little utility? Why hadn't she just thrown on sweatpants or snow pants?

The pounding continued, directly behind her now, and she realized that it was now off-beat. Her own heart was making plenty of noise, but it was a triplet rhythm, whereas the scraping-pounding sound from behind her was more of a military march.

She felt her breath giving out, her body simply unable to continue at this pace. She had never been athletic, and she hadn't spent nearly enough time in the university gym, only going when she believed that cute guy from her European History course was...

The pounding stopped. The scraping stopped. Her heart continued to beat.

She kept running, but she slowed. *Why had it stopped?*

She wanted to continue on; she could see the lights of the inn in the distance, just beyond the tops of the pines that lined the descending hill in front of her.

But she had to know.

She needed to know what it was that had made the noise.

It had stopped only a half-second before, but she had continued moving forward. She slowed now, stopping in the middle of the road.

Then, just as slowly, she turned.

She looked behind her, seeing what it was that had followed her out of the woods.

And she screamed.

CHAPTER 2
BEN

THREE DAYS AGO

Anchorage, Alaska

Ben held up the package of hand warmers, wondering if the people who had designed them had ever truly experienced cold. He sighed, then mumbled under his breath. "Five dollars for a pack of these things?"

He tossed the orange pack of hand warmers back into the bin on the shelf and moved on. He needed a few more supplies, mostly small items and refills for his first-aid kit, to fill out his 'bug-out bag,' a precaution in case he had to leave the cabin quickly and a ready-to-go survival pack.

He liked to keep it full and prepared for anything, but he really enjoyed the process of shopping for the items he kept inside it. He was in Anchorage, at one of the big-box sports and outdoor stores, and he'd just been wandering through the single aisle of clearance items, hoping to find something useful that he didn't have yet.

So far, it had been a bust.

He'd stocked up on first-aid gear and more gauze, finding his supply dwindling, especially after a surprise rescue mission had taken him on snowmobile up into the mountains behind his land. He'd had to rescue the pilot of a downed plane, treat his injuries, then help him retrieve data from the crash site.

His kit and gear had performed well, but he had left the mountains short on some critical supplies.

Harvey "Ben" Bennett, the leader of the newly formed Civilian Special Operations, was a bear of a man. Tall and thick, with brown hair and brown eyes, he looked like an enlarged version of an average American man. He kept the hair short enough not to have to worry about it, and he wore clothes that allowed him comfort and utility, which fit in well in the backwoods of Alaska.

The lingering winter was still pressing down on the area, so today he had on a wool base layer underneath a red and brown plaid long-sleeved shirt. A heavier coat rested on the passenger-side front seat of his SUV, but the early afternoon sun had warmed him enough that he'd gone into the store without it.

His phone buzzed in his pocket. He kept it on silent, and there were only three callers that he allowed through to actually vibrate the phone's ringer. One was Julie, the caller now.

"Hey," he said, bringing the phone up his ear.

"You still shopping?"

"About to head out. They didn't really have anything here — I'll just order online. What's up?"

Julie paused, and Ben could hear her clicking around on her laptop. His wife was one of the CSO members, and she'd recently taken a role as a sort of intelligence and information technology officer. She had a degree in computer science and had worked for the CDC as a computer information systems researcher, where she had excelled before meeting Ben.

"New job," she finally said. *"Just came in, Mr. E vetted it. Looks legit to me."*

"What is it?" Ben asked, switching his phone to his other hand as he pushed his near-empty cart toward the checkout area.

"Apparently we're being asked to meet with a woman, Eliza Earn-

hardt, who claims she has information on a company that's doing some... how did she put it? 'Questionable research.'"

"'Questionable research,' huh?" Ben said. "Sounds fun. What sort of questionable research?"

Ben could almost hear Julie shaking her head. *"Didn't say."*

"They never do. Must be legit — no one ever shows their cards on the first hand."

"It would make them a poor poker player," Julie said.

"Anyway, what's the plan? Is there a meeting set up?"

"Mrs. E is working on it; I'll have more for you when you get back."

Mrs. E was another member of the CSO, the wife of the man who had brought them all together. She and her husband had run a massive communications conglomerate and had invested heavily in satellite communications and technology earlier in the decade. Now, with Mr. E's health issues and reclusiveness preventing him from participating in the day-to-day dealings of his company, they had turned their sights on more philanthropic efforts.

"Okay, well I'm checking out, then I'll be heading home. Give me an hour."

"You got it — I'll send Reggie a text; I think he's somewhere in the lower forty-eight."

"Sounds good, Jules. Thanks."

He hung up and pushed the cart toward the counter. The young blonde-haired girl behind the counter looked to be no older than fourteen, and she gave him a wide, braces-covered toothy smile as he neared the register. He'd seen her here before. Nice girl, probably working part-time on weekends and in the summer.

"Find everything okay?" she asked.

"Not really," Ben said. "I think you guys are out of milk and cheese."

The grin faded and was replaced by a mix of confusion and terror. "Uh, sir... this is a *sports* store. We sell *outdoor* products."

Ben nodded slowly, looking up at the ceiling and really trying to sell the ruse. "Ah, that must be why. Okay, thanks."

He held back a smile as she passed the two items he was purchasing over the conveyer belt, but she did a poor job of hiding her eye roll.

CHAPTER 3
LARS

THREE DAYS AGO

Grindelwald, Switzerland

Lars slammed the receiver down onto its cradle. It was a satisfying experience; pressing the 'END' button on a cellphone lacked the impactful tactile feedback of smashing a mechanical device into another one.

He'd had the old-school phone installed here for personal reasons. His team and the contractors who'd built his office in this brand-new building didn't know what that reason was, and he had no interest in telling them. The office was *his*, and he'd put it together *his* way.

But that way — the way he'd set up the space — wasn't *just* his way. It was his grandfather's office, or at least an exact replica of it. Down to the type of now-ancient telephone he'd purchased from an antiques collector in Prague, everything matched his recollection of his grandfather's study from when Lars was a boy.

His grandfather's own office had morphed over the years into a more modern, more practical suite, from which he ran his EKG empire. Baden Tennyson, the 'Baron of Biology,' was a man exceptionally gifted in not just the pursuit of science but also in the art of building empires. Baden Tennyson had grown his company into a worldwide powerhouse of research and development in the biological sciences, and he had formed strong alliances with multinational pharmaceutical companies that paid him and his company attractive dividends.

Lars, the 'golden boy' of the family and longtime expected successor to his grandfather's throne, had spent his formative years as an Army doctor, then transitioned into medical research. Finally, he had been deemed by his grandfather old enough to lead an entire division of EKG. That age — thirty-four — was far later than Lars would have wanted, but he wasn't going to argue with his grandfather. It had taken a lifetime, but Lars finally had gotten the coveted position of Director and Lead Researcher at the brand-new division of his grandfather's company.

Lars had been involved with every aspect of the growth process of the new division, from selecting a proper secluded location to hiring each of the employees and security team members. Lars was a perfectionist, and he now had the blank check and blessing from his idol to build exactly what he wanted. This division was Lars' pride and joy, and he fully intended to make it his grandfather's as well.

Everything about this room needed to reflect his passion for his job and his desire to follow in his grandfather's footsteps. He had no desktop computer in here — though he carried a laptop with him wherever he went — and most of the modernized equipment he needed for the more mundane aspects of his job he kept in his assistant's office next door. He took notes on a yellow legal pad, using a replica of a 1959 fountain pen he'd once seen his grandfather use. He'd even had a doorbell-like intercom system put in, but it was rarely used.

Lars Tennyson stood and stretched. He needed a break, but now was not the time. There was work to be done, and that work was now reaching the point of no return. If they stopped the research, they couldn't resume it later. It was all or nothing, now or never.

He strode through the office, admiring the way his shoes sunk into the soft, plush orange carpet — so unlike the shiny tiled floor throughout the rest of the building — and knocked on the door of his assistant's office.

He didn't wait for a response. Lars flung the door open to find his plump, round assistant, Roger Dietrich, panting and surprised, the cheap big-box store-purchased desk speaking volumes about the man sitting behind it. Efficient, practical, savvy.

"Lars — what's up?"

"We need to move to the next phase of research. Today. *Now.*"

"Wait, wait," Roger said. "It's too early — I mean, Dr. Canavero was supposed to have a scheduled call —"

"I was just on the phone with him," Lars snapped. "He informed me that there have been delays and that he is choosing to hesitate instead of choosing to push forward."

"And you told him —"

"I told him *nothing*," Lars said, recalling how he'd hung up on his head physician in mid-sentence. "But as I recall, *I'm* in charge of this research. *I'm* responsible for its success."

"Yes, but —"

"I need you to explain to Canavero how important this test is. How crucial it is to our success. Without a successful trial *this week*, our research is thrown back *months.* Potentially years."

Dietrich's jaw and jowls danced along as he nodded to Lars' words. His tiny, beady eyes bore into Lars' soul, seeing and understanding exactly what his boss was telling him. His assistant was a man of many talents, but it was his loyalty to his boss and the company that Lars cared about most.

"I understand. I'll have a word with the team."

Lars nodded once. "This *needs* to be finished this week. It *must* be."

Dietrich's face remained blank, expressionless. Those eyes kept boring into him. Reading him.

Lars felt his hands beginning to shake.

"Dietrich," he said, his voice nearly a whisper, "this must be completed on time. Do you understand?"

Dietrich stared at him longer, then finally swallowed. "Yes. Yes, I do."

"Good," Lars said, gathering himself. "Get to work. I must be in Bern by tomorrow morning, so I'm going to prepare. You have my full authority to do what it takes to get this process moving once again."

Dietrich forced a brief smile, and then his head fell back to his computer screen. Lars wasn't sure what the man was currently working on, but he had a feeling it was some sort of spreadsheet, some number-crunching program that would somehow keep all of this running.

Lars successfully pushed back the anxiety and regained his composure. If there was anyone in the world he could trust with his insecurities, it was Dietrich. They shared so much — everything, really. But in the office especially, he preferred to keep his emotions in check. It was a safer route to success. There was enough to worry about without his personal feelings being laid bare.

He smiled at his assistant, then turned to leave.

CHAPTER 4
DIETRICH

ROGER DIETRICH FELT the warmth slide over him as he sat still in his office chair. Lars always had that effect on him. He'd been the man's assistant for over a decade, first meeting the younger Lars as he finished his graduate degree in Animal Behavioral Science back in France. Dietrich, a German transplant, had been working toward an MBA at the same time, and the two had found each other in the university's library.

It had taken more courage than Roger had thought possible to actually get up and walk the expanse of the library's open area to introduce himself. He'd imagined every eye in the room staring at him the entire time. Judging.

Their relationship grew slowly from that point, based on mutual respect for one another as well as a mutual fear for what it all meant. They were careful, trusting but hesitant, until one day they looked back and they found they had a decade together under their belts.

Dietrich smiled and then focused again on his work. Lars' was the typical type-A personality, the stereotypical entrepreneur — full of vision, dreams, and strategies, but desperately in need of the calmer, more thorough presence close at hand to keep them balanced. Roger Dietrich was like Lars Tennyson's hands — the younger man had the mind for the job, but Dietrich was the worker who saw them to fruition.

And they made an incredible team. Able to finish one another's thoughts, they understood the ultimate goal here and believed in the project. Roger was committed to Lars' success, as he knew his partner's success meant his own. They were both driven, but their individual accomplishments were much better enjoyed together.

Roger minimized the spreadsheet he'd been working on — a hypothetical budget for the next quarter, which wouldn't be due for another three weeks — and opened his email client. Lars was on a tear, and he wouldn't stop until Roger had proven to him that things were still under control.

Half of Roger's job was planning, building projected income and expense calculations, and generally managing the staff and medical professionals they employed in the new division.

The other half of his job was corralling Lars. Like any visionary leader, Lars could get his head in the clouds — or the sand — and need a gentle hand to pull them back to reality. Roger wasn't sure if this situation was similar, but he'd find out.

He began typing an email when his phone rang. He pulled it out of his pocket. *Dr. Lucio Canavero.* Canavero was the head of medical research in the wing, and a world-renowned physician and surgeon.

"This is Dietrich."

"Have you spoken with Mr. Tennyson?"

"Regarding?" Dietrich asked. He never liked to play his hand too early. Perhaps this was nothing more than a check-in, and therefore there would be no need to alarm the caller.

"I was just on the phone with him, trying to explain to him that we are not going to be able to hit our target deadline."

"Ah, yes," Dietrich said. "This is concerning. Mr. Tennyson was just in here, asking me to verify —"

"I am verifying it now," the doctor said, his voice alarmed and frantic. *"We are not going to be able to hit it."*

"And for what reason? Mr. Tennyson would like to know. We were under the impression that your team was proceeding quickly, moving through the phases as planned."

"But, there has been an incident."

Dietrich's blood ran cold. In their line of work, 'an incident' never meant something good. He gripped the phone tighter and lowered his voice. "What sort of incident, Canavero? Lars said he spoke with you, and that you were choosing to hesitate on the next phase. Has the surgery not gone according to plan?"

There was a pause. *"The surgery has proceeded as we have planned."*

"That's excellent news."

"Fine, but the post-surgery rehabilitation has... stalled."

Dietrich frowned. "Stalled? In what way?"

"Well, it appears the subject has stopped responding to outside stimulus."

"How — how is that even possible? The subject is no longer alive?"

"Well, yes. The subject is alive, but... we cannot get a reading on — hold on."

Dietrich sighed. If there was anything he and Lars had in common, it was their impatience. He rolled his eyes as he waited for the doctor to return.

He did, breathless. *"Dietrich — the subject — appears... is moving. Responding to —"*

"Wait, slow down. You're cutting out." Dietrich tried to push the volume controls on the side of the phone. It didn't help.

"Response — status unknown. Subject appears to be — subject..."

Another pause, but it sounded as though Dr. Canavero was still on the other end, still breathing heavily. Still —

There was a crashing sound. *Was it just in the phone? Was it somewhere upstairs?*

"Dr. Cana — Dr. Canavero, can you hear me? What happened —"

"Code Four! I repeat, Code Four," the man's voice screamed into the phone. It wasn't the doctor's voice. It wasn't a voice Dietrich recognized.

He listened on, waiting for some semblance of normalcy to return.

It never did.

He heard another crash, followed by a deep, heavy thud. It was directly above him. The drop ceiling in the office shook, and he wondered what sort of force it would take to shudder the concrete slabs in-between each floor.

He stood up, listening partly to the phone's speaker but also to the world around him. He and Lars shared the double office space in the back corner near the southeastern side of the building. Directly above them were the labs, the containment cells, the —

No.

There was no way this could be happening. No way an actual Code Four had just been announced.

And then he heard it. It started on the floor above him, the deep thudding sound increasing in speed and volume. Then the sound a few seconds after, this one unmistakable.

Alarm klaxons.

Again, on the floor directly above him, then down through the stairwells and finally throughout the entire building, including the first-floor offices and conference rooms where Lars and Dietrich and the other staffers worked.

They blared through tiny hidden speakers, the noise far louder than Dietrich would have guessed. He wondered if Lars had left yet. He would know soon, regardless. The man's phone would alert him to the Code Four and ask for permission for the next protocol.

Lars would not give that permission. He needed this — *they* needed this. They hadn't fully lost control. Not yet. Lars would try to stop it, to regain their control over the situation. Whether it would work or not remained to be seen. Lars would expect to hear from Dietrich within minutes.

But Dietrich had another call to make first. One that would potentially change the narrative going forward.

Dietrich slammed his computer shut and tossed it into the leather shoulder bag. He threw it over his shoulder as he hung up the call with Canavero and started another, all with one hand.

He was running before the bag had settled at his side.

CHAPTER 5
BEN

"SHE'S AN ACTIVIST. Or was — I'm not sure," Julie began.

Ben was seated in the new section of their cabin, an entire wing that completely destroyed the idea of a 'cabin' altogether. Two levels, a meeting room, an entire communications space full of satellite imaging and GPS technology, as well as myriad computer parts Ben hardly understood, and rooms enough for the CSO as a whole and guests.

Reggie, Ben's best friend, was on one of the screens, joining the meeting via remote connection from wherever he was in the world. When he was in town, he usually stayed at Ben's and Julie's, in one of the CSO rooms, and had been turning the main conference room Mr. E had installed into a makeshift 'man cave,' complete with pool table, beer fridge, and gaming consoles.

"I thought her husband was the activist?" Reggie asked.

"He was — they both were. Eliza and her husband, Jakob Earnhardt, were some sort of animal rights activists working to bring more scrutiny to European companies. Her husband was a professional lobbyist as well."

"One of those guys who's paid to get Congress to do what companies want?" Ben asked.

"Yeah, but he operated in Europe."

"Sounds like a conflict of interest," Reggie added.

"Well," Julie explained, "the way she said it, it made it seem like her husband was working on the same side as their animal rights friends — trying to lobby local and regional governments and corporations to tighten restrictions and provide more transparency to their research."

"On animals."

"Yeah, I think."

"And her husband's dead?" Ben asked.

"He died in a climbing accident a year ago."

"So, she wants us to go to Switzerland and help her nab this company?" Reggie asked.

Mrs. E piped in from another monitor. *"What company is this, again?"*

"Well, as far as I can tell, it doesn't exist. My searches pull up a few news and web references, but there's nothing substantive. Best guess is it's just a small division of a larger company, and they want to keep their investments separate."

"Well, if they're torturing animals, I wouldn't doubt it," Reggie said.

"We don't know they are," Julie said, "but Eliza believes they're doing *something* they're not supposed to."

"And why call us?" Ben asked. "The CSO is about as far away as you can get from on-the-ground help. Can't she call the local authorities?"

"She has already," Julie said. "They told her there's an 'ongoing investigation.'"

"Which just means there's a single-page form filled out in the middle of someone's pile on their desk at the precinct," Ben said.

"Exactly," Julie said.

"What about something higher up?" Reggie asked. *"Something at the state or national level? This is Switzerland, after all — I would*

think a country with a high enough respect for its own internal affairs would want to know what's going on inside it."

Julie shrugged. "I asked her that, too. Eliza just said she's tried all the options she has access to. She feels there could even be corruption at that level, or — and this is where she mentioned her husband's line of work — it could be as simple as money changing into the right hands. Enough of it and the hand chooses to ignore what the other's doing."

"That's a good way to put it," Ben said. He could think of at least three scenarios where they'd run into that exact sort of sabotage; governments and corporations and individuals escaping justice simply by having enough money to pay off whoever got too close.

"Okay," Reggie said. *"It definitely sounds like something I'd be interested in checking out, but the timing ain't great. I'm not sure I can get away from what I'm doing down here."*

"What *are* you doing?" Ben asked.

Reggie glanced off-screen. "Well, I, uh... let's just say it involves *a girl.*"

Ben smiled, then nodded. His friend had had no flings or girlfriends since he'd known him besides the relationship he was currently in. He'd been married before, long before Ben had met him, so he knew Reggie was a bit standoffish toward serious relationships.

This woman, however, was quickly becoming someone they all assumed would last in his life. Dr. Sarah Lindgren, a renowned anthropologist and daughter of famous archeologist Dr. Graham Lindgren, was a Swedish-Jamaican American who had helped the CSO on and off for the past few missions. She was busy with her teaching and speaking schedule, but she had come to Ben and Julie's wedding and was currently in the states.

After publishing a book with their new friend, Victoria Reyes, Sarah Lindgren was busy with speaking engagements and university book signings.

Ben hadn't realized that she and Reggie were together, but it made sense. After their debacle in Peru, the CSO had agreed to a well-deserved two months' vacation, barring any life-threatening attacks or nuclear war.

He could have talked Reggie into returning to work and cut his vacation short, but Ben knew the man needed time with Sarah as well — and besides, what Eliza was describing simply didn't seem like the sort of mission that required all hands on deck.

"That's fine, brother," Ben said, winking at the screen. "We'll be alright without you. Julie and Mrs. E can stay here and offer communication support as needed, and I can fly over and meet with her."

"You want to go alone?" Julie asked.

"No, but it doesn't make sense to have us all come out. If we want to investigate further and need more help, we can always get you a ticket, too."

The CSO had been formed to tackle problems brought to them by anyone who needed to find a good solution to something that couldn't be solved through 'normal' channels. Normal, in this case, typically meant finding things that had been lost, or hunting down organizations and groups that the governments wanted to have no part of. Sometimes it was finding lost treasure, and sometimes it was preventing someone from doing something that would have devastating consequences.

Julie held up her hands. "Fine by me — I'm more than happy to sit behind a computer screen for a bit and let you have all the fun."

Ben smiled at his new wife. "Yeah, 'fun' is *exactly* how I'd describe what we've been through."

Mrs. E jumped back into the conversation. *"I will speak to my husband about tickets, and get them set up for you. Expect an itinerary by the end of the day today, and a flight sometime tomorrow afternoon. Will that be enough time to get ready?"*

"Not sure there's anything to get ready," Ben said. "I'm just meeting with Eliza, and we'll probably go try to knock on some doors or something."

"Still," Mrs. E continued. *"I would like to get you some sort of support in the field."*

"You talking the *human resources*-type support or the *bang bang*-type?"

Mrs. E smiled onscreen, her shaved head tightened and pulled back behind her eyes. *"Both, perhaps."*

"Sounds good," Ben said. "All right, let's roll."

CHAPTER 6
ELIAS

THE MORNING WAS NOT TURNING out to be as easy as he'd hoped. Elias Ziegler checked his rifle out of habit, the third time this hour. He ran a full diagnostic, even wishing he'd brought along his field mat for cleaning. He usually preferred German-made guns and pistols like Heckler and Koch and Mauser, but that was mostly out of loyalty to his country as well as his training during his time with GSG-9.

The *Grenzschutzgruppe 9 der Bundespolizei,* or the Border Protection Group 9 of the Federal Police, was an elite tactical unit of the German Federal Police, created after the devastating events of the Munich Olympics in 1972. Elias had joined the unit after his military career at 35, then served an additional ten years, rising in rank as he served in the unit's Regular Operations group.

After retirement, he'd moved around Europe a bit, finally settling in a one-bedroom apartment in France. He spent little time there, opting instead for a semi-nomadic lifestyle running around Europe on work-for-hire missions and odd jobs that required a special sort of skill set.

That skill set was what he'd been hired for today, and it was going to be a bust unless he could lengthen the contract. His orders were simple: hunt big game in the foothills of this region, and don't come back empty-handed. The trouble was that there really *was* no big game in this region — ibex, chamois, red deer. Sometimes there were reports of brown bears wandering into the region, but these were unfounded and mostly around the borders.

He'd pressed the company for more details, but they were unsurprisingly vague. He'd assumed they needed some sort of "animal control" service, and that assumption had all but been proven accurate when he realized he wouldn't have to prove his hunting license and pay the annual fees for hunting. The canton rules here had even been waived — or at least, that's what they'd told him.

Elias sighed and checked his rifle again, then decided to pack up and head back to the tavern. The weather was getting warmer this time of year, but the springtime evenings in the foothills of Switzerland were chilly to the point of his wanting to call it early.

He rummaged around in his pack, discovering that he'd already eaten the last of his protein bars, then decided he would, in fact, be heading back early. He'd call the company tomorrow morning and complain that they hadn't given him enough information — simply walking around their land and looking for animals to shoot was a terrible hunting strategy. He needed more. He needed to know what tracks to follow, what droppings to examine, what eating habits and water needs they'd have.

Elias had come from a long line of hunters. His father and grandfather had taught him and his brothers how to hunt, and even the Ziegler women had shown a proficiency for handling weapons. The war had ravaged his homeland as well as his family history, and it had taken him a good bit of political maneuvering and distancing from his family tree to get back into the good graces of his countrymen after WWII. His father had died fighting for the wrong side, and thankfully Elias had fallen far from the tree when it came to political leanings.

He stood and stretched. Tomorrow was another day, and he

was confident he could get the contract extended. He'd be paid half for his work so far, but he really wanted the bounty they'd promised by delivering on the contract. His contact at the company had even suggested to him that they could prepare an outfit to help search the countryside for the animal—two additional men, including one who would cook and provide quartermaster duties.

He had answered that he preferred to work alone, but now he was second-guessing himself. Elias' stomach grumbled. *It would be nice to have a fresh, hot meal to come back to.*

Much of hunting like this was waiting, following, camping, and more waiting. The moment of pulling the trigger and bringing down a wild animal was a moment one had to earn, and that moment could take days to achieve. He enjoyed being alone, out in the woods, but his age was beginning to make him long for shorter, simpler days. Trekking through densely forested areas in search of wild game might be peaceful, but it wasn't easy.

He stood, stretched, then began packing away his rifle. *Time to call it,* he thought. He could almost taste the Bavarian beer selection awaiting him at the themed tavern just down the hill from his campsite. He might even splurge and use the per diem the company had allotted him for one of the massive turkey legs he'd seen smoking behind the bar.

With a mind toward food and drink, he closed his pack, slung it over his shoulder, and turned.

He heard a click. A tiny, fragmented sound that was at once perfectly at ease in the midst of the forest around it, and yet something so foreign it caught his attention.

It was the clicking sound of a breaking stick, one that would have been as thick around as his thumb, and therefore strong enough to withstand a good bit of pressure.

He waited. Still turned away from the noise. He had a better sense of presence and space sometimes *not* using his eyes, and besides, it was growing darker by the minute. He didn't want to ruin whatever chance he might have at bringing in a kill.

He and the stick-breaker waited there like that, for well over a minute, Elias barely breathing and the creature — whatever it was — not making another sound.

For all he knew, the thing could have been creeping up on him, ready to pounce, but he sensed that anything large enough and careless enough to break a stick beneath its feet either was no danger to him or something that would start an attack loud enough for him to react.

Elias waited more, then risked a glance over his shoulder.

Nothing.

The silence and stillness of the Swiss Alps foothills greeted him, staring back at him as it had for hours, only now darker and colder. He squinted into the spaces between the trees, and —

There.

No, his eyes were playing tricks. What he had thought was a shadow, a looming creature standing taller than him on two feet, was nothing but a simple illusion cast by the twisted branches of the trees. He even identified the branches that played a part in the trick, seeing the trunks and the wide spaces between forming the shadow he'd seen before.

Time to go, old man, he told himself. He turned back once more, then again twisted his head around to peer on the creature-looking shadow.

It was gone.

See? he told himself. *Nothing but a trick of the imagination.*

CHAPTER 7
BEN

IT HAD BEEN a full day of traveling before Ben arrived in the small town of Grindelwald, Switzerland. Flights to Geneva, then to Berne, then a long, meandering train ride to Grindelwald. Upon arrival, Ben had wanted nothing more than to take a long nap — the train offered no comfortable seating, and he hated flying — and get a bite to eat.

But when he'd stepped off the train and seen the mountains, or 'horns,' as they were called here, he was stunned. He'd traveled quite a bit during his stint with the CSO, and he even lived in one of the most picturesque states on the planet, but he had never in his life seen a village so beautifully spaced beneath the towering mountain range. Idyllic and perfect in its color and landscape, Grindelwald had had that same effect on myriad people traveling to the area for skiing, climbing, and sightseeing. It had long been a national treasure, and even an international tourist destination.

And part of that appeal, Ben now knew, was that the city maintained a relatively small population of around 4,000. Mostly related to tourism and hospitality, the inhabitants also had a comely, homegrown feeling to them, and it hadn't taken Ben long to discover that. He'd asked around for directions to the small inn Mrs. E had booked for him, and he was met with a delighted response offering not only directions to the inn but directions to every other tavern and pub and restaurant in the area worth visiting while he stayed.

It turned out that the inn was near the station, so he'd decided to walk the three blocks instead of hitch a ride, and he was glad he did. He felt as though he'd been thrown back in time to a place where life was simpler and peaceful. The floral arrays and foliage were in full bloom, and many of the storefronts and second- and third-story porches had been decorated with glorious springtime flower arrangements.

The main road through town was paved, but it didn't take much for Ben to imagine cobblestone or even dirt pathways between the buildings and horses in place of the cars. It looked to him like one of the many tiny ski resort towns back home, without the garish displays of wealth and privilege. A sports store sold new and second-hand ski and climbing gear, and small grocers on both sides of the streets offered in-season fruits and vegetables for prices in currencies Ben didn't understand.

The whole experience was breathtaking, and he had immediately wished Julie had come along. There was still time to have her fly out, but he wouldn't waste the CSO's resources on it unless she truly was needed here.

The inn looked like the sort of thing he'd see on a postcard, and the old man at the front desk — the owner and tenant, he assumed — was equally delighted to see him as the woman who'd given him directions. He walked Ben up to his room and gave him the same spiel as the woman: where to eat, where to drink, where to ski.

Ben smiled along, then dumped his single backpack on the twin bed and turned to the small mirror in the room. He felt as though he hadn't showered in weeks, but he didn't look it. His eyes were heavy, but he'd decided to get something to eat first, then come back to the room to relax and meet up with Eliza tomorrow morning, first thing.

He called Julie, checked in with her and shared his experience so far, then headed out to find one of the three pubs the locals had recommended.

He'd ended up in one simply called *Downtown Lodge,* right across the street from a similar-looking inn called *Alina's*, both quaint-looking single building bed-and-breakfasts. This one had a small tavern on the ground floor and an inviting, warm orange glow spilling out the open front door.

Ben pulled the jacket he was wearing up over his neck as he finished the last of the beer. It was cold, now that the sun had gone down, and he'd even seen on the forecast that there might be a bit of snow during the week he was here. Not uncommon for this time of year, but he'd half-expected the weather to be warmer than it was in Alaska. Right now, it felt as though it was going to be difficult to keep warm walking around town. He made a note to purchase a ski jacket, or something heavier than his light coat, tomorrow before meeting Eliza.

"Get you another?" the barman asked. His English was perfect, and Ben had a hard time believing the man was from Switzerland.

He nodded, then put a credit card down on the table. "Keep it open, too, if you don't mind."

The older man winked at him. "Already have, son. Usually slow this time of year, so the only people coming around are looking for late-season skiing or early-season flowers. Either way, it's quiet enough that we typically don't worry too much about tabs."

Ben frowned. "It's *free* beer?"

The man guffawed. "No, certainly not. I just mean we don't worry about the tab until you leave."

"That's... what a tab's for, right?"

"No, leave the *town.* You're staying over at old Ringgenberg's place, yeah?"

Ben nodded again.

"Leaving Friday?"

"How'd you know?"

"He was just in here earlier today. Said he had an American coming later, so he had to get back to the counter before you arrived. Said you were from Alaska."

"I am."

"And yet, you seem cold."

Ben laughed. He liked the guy. He was funny and warm, and he seemed like he genuinely enjoyed Ben's company. He nodded. "Yeah, I'm chilly. I packed for *cool*, but I have to admit it's getting *cold* out there."

"Stop by *Roth Toni* tomorrow. The sports shops will get you — out of town tourists and all that — but the little shop down the way carries cheap coats and things."

"Thank you, I really appreciate that," Ben said.

The barman performed the obligatory *Karate Kid* wax on, wax off movement, making a circle on the bar top with a dishrag, then leaned in closer to him. "May I ask what your business will be, here?"

CHAPTER 8
BEN

BEN WASN'T sure how to take it. His voice was a bit lower, and the man seemed to want to keep this portion of the conversation to himself. Still, there were only three other people in the bar, all men. Two were sitting across from each other at a table; the third was drinking a whisky at the opposite end of the bar. None of the other patrons seemed to care about Ben or their conversation.

"Uh, work, actually."

The man raised an eyebrow. "Not many come out here for *work*, son. What type of business are you in?"

"Well, I, uh, help people with… things."

"I see. An Alaskan CIA-man."

Ben laughed again. "No, unfortunately, it's nothing as cool as that."

"How 'cool' is it, then? Do tell; I'm just an old fart running out of good bar stories."

Ben leaned a bit closer and shifted on his stool. The man seemed harmless, and Ben knew there wasn't really any information he could share that was sensitive in any way, perhaps besides the names of the involved parties. "I just got a call that someone around here might need my help. I work for a new group called the Civilian Special Operations."

"Special Operations?" the man asked. "Oh, that sounds *serious.*"

"Trust me, the *civilian* part keeps it pretty tame." It was a lie, but it was a safe one. "We mostly help people find things that have gone missing, or make things right that have gone wrong. As long as we're helping people and not hurting them, we'll take the job."

There was a bit more to it than that, but again Ben decided it was probably not worth offering up extra information.

The man nodded slowly, still smiling. He placed a basket of fries in front of him — Ben hadn't even noticed the younger man deliver them — and then offered him another beer.

Ben waved it off, knowing that two beers was about his limit.

The bar owner worked down to the other side of the bar and refilled drinks for his patrons, then moseyed back to Ben.

"I'd better be going," Ben said, once again offering his card.

"Don't worry about it," the man said. "Stop by before you leave Friday, and we'll settle it."

Ben thanked him and stood up.

"Oh, son — before you go."

"Yeah?"

"You might stop by *Alina's* across the street. Talk to the owner there. Man named Hugh. Nice guy, and I'm sure he'd like to meet you."

Ben frowned. "He'd like to meet me?"

"I'm sure of it."

"And... why is that?"

"Well, you're in the line of work that helps people, right? 'Finds things that have gone missing?'"

Ben sighed. He knew he shouldn't have opened his mouth. *Now he's going to want me to find his prized Mustang convertible or an old baseball card,* he thought.

“I don’t know,” Ben said. “I’m not sure I was clear when I said that, and —“

"I believe you were, son," the barman said. "He's got a daughter. Came home to see them after being away at university for a while. Thing is, she never showed up."

Ben cocked his head.

“He’s been beside himself trying to sort it out, and the police here just don’t have the resources to help. They say she’s probably just waiting it out in a bigger city, meeting up with friends from school.”

“But he doesn’t think so?”

The man shook his head. "No one thinks so, son. She was scheduled to be in town a couple of nights ago, and someone even said they saw her getting off the train."

“And she never arrived at her folks’ place.”

“That’s right. No reason to expect she’d change the plans, and her father’s been pretty worked up about it. Actually I’m surprised he’s got the shop open today — his wife and her grandparents have gone up to Interlaken to look for more help.”

“Sorry to hear that,” Ben said.

“Right, we are too. Nice girl.”

“Is... there anything else?”

“Well, no. Just go talk to him if you get the chance.”

Ben nodded, still feeling like he shouldn't have offered up information about his line of work. He wished he could help, but there were other matters here he needed to attend to. If the local police couldn't figure it out, why should he be able to?

But he also liked this man, and it wouldn’t hurt to just check in.

"Okay," he said. "I'll go see him. Tomorrow morning, after a meeting."

The man’s face lit up. “Wonderful! I’ll mention it to him. Thank you, son.”

CHAPTER 9
DIETRICH

"THIS IS A MESS," Lars said. "This is an absolute mess. I thought I paid people like you to fix messes like —"

Roger Dietrich held up a hand, and Lars stopped. He was seated across the table from him, and for the last half-hour he'd been silently and patiently listening to Lars berate him and the rest of the staff.

No one else on the planet could have gotten away with this, but Dietrich wasn't afraid of Lars.

"I am not a lowly scientist who works for you, Lars," Dietrich said. "Do bear that in mind. We are on the same team."

Lars' mouth opened, then closed again. He nodded. "Yes, I'm sorry. I apologize. I am just at my wits' end. Dr. Canavero had everything under control. I cannot understand what could have happened. How this could have —"

"We will have it under control," Dietrich said. "Remember that. We *will* get back on track, Lars."

"It will be too late."

Dietrich shook his head. "It won't. Our hunter is out there now, working to resolve this as quickly as possible."

"He is taking too long."

"We haven't even told him what it is he's hunting for," Dietrich argued.

"And we *cannot* tell him. It's too risky. If my grandfather finds out anything —"

"Lars, he won't. No one will. You did the right thing. Shutting down was the correct move, and no one's the wiser."

A few days ago, they'd shut down the new research division, sending all but a handful of the staff and scientists away on leave. They had the funds to keep them on payroll, but Lars didn't want his grandfather to suddenly appear and ask for details. They needed to keep this quiet, so they offered their staff a 'surprise vacation' package, including per diem.

Many of them had chosen to go skiing in one of the many nearby ski towns, with the requirement that they should be prepared to return to work in one week. Many of the scientists, privy to the events that had taken place a few days ago, had also been paid for their silence.

The building was now running with a skeleton crew of security guards and specialists and doctors — only the necessary staff to keep the place running for a week.

But Lars needed to get this matter resolved. He didn't have a week. Dietrich knew the man was stressed, but he had done a good job of hiding it.

So far.

Dietrich had known this man for a decade, and so he was able to see when the cracks began to appear. They were small, mostly unnoticeable now, but the next few days would be trying.

"What do you want to do?"

Lars sighed. "We need to join the hunter. We need to go into the field and get this resolved. The sooner we can get out there and —"

"You want *us* to go out there with him? Lars, he's a professional! We can't expect to —"

"You can stay here if you want," Lars said. "I am going with him.

The more we have searching, the faster we can find it and return it to the lab. The faster we can continue with the operation."

And the faster we can solve the actual problem, Dietrich thought. *The faster we can move to the* real *test.*

"Inform Mr. Ziegler that we are adjusting his schedule. His directives will be made clear tomorrow at this time. Hopefully, he is still close enough to return by then."

Dietrich was making notes on his phone as Lars spoke. "Here?"

"Here, at the coffeehouse. That is fine. I trust you can outfit us by tomorrow as well?"

"I believe so," Dietrich said. "There are a few shops in town, and we won't need much. We already have the weapons we will need back at the office."

"Good," Lars said. He reached over and placed his hand on Dietrich's, and Roger felt the warmth rising in him again. It wasn't often that Lars displayed any outward signs of affection, and it was even more rare in public. There were no other patrons in the coffeehouse, but Dietrich knew it was still a sign of distress for Lars.

This *must* be completed. It *must* be finished successfully and on time. There was no other option.

"This hunter: Elias Ziegler. He is still worth retaining?"

Dietrich thought for a moment, then nodded. "I do. He is subtle, discreet. He will likely demand more money, especially since we are giving him almost no information to go off of. But he is good at what he does — better than we would be, for sure. Let's let him continue, with our oversight."

"If he does not perform..."

"If he fails, we take matters into our own hands," Dietrich said. "Let me handle that. You need to focus on the upcoming trials, once we resolve this matter."

CHAPTER 10
BEN

BEN SHOOK HIS HEAD, both to calm his nerves and to shake off the last of the early-morning jitters. He wasn't awake earlier than he normally was, but a six-in-the-morning alarm clock *after* a full day of travel always seemed too early.

Nonetheless, he was awake, and it was time to work. He downed his third cup of coffee — one in the inn's bedroom, another while visiting with the owner of *Alina's*, and now this one.

He was sitting in a comfortable chair in one of the many cafes that lined the main thoroughfare of Grindelwald, the same road that his own inn was on, and the one *Alina's* and *Downtown Lodge* was on as well.

He sipped at this cup, finding it notably better than the first two. Or perhaps he was more awake, and his senses were finally more adept. Either way, he enjoyed the cup. He shivered out the last of the chills — the morning was a bit colder than the evening had been, and he still had yet to visit the store the barman had recommended last night.

"Mr. Bennett?"

He heard the voice from behind him, and he turned around, nearly spitting out his drink. The woman who'd spoken was *incred-*

ibly beautiful. Bright-red hair that fell straight halfway down her back, and a body that seemed to have been chiseled into the perfect shape.

He stood, trying to pretend away the shock.

"Hi," he said. "Call me Ben. You must be Eliza Earnhardt?"

She smiled, shocking him once again. *Get a grip, man,* he thought. *You've seen beautiful women before. You're* married *to one, for Christ's sake.*

"Thank you for meeting with me," she said, coming around to the front of Ben's chair, where there was an identical one waiting. "I am sorry you had to fly all this way, but you're the only one I could think of to help."

Ben sat again, offering her a drink. She waved it off. "Why is that, may I ask?" he asked. "Why we're the only ones you could think of?"

"Oh," she said. "It's not that you're the *only* one, it's just that I've tried everything else. I explained part of it to Juliette, your wife. I have heard of the CSO from your work here in Europe."

'Work' is not usually how people describe it, Ben thought. *She's trying to flatter us.* The CSO had been in the news a bit over the past year, mostly for disrupting peacetime investigations into international museum fraud in Athens, and then ousting a good-standing Minister of Antiquities in Egypt. They weren't sorry for those things — what they had prevented would have been far more disruptive — but still, it was sometimes difficult to explain to people that they really were the 'good guys.'

"Thanks," he said. "Yeah, she mentioned that you've tried the police? And government?"

Eliza seemed slightly offended by the mention of the police. "They're as much a mess to deal with as the government. Both are useless."

"When it comes to bringing this company to justice?"

She didn't answer.

"I see," Ben said, smiling. *She definitely has it out for the govern-*

ment. He'd met people like that before. They lacked trust in most organizations and official authorities, and they were quick to question anything that smelled like bureaucracy. Knowing that she and her late husband had been lobbyists *against* most governments and corporations seemed to fit perfectly.

"I called you because I know you do not worry about things like laws and rules."

"Whoa, whoa," Ben said, smiling. He leaned forward in his chair. "It's not that we don't *worry* about them — we just don't let them get in our way when we know there's right and wrong, and we believe we've found the right."

"I know what's right and wrong here, as well," she said. "And I want you to help me do what's right."

"And what's that?" Ben asked. He could already tell that this woman was smart, to-the-point, and incredibly adept at navigating a conversation to her point of view. And she was doing it all in English, a language he knew was her second or third. He wanted to remain out in front, to ensure he got the questions answered he needed.

She took a breath. "You spoke with Alina's father this morning?"

Ben couldn't hide his surprise. "Y — you heard about that?"

She smiled, an honest, genuine grin. "Sorry. It's a small town. Grindelwald may have four-thousand people, but the ones you'll actually run into here in town are well-connected."

"You're one of them?"

"I'm not, but I've lived here long enough that they trust me. And it's not espionage, Ben. There's just usually nothing better to do than discuss Ms. Allworth's latest batch of honey or Ruegsegger's latest goat-breeding troubles. Trust me, when something like Alina's disappearance comes through, *everyone* knows about it."

"Right," Ben said. "Although goat-breeding stories are quite popular back home, too."

She laughed, and her nose rose up a bit. Her teeth were as perfect as her figure. She shifted on the chair, throwing a long leg up and over her other knee.

"So, yes, I did see him," Ben said. "He was... distraught."

"Of course," she replied. "This is his daughter. She has been missing now for, what? Three days?"

"Two," Ben said. "And she was coming back from university in Geneva."

"Her father's land backs up to the hill just out of town," she said. "EKG owns that land."

Ben frowned. "You think EKG — the company you want to go after — has something to do with Alina's disappearance?"

She shrugged. "No idea. But once I give you all the information, I believe you will find the entire thing suspect, as well."

"Okay," Ben said. "I'll bite. I'm here, after all. I flew around the world to meet with you because my wife and coworkers say your story checks out. But you wouldn't tell us what you really *want*. 'Investigating a company' isn't really something we're equipped to do, and yet you were adamant that we were the right ones for the job."

Eliza got serious, the color in her face fading a bit. She flicked her eyes left and right, then stared holes through Ben. She leaned forward, her face inching toward his.

"Ben, I want you to find the people at the company — at EKG — who are responsible for killing my husband."

CHAPTER 11
ELIAS

ELIAS ZIEGLER CROSSED the street and entered the small cafe, five minutes exactly before the scheduled start of the meeting. He'd been instructed to meet there at nine o'clock in the morning, ostensibly to discuss 'options' with the company that had contracted him.

He stepped over the ancient wooden threshold and entered an equally ancient cafe, tiny and smashed together in the style of every other European cafe. He didn't like these sorts of places. Besides being too small for a man of his large stature, it was simply uncomfortable for him to be in such warm, inviting places. He never knew how to act.

"Coffee, sir?" a young barista asked as soon as he'd entered the building.

Elias ducked his head to dodge a low-hanging light fixture and eyed the space. There were two other men sitting in a corner booth around a circular table, engaged in conversation. A woman stood behind the barista, cleaning something.

The kid repeated the question in German.

"Uh, coffee, yes," Elias said. He cleared his throat. *When was the last time I've spoken?* he wondered.

"You... want a latte? Perhaps something —"

"Coffee. Black. Hot."

The kid swallowed and nodded quickly, no doubt taken aback at the attitude of a man who had to be the only person in this village who wasn't excited to be there.

The woman continued cleaning with one hand but reached out and grabbed a short, stout coffee mug with her right hand and flipped it up and began pouring the drink.

The kid regained his composure. "That — that'll be four francs."

Elias was stunned. *Four francs? What the hell have I stumbled into?* He longed for the days before the Americans had discovered cafes and cappuccinos, before they created expensive desserts out of what used to be simple hot beverages. And he longed for the days before America exported those same abominations back to Europe, where they'd come from. It seemed everyone in the developed world felt better about themselves by being able to afford an outrageously priced coffee.

He slapped the bill and coins on the counter and sighed, trying to pass off his impatience at the young man in the hopes that the kid wouldn't ask him any more questions.

"Are — are you in town for long?" the kid asked.

Apparently, his purchase of the coffee had signaled to the kid that Elias wanted a longer conversation.

The woman placed the cup of coffee on the counter with a brief smile; then she turned back to cleaning.

"No."

He turned and left the kid, shocked, at the counter. Elias walked briskly toward the corner of the room, opposite the two men already seated.

"Elias Ziegler?"

He stopped, waiting. The man repeated the name. Elias turned slowly, eyeing both men.

One was seated facing across the table at the other man, whose legs were poking out from underneath the table and facing him. He was the one who had spoken. He wore an expression of intrigue and anticipation. One eyebrow up a bit, a few wrinkles cutting across the front part of his newly balding head.

He looked like a banker who had allowed himself to be carried fully into the expectations of his industry, to let himself be mired in the details and drudgery of numbers and accounting and spreadsheets, and completely forget that there was supposed to be something resembling a human on the outside.

His hair, what was left of it, was slicked back, and wiry glasses curved around his eyes and nearly all the way around his ears. Elias sized him up while he stepped toward the two men. Slightly overweight but certainly not obese, the man looked as though he'd never been in a gym in his life but had been hounded by his wife to eat better.

The other man looked a bit more palatable. Similarly slicked-back dark-brown hair, wearing a turtleneck sweater underneath a puffy gray winter down vest, slacks and sock-less shoes. Sneakers. The man looked like a French mountain climber: in shape, but woefully out of style.

"I'm Ziegler," Elias said. He approached the table. His hand went involuntarily for his back, where he kept an H&K VP9 tucked into a belt holster. He knew these men were here for the meeting, which had been sanctioned by the same company that had hired him, so it was unlikely they would attack him for any reason.

Still, old habits died hard.

He brought his hand back out to shake the first man's — the banker's.

"Mr. Ziegler," this man began in German, "my name is Roger Dietrich, this is Lars Tennyson. We are with EKG."

"And in what capacity are you with EKG?"

"I work with the research wing. I am Lars' assistant."

"I see."

"Thank you for meeting with us," Dietrich said. He motioned

with an upturned palm for Ziegler to sit. Elias considered opting out but didn't see any benefit to remaining standing. There was no one else besides the kid and the woman in the tiny cafe. "I hope you are enjoying your coffee."

"It's coffee."

"Right. Well, anyway, thank you again. I wanted to let you know of some progress we've made with the project."

Ziegler was legitimately confused now. He knew the 'project' was this hunting trip they had funded. They wanted Ziegler to find — and kill — something in the foothills of the Swiss Alps, specifically in the wide, expansive tract of land the company owned in the region.

So far he had not been successful. But it had only been three days, and they hadn't explained what exactly it was he was supposed to *hunt.*

"I take it you're going to tell me what the hell I'm supposed to be looking for out there?" Elias asked.

The two other men exchanged a quick glance, and the banker-looking one spoke. "No, unfortunately. We can't discuss that here. When we get into the field again, perhaps we can —"

"Into the field again?" Ziegler asked. "I thought this project was over? I was going to come back and complain that you haven't given me enough time."

"That's... part of why we're here, Mr. Ziegler. You see, the company feels the same as you — this project must be continued."

"I agree."

"Right. Well, we would like to extend the length of the project, and offer some assistance."

"Sorry, I don't follow."

"Three more days — another expedition. This time, you'll have help." He looked across at Lars, then back to Ziegler.

Elias paused, taking a long look at Dietrich and Tennyson. "You?"

"Yes, Mr. Ziegler."

"No."

"I — I'm sorry?"

"I work alone. I believe I made that clear to your bosses when I accepted this contract."

"You did, Mr. Ziegler. However, with the most recent course of events —"

"What events?"

"I mean with your... *failure*, as of yet, to produce on the contract's final deliverables, we —"

"Shoot straight with me, son," Ziegler said, cutting him off. "I shoot straight when I'm shooting *and* talking. That's why you hired me. Now, you're pissed because I haven't given you... whatever the hell it is that's out there, that your bosses are worried about. *I'm* here because I'm telling you I *will* find it, and I *will* deliver it to your doorstep. That's a fact."

"Right, that's what I'm getting to. We just feel that it would be prudent for us to offer our —"

"I work alone."

"— *Give* our support while in the field for another three days."

Lars leaned forward, speaking for the first time. "The support is not optional, Mr. Ziegler." He wore a constant half-grin, a smug know-it-all look that Ziegler immediately hated. *Definitely French,* he thought.

Elias sighed. "I'm not being given a choice, am I?"

"Well, Mr. Ziegler, you are free to turn in your contract and return home. We can find another —"

"I can find it. Whatever it is. But it's going to cost more."

The small man nodded, his glasses falling a few centimeters down his nose. "Good. Yes. That is the second topic we wanted to discuss with you. I have authority to triple the contract's price upon —"

"I accept." Elias took a quick sip of his coffee, then began to slide out of the booth seat.

"That — that is it? You are fine with the terms?"

Elias sniffed, looked at each man once again, then curled his shoulders inward. His massive frame seemed to roll in on itself, consuming the entire table. The two men sat back a bit in their seats. "I am decidedly *not* okay with this 'support' you think you are offering me. But I will hold you to your first words. You will tell me *exactly* what it is I am to be looking for out here. This isn't a lazy camping trip for me. I want to produce results, gentlemen, and I will, once I have the right information."

He once again slid out of the seat and stood, now towering over the table. "Is that clear?"

Dietrich and Tennyson nodded simultaneously.

"We — we'll email you the meetup time and location," Lars called out.

Elias didn't bother shaking their hands as he left.

CHAPTER 12
BEN

"WAIT," Ben said. "You think they *killed* him? You told us it was a climbing accident."

She nodded. "I know they did. EKG was where I worked for seven years, at their old headquarters in Austria. My husband and I bought into the business model, the research, all of it. Until things started to change. He had a career in lobbying, mostly working for organizations similar to Greenpeace and PETA, stuff like that.

"Things at the company began to shift toward animal research and testing, which is always a little touchy."

"Yeah, I'd have to agree with that," Ben said.

"But we knew that it was necessary, too. In certain forms, and in specific, very *regulated* ways. My husband was an expert on that sort of thing. Legislation necessary for proper testing and research. Treatment methodologies that allowed *all* parties to benefit."

"Like not killing animals."

"Right. These aren't new ideas, either. We've been able to perform 99% of our research *without* harming or even stressing the lives that are used during the process."

"I see."

"So when things at EKG started to change — namely, the

company splitting off a small section of its overall research and development laboratories and moving them here — my husband and I were concerned."

"Why?"

"Because they did it in a way that was... strange. I was working in that department, and the way they explained it was by issuing a memo. Via email. It said something to the effect of, 'we're moving. Some of you are fired.'"

Ben laughed. "Sounds like they *didn't* really inform anyone as to their intentions."

"Exactly. And that was internal, to their own staff scientists. You can't imagine how vague and nondescript they were toward the general public."

"I bet."

"Anyway, after this happened, about the time they started building the headquarters for their division here, I stepped down. My husband was doing well, and I had concerns as to the integrity of the company and their direction anyway. I thought I would dip my hand into some of the work he was doing — he had too much of it for one person, anyway.

"We made a hell of a team, Ben. We brought companies to justice, small and large. We got *millions* paid out by organizations that had refused to abide by well-established rules and regulations all over the world."

"Sounds like you played lawyer."

She nodded. "We used paralegals for most of it, but that's essentially what the work was. Writing letters and threatening massive class-action suits if they didn't pay up. But the *real* work was in getting them to change. To actually *care* about this stuff."

"Did they?"

"Some did, not many. It was exhausting work, but it was only rewarding when things changed. Money changing hands is only fun when some of it lands in your lap, and not enough of it did for us to be able to be swooned by it."

"Not necessarily a bad situation, though. You were in it for the right reasons."

"Right, exactly. But, like I said, it was exhausting. The sheer amount of work it took to even get a *payout*, much less a change in policy or practice, was daunting. And we never did get many answers about *this* place. About my old division that moved to Switzerland."

"So, how did your husband die?" Ben immediately regretted asking. It felt harsh, forward. But it didn't seem to bother Eliza.

"It was a climbing accident, just as I said on the phone. But I have reason to believe the company orchestrated the entire thing. They killed him, Ben. *Murdered* him because of the work *I* had been doing. We wanted to stop it, but we were never going to do more than bring lawsuits and letters up against them. They... took it to the next level."

"Yeah," Ben said. "I'd say killing him is a definite leveling-up. But... how? They made it look like an accident?"

She seemed as though she were about to cry, but she held it together. "Yes, that's what I believe. He was found at the bottom of a wall we've climbed together many times. It's an easy face, typical aid climbing, and he fell on the abseil — the rappel."

"How do you know there was foul play?"

She paused. "That's just it. I can't *prove* it. There was nothing that suggested anything outside of an accident."

Ben's face must have betrayed a bit of his feelings of disbelief.

"I know," she said. "I know how it sounds. It's crazy, but... I *know* they got to him. They made it as accidental as possible. Slipped cam, shortened rope, something. I *know* it happened. About a year after it happened, I was slated to speak at a university, to give a presentation I've done many times. A day before the event, the university called to cancel, citing 'communication misunderstandings.' But I believe that, too, was the work of the company. They wanted to silence us, and they have."

"Why?" Ben asked. "Why would they — the company — go through the trouble? It's one thing to be against what you and your husband did for a living, but it's another thing entirely to actually *kill* him. That's, like you said, 'next level.' Why would they be so upset about your work?"

Eliza shifted in her seat again, signaling a change of subject. "Harvey — Ben — do you know the name Lucio Canavero?"

Ben shook his head.

"He's a doctor. A scientist, really. He was recruited by EKG a few months before I quit, but he was very quickly made head of the entire medical research component of the division that was to move out here. He was given carte blanche to carry out his research, and I assure you, there was plenty of money there to keep him happy."

"What sort of research did he do?" Ben asked.

"Animal testing, just like everyone else in the department. Like I was supposed to do. But his work was, well, *controversial.*"

"In what way?"

"Here," she said, "give me a moment." She pulled out her phone and flicked around the home screen until she found a folder and opened it. Inside was a photo app, password protected. She placed her thumbprint over the phone's main button, and the app opened. "It's not the most secure method, but it will do for now. Take a look. These were sent to me by an acquaintance I used to work with. I haven't been able to get ahold of him to confirm anything, and I fear the worst."

Ben took the phone, holding it gently in his open palm. His finger hovered over the first image's thumbnail, but before he pressed it he looked up.

"These — these are *real*?" He asked. "And this is what Canavero's new division, and EKG, were working on?"

She nodded. "What they are *still* working on, Ben."

He swallowed, almost wishing he had turned down the offer to help this woman. But something was driving him forward. Something horrible, and yet something intriguing.

The truth.

Could this be real?

He clicked on the first image, and his hand shook, nearly dropping the phone.

CHAPTER 13
BEN

THE IMAGES WERE all close-up pictures, taken by the staff and their boss, Lucio Canavero. They were all pictures of the inside of a medical facility, but unlike a hospital, most of the hallways and corners of rooms were dark, with only a single bright light source directly above the operating tables.

And the operating tables were exactly that — sterile, cold steel tables. Besides medical implements and instruments, there was nothing about the pictures that made him think he was looking at the inside of a state-of-the-art research laboratory.

But it was the *subjects* of the pictures that had appalled Ben. He flicked through each image, pausing for a few seconds on each one, sometimes pinching and pulling his fingers apart on the screen to enlarge them and see more detail.

Each of the pictures was of an ape — a chimpanzee, Eliza told him — in different stages of 'testing.' Its eyes were closed in each of the images so far, yet Eliza told Ben that the ape, a young chimp by the name of Apollo, was very much alive.

Worse, she told him that Apollo had not been anesthetized before the operations had begun.

In the first picture, Apollo lay on the metal table, its thin arms and legs strapped down with thick leather bindings. Its head was straight and even, held in place by a form-fitting Styrofoam headpiece that was also attached to the table.

The next few images showed Apollo again, but with the additions of human hands and arms as they worked on Apollo's body, attaching and applying tubes and different salves to the chimp's hairy frame. One tube ran into the chimp's chest cavity, inserted and attached after a 'researcher' had cut a two-inch hole near the animal's sternum.

Another image showed some sort of liquid coursing through the semi-opaque tube, which was coiled around a rectangular white machine that sat nearby on the table.

"Keep going," Eliza said.

Ben didn't want to, but it was important. He'd flown all the way here for this, even though he hadn't known it at the time. He was horrified, but it wasn't just the images that terrified him. *Whatever they were working on was important enough to* kill *over*, he thought. The realization caused him to look up.

Eliza was nodding, a concerned look in her eye. "Yes," she said. "This is all true, Ben. Keep going. You must know what they are doing."

He did. The next images showed the chimp's head being turned sideways, a larger human hand beneath it, cradling it.

And then the true horrors began. Ben watched as the cameraperson began taking pictures more and more frequently, judging by how little Apollo's head was moving around on the table as the doctors and aides performed their operation.

And that operation seemed to involve *cutting across Apollo's neck*. Another person's hands held white cloth that caught most of the chimp's blood, but Ben was surprised to see that there wasn't much of it — perhaps a pint or two.

"They've lowered his body temperature," Eliza said. "It's off-screen, but there is a machine pumping saline into the chimp's bloodstream, essentially replacing his blood."

"*Replacing* it?" Ben asked.

"Yes," Eliza said. "They call the procedure *Emergency Preservation and Resuscitation*, or EPR. It's a new technique, but American doctors have been using it on gunshot and mortal wound victims. It almost 'suspends' them, slowing everything down in the host's body so that doctors can remove dangerously sick organs or fix excessive bleeding injuries."

"That's... incredible," Ben said. He couldn't think of a better word. What he was seeing was, almost, *not* credible.

"It truly is remarkable," Eliza said. "And it works, which is even more remarkable."

"And why are they doing it to Apollo?" Ben asked. "I didn't see any gunshot wounds or anything."

"Keep looking," she said.

He did. The next few images were at a slightly different angle, but still looking down toward Apollo as his neck was cut entirely through.

They severed his head.

The surgical procedure ended with Apollo's head *completely removed* from the spinal cord and neck, and with someone's hands cupping Apollo's cranium and lifting it off the table.

The head disappeared but was then replaced in the next image.

But something seemed strange, off. It was...

"Oh, my God," Ben whispered.

"Yes," Eliza said.

"That's... that's *not his head*."

There was another chimpanzee head in the image now, but it was clearly the head of a *different* chimp. Apollo's body lay still on the table, but a new cranium lay where the young ape's head had been.

"What are they going to do?" Ben asked. But he kept sliding to the next image, in part hoping the sequence had finished and simultaneously wanting to know the ending.

That ending came soon.

The next sequence of images was of Canavero and his team working on *reattach*ing the new chimp's head onto Apollo's body. Ben watched in silent suspense, partly knowing how it would end.

The final image was the most terrifying of all. The Frankenstein-looking wound on the young chimp's neck stood out in the image, bloody and scabbing over, the thick sinewy threads crisscrossed in 'X's around his neck, but it was the chimp's *face* that caught Ben's attention.

The chimp's eyes were open.

CHAPTER 14
ELIZA

ELIZA WATCHED THE MAN — Harvey Bennett — as he browsed through the images, his eyes scanning and catching every detail. She had been hesitant to reach out, but she was now glad she had. This man was thorough, and he was slowly coming around to her side.

She wasn't lying to him — she *did* believe that EKG had killed her husband. She had never been able to prove it, but she knew Ben and his team at the CSO didn't work through normal channels. They would vet her case, for sure, but they would find her correct in her assumptions.

This company needed to be taken down.

She had spent the latter portion of her life attempting to bring down companies just like this one, and her husband had given his entire life for that same purpose. They had succeeded many times, but they had also never come up against a company such as EKG.

She knew from her experience and time working at EKG's old headquarters that there was something *different* about them. They didn't care for conducting research through typical, peer-approved channels, nor did they care for the methods and means they took to get their results.

They cared for *results*, and that was it. Nothing else bothered them.

The company had been started many years earlier, just after the end of World War II, and it had changed hands many times. She knew that the latest owner, an investor and amateur scientist, was interested in using the company's results as his personal profit engine — a story unfortunately not uncommon, as she and her husband had found.

But he had even fewer scruples than others similar to him, Eliza had eventually learned. The man simply didn't care for anything but profits, and the results that drove them.

She had realized her mistake of accepting the high-paying job almost too late, but she had been able to quit without direct repercussions. When she discovered that they were going to move Canavero's division to Switzerland, her and her husband's plans began to take shape.

Her husband, unfortunately, had paid the ultimate price.

They were going to burn, and she would do all she could to see that it happened.

"I don't understand," Ben said. "This chimp — Apollo — or whoever it is now, is *alive*. How is that possible?"

Eliza forced a smile. "I assure you it is very possible. EKG has been performing experiments just like this one for years, and most of them, unfortunately, did not end nearly as well."

"Is it... capable? I mean, can it —"

"It is a full chimpanzee," she said. "A functional being, completely capable of anything Apollo was able to do."

"But its brain —"

"Is different, yes," Eliza said. "And that invokes a major ethical concern. But the technology — the science involved — is all quite real. The process of cooling the blood with saline, which slows cellular activity enough to perform surgery such as this, is coupled with a new technique developed by Canavero using polyethylene glycol, or PEG, which conserves nerve cell membranes. That's important because it allows the spinal column and cord to be cut without damaging it. It will re-fuse afterward. They use a negative pressure device to urge the areas to heal, and it's been proven quite effective."

"I just..." Ben wasn't sure what to say. "I just didn't realize any of this was *possible*. It seems like something out of science fiction."

"All of science fiction is just truth before its time," Eliza said. "I can assure you, this research EKG is doing is based on mountains of prior research, both by them and the companies and scientists that have come before. They're standing on the shoulders of giants, and to be honest with you, Ben, this progress doesn't surprise me."

"It doesn't?"

"No, not at all. I've seen the same sort of surgical prowess used for similar experiments on mice and rats, and some other small mammals. This — this is big, for sure, but it's nothing, Ben. It's nothing like what's coming."

She watched the man in front of her. He seemed to be chewing on something as if he were deep in thought. She expected a certain question; everyone she'd brought this up to had asked it. He might still ask it, but for now she could see that he was working through a much deeper emotional reaction to all of it.

"All of that stuff... taking actual *heads* off. Transplanting them. It's... considered scientific advancement?"

"Well, sure," Eliza said. "It advances our understanding of what's possible."

"And scientists are *okay* with it?'

"'Scientist' only means that a person is engaged in the research and study of something, and that they have determined to abide by the rules established by previous scientists."

"The scientific method."

"Precisely, Ben," she said. "Scientists come from every walk of life, and they are impossible to categorize. For some, the promise of solving a problem is enough motivation. For others, it's money."

"Money was their motivation for doing this?" Ben asked.

"Well," Eliza began, "yes. But — I don't think I mentioned it before. Apollo, the chimpanzee in these photos, was paralyzed."

"Paralyzed. As in, he couldn't move?"

She shook her head. "From the neck down."

"And... after?"

"He was able to move as if nothing had ever happened."

"Wait a minute," Ben said. "So Apollo, previously, couldn't even move? And then they swapped his head with another chimp, and he... *could* move? Like, he could walk, move his arms?"

"Oh yes, Ben. He could do anything his fellow chimps could do."

"So he's okay, now?"

"Well, no. They terminated the experiment after 24 hours of close examination."

"They killed him?"

"Euthanized, I believe, is the word they used. But yes, they put Apollo down after a day of study, for ethical reasons."

"Good to know they're taking ethics into consideration."

Eliza laughed at that. "Right. My thoughts exactly." She liked Ben's tone, his sarcasm. He was easy to get along with, and in that way he reminded her of her husband. "Ben, I'm not worried about their experiments on *chimps*."

"Why not? It seems a bit... rushed, to say the least. I'm no doctor, and I don't think I'd know the business end of a scalpel, but it seems like EKG should be stopped. At least slowed down a bit, right? To present this stuff to a... a board, or something? Isn't there something like that out there?"

"Yes, absolutely," Eliza said. "And peers — other scientists and doctors — have weighed in already. Many feel as you and I do, that this research is moving along too quickly, that there are ethical considerations as to the nature of a chimp's soul — their *being* — that should be answered first."

"Wait a minute," Ben said.

She saw it in his eyes. The moment. The single spark in his mind as he put it all together, finally understanding what this was all about.

"Go on, Ben," she said, urging him along.

"You said... you told me you're not worried about their experiments on *chimpanzees.*"

"Correct."

"Which means... you're thinking they're testing —"

"I'm not *thinking,* Ben. I have *proof.* My research in the division just before I left was related to all of this; I just didn't know it at the time. Researching serums and chemical compounds that would help the spinal column of a vertebrate animal heal, discovering and testing new medicines for the treatment of mortal lacerations, all of it. I had no idea it was for *this,* until right at the end. My husband and I were able to put the pieces together. He died because of it. And that's why I want to take them down."

Ben sucked in a deep breath, a quick, sharp inhalation. He held it. Looked around, then leaned close. Exhaled, then met her eyes.

"If — what you say is true, if you're telling me right now is actually what's going on there, then... I'm in."

She nodded. "It's true, Ben."

"My team back home will want to know. They'll need to verify it first, but... if you're telling me what's *actually* going on there is..."

"Go on, Ben."

"If you're telling me that they're trying to do this — experiment... the thing they've done to Apollo — on *humans,* then I'm in. They must be stopped."

She met his gaze and held it, their eyes locking. "They *must* be stopped."

CHAPTER 15
DIETRICH

"HELLO?" Roger Dietrich said, answering the phone. It was a single word, and yet he knew it sounded abrupt. *Good,* he thought. *Very well.* He was growing quite tired of these 'check-ins,' and even more tired with his lessened role in it all.

"Yes, hello. You have met with the team?"

"More than once," Dietrich answered, rolling his eyes. He looked out the window, seeing the beautiful snow-riddled landscape of Grindelwald and the nearby foothills of the Alps. It was truly a striking, remarkable locale, but he had seen plenty of beautiful, striking locales in his time.

"And?"

Dietrich clutched the phone tighter with one hand and squeezed his other fist into a white-knuckled ball with his other. *I don't have time for this,* he thought.

He took a few deep breaths before answering to calm himself down. He was typically an impatient man; he hated waiting on anyone with lesser intellect. Still, he knew his tendencies were against reacting in a rash, thoughtless manner, but lately his ability to withhold his impatience was growing thin. He had trained his entire life to keep these sorts of emotions in check, and he needed to tap into his vast reservoir of practice and study now.

"And *what*?" he asked, still unable to hide the annoyance in his voice. "We met, we discussed deliverables and expectations, and we are prepared to move out."

"I see."

He shifted in his chair. He was sitting in the lobby of the small hotel, one of the only buildings in the town that looked as though it had been built this century. He knew the history here — he had done his homework long before allowing the division to be built out here in the middle of nowhere. He knew that Grindelwald was part of the Canton of Berne, Switzerland, and that it was an ancient city — first inhabited during the Neolithic Age.

But he wasn't here for the history. He had a job to do, and these check-ins were growing mundane. He understood that the company expected him to find its asset, and that the stakes on this particular mission were high, but that didn't negate the fact that he often worked alone toward this goal. He *preferred* working alone.

Hell, he was *best* when he worked alone.

Lars was a good man, and he enjoyed his work with him, but Dietrich had no plans to be his assistant forever. Dietrich was capable of not only carrying the company on his back, he was capable of furthering his own plans at the same time.

And every now and then, a job would appear that was simply too lucrative to the company to turn down.

The type of job Lars couldn't know about.

Dietrich wanted the money, but as much as that, he wanted the *thrill*. He'd been doing this job for too long. The corporate espionage, the logistics, the research, the planning — all of it was part of the game. He *lived* for the game.

"Is there anything else?" he asked, already knowing the answer. Just because these calls had grown redundant didn't mean the company wasn't still seeking out new information to pass along.

They were efficient and brutal in their effectiveness. He had to admit that, and if he were honest, he respected that about them.

They wouldn't call for no reason.

"Yes," said the voice on the other end of the phone. *"There is new information."*

"What information? Can you just email it?"

"We already have, but I want to ensure that it reaches you directly as soon as possible."

"I see," he said. He'd always hated the types of people who would send an email and then immediately walk down to his office to see if he'd read it yet. This was the virtual version of that, apparently. "And what is this information?"

Bureaucratic annoyances aside, anything that required both emailing *and* calling him directly meant that it was likely mission-critical information.

"You met with your team today, correct?"

"Yes, I already said that."

"And you are prepared in every way?"

"Again, yes."

What is the point of this? he wondered. They were conversing in his native tongue — German — and he thought of a slew of German insults, but held his breath instead of speaking them aloud.

There was a pause.

"Yes, well, there has been an, uh, alteration. In mission parameters."

He appreciated that this man was attempting to communicate using terms that sounded militaristic, but it was still annoying. Especially since neither he nor this person had ever served.

"Fine. What are the changes?"

"There is now third-party involvement."

"What is that supposed to mean? I am not here to play tour guide."

"I am hoping you can nullify their involvement."

Dietrich paused. Waited a moment. Then another. *Calm down,* he willed himself. *Just breathe.* "What is that supposed to mean? 'Nullify their involvement.'"

"It means I am authorizing any and all force necessary. This third party — a group of at least two, I believe — is not, *under any circumstances, to be allowed to discover any information regarding EKG and its interests."*

"Right," he said. "Okay, you've got some prying eyes. I can prevent them from prying. But you sound like a lawyer now, and I don't feel like calling mine. Can you dumb it down for me?"

"I am authorizing the use of full force — any and all necessary — to stop this group from trespassing on company land. Any information they are able to extract while on our grounds is cause for their immediate termination."

"That's... very clear," he said. *Except that we have already sent most of the guards away.* "Thank you. And who exactly is this 'third party'?"

"I am unsure of the exact personas involved, but they are with a group calling themselves the CSO."

"CSO?" he asked. He'd never heard of them before. *Must be a new security firm.*

"Based out of the United States. The Civilian Special Operations."

CHAPTER 16
BEN

BEN PRESSED "*END*" on the iPad's screen and looked around to make sure he had everything he would need. After connecting with Julie and Mrs. E through the secure network calling app Julie had installed on his iPad, he'd suddenly felt better about Mrs. E's offer to secure some weaponry for the field.

He had been instructed to visit a local hunting outfitter; Mrs. E had set up an appointment for that morning when he would be introduced to the owner and his nephew. The nephew, a young man by the name of Clive Vanderstadt, would be going with him. He was a reputable hunter and outdoorsman from the area, and Mrs. E assured Ben that he would be a good asset to have out in the wild.

Ben wasn't sure how "wild" they were going to get, as it seemed the hike over the ridge from the village to the edge of EKG's property was fewer than ten miles. Still, he didn't turn down the support.

And he certainly didn't turn down the offer for the elder Vanderstadt to supply him with what Mrs. E had described as a "military-grade rifle." He would get the details later, and stock up from Vanderstadt on whatever else they needed.

He was shaken up a bit about the young woman's disappearance. The young woman was pretty, smart, and well-liked in the community. It seemed unlikely that she would have been involved with thugs or any less-than-reputable folks, especially in a place like Grindelwald.

While Grindelwald was a tourist town, inviting people from all over, the core population was made up of the steady, consistent type of people Ben knew well. They seemed to all know one another, and any disputes between residents were usually resolved in-person and without much fuss. The local police had an easy job; most of their days were spent directing traffic at busy intersections or passing out parking tickets to rented tourist vehicles.

But Julie had told him about something *else* that she'd discovered: Alina's disappearance wasn't the only one. In the past month, there had been *three* strange disappearances. It had taken a bit of digging — Grindelwald wasn't often in the Swiss national news — but Julie had uncovered a case two weeks ago of a man who had gone missing. He was somewhat of a nomad, living in and between nearby towns without much to his name, and he was normally seen around Grindelwald for a few weeks at a time before disappearing again to another nearby town.

But no one in Grindelwald had seen the man in months. After leaving the town of Lütschental and heading up the highway toward Burglauenen about three weeks ago, he had never appeared in Grindelwald. The townspeople had talked and called around, but the man seemed to be gone.

A week ago a dog had gone missing as well. A family in Grindelwald had posted signs everywhere in town regarding the disappearance of a Bernese mountain dog. The animal hadn't returned home after a day in the open backyard, and the owners were distraught. The dog was too young to have wandered off and too old to have gotten lost.

Alina's disappearance combined with the lost dog and homeless man gave Ben a bit to worry about. He was pretty sure EKG had nothing to do with any of the cases, but what Eliza had told him the previous day about the company and their research was still weighing on his mind.

There was something going on at that company, and he wanted to find out what it was. He wanted to bring them to justice, to allow Eliza to do her job and bring attention to their research and to the proper authorities. If possible, he wanted to shut it down.

There was a road that led to EKG headquarters, but it would be a huge risk to use it to gain access. There were multiple guard towers and camera surveillance along the three-mile route, as the company's access road that split off from the single-lane highway nearby was completely located on EKG land. Besides that, there were two rows of razor-wire fencing on the front side of the building, situated like two large rectangles with — again — more guard towers.

The map view Julie had sent him was enhanced far more than what the typical consumer-grade satellite imagery would pull up, so he had scanned through the images to determine the best entry point. If they wanted to remain stealthy and under the radar, their best option would be to travel over the back areas of the region, staying along the ridgeline until they reached the edge of EKG's land. The forest would provide plenty of cover, but there had also been reports of guards patrolling this land as well.

Which meant they'd need to be armed.

Still, Ben felt like the best option was to travel this route, staying hidden in the trees until the final stretch, then using wire cutters to gain access to the grounds. After that, they would need a good bit of luck and some skill to get into the building itself.

Ben adjusted his shirt and pressed his palms down the front of it. He didn't bother looking in the mirror as he left the room — he knew what he looked like, and he knew he wasn't bleeding. Nothing else could be done about his appearance. He'd never been vain, and he'd never cared much for appearances. Julie seemed to think he was good-looking enough, and that's all that mattered to him.

He pulled his large frame through a door barely tall enough to walk through without ducking and plodded down the stairs and out the front door of the inn. So far, Ben loved this little town, but he got the feeling it had been built for smaller people.

The outfitter was off the main street, but it was still only a three-block walk from his hotel.

The morning air was crisp and delicate, and it smelled faintly of apples. He wondered how this place hadn't been completely consumed by outsiders, turned into a living postcard. He assumed the winters must have been brutal enough to keep away all but the most determined settlers.

The mountains, craggy and pointed, rose up and towered over the town in the distance. It reminded him a bit of his own home, back in Alaska, the tips of the peaks covered with snow, then dark gray bare rock until the mountains rounded and touched the ground, where trees and foliage sprung up to fill every cavity and patch of earth.

The walk was indeed short, and Ben pushed the door of the outfitter's open, a bell jingling above the door frame.

"Hello!"

He was greeted in English, and Ben waved at the large, jolly-looking man stacking boxes against the far wall.

"You must be Mr. Bennett," the man said, his German accent as thick as his gut. "I am Olaf Vanderstadt."

Ben nodded. "Thank you," he said. "I hope this is okay, coming in before you're open."

The man dismissed the statement. "Nonsense, young man. Anyone who's a friend of Hugh's is a friend of ours."

Ben frowned, not realizing this man was friends with Alina's father, the innkeeper. *I should have known,* he thought. "Right — well, I'm hoping we'll find her out there."

"My boy will be there to help," Vanderstadt said. "Clive!" he shouted over his shoulder.

A spitting image of the large, round man, though much thinner and younger, appeared from a back room. He smiled and nodded at Ben as he walked over. His gait was angular and forced, like a grasshopper trying to walk on its back feet. He was thin but not ungainly, with a head of light-brown hair that was combed to the side.

His face was smooth, with a day's worth of stubble covering a broad chin. Ben thought the man looked like a fresh military recruit — strength hidden beneath innocence, potential yet unrealized.

He strode up to Ben and extended his hand. The force of the man's grip nearly crushed his, but Ben only saw genuine kindness in his eyes. "Good to meet you, sir," the kid said.

Ben laughed. "Please, no 'sirs' around here but your uncle, yeah?"

The older Vanderstadt chuckled. "No 'sirs,' in that case. I'm much too young and spry to be a 'sir.'"

"I was told by your team that you are... looking for something out there?" Clive asked, tossing his head a bit to motion over his shoulder. It was in the direction of the mountains Ben knew were looming over the town — the direction of EKG's land.

"Well, we'll be looking," Ben said. "Though I'm not sure for what. I'm assuming some light rifles, possibly sidearms, things like that?"

Clive and his uncle looked at one another, and the older man nodded. Clive walked briskly over to the front door and flipped the sign so that the side that said "CLOSED" pointed out toward the street.

"For this, my friend," Vanderstadt said, "we must come to the back of the store."

CHAPTER 17
BEN

BEN WASN'T sure if it was illegal to buy and sell firearms here in Switzerland. Every country was different, but in his experience, in one way every country was also the same: if you had money, you could find just about whatever you wanted.

It appeared to be no different in the town of Grindelwald, as the Vanderstadt men had led Ben to a small, closet-sized space off the back of the main store. It was the same room Clive had appeared from earlier, and stepping down the single step into the room, Ben looked around.

Shelves, full of boxes and crates of gear and supplies for the store, rose along two of the walls. A window sat at the far side, but curtains had been drawn to cover the interior of the room from prying eyes. Another row of shelves lined the wall below the window.

On the opposite short side of the room to Ben's left sat an old wooden desk. It was about six feet long and three deep, and on top of it sat a couple of boxes and gun cases.

"Your contact tells me she prefers you are better armed than you might think necessary," Olaf said.

Ben smiled. *Sounds like Mrs. E,* he thought.

"This is a Heckler & Koch HK416N, used by the Norwegian Army. I am also including an Aimpoint CompM4 sight and a vertical foregrip — you can remove it if you'd like — as well as four additional magazines of NATO rounds. It is heavy, but you will be traveling light otherwise. My son can carry additional gear as well, if necessary. You will each carry one of the rifles, and you will have this —" he pointed to the smaller case — "as a sidearm, just as you have requested. H&K USP."

"Ammunition?" Ben asked.

"For the pistol, a few magazines. 9mm, so they are light."

"Very good," Ben said. "How much?"

Olaf Vanderstadt frowned. "I do not understand."

"Money," Ben said, waving his hand over the cases. "This stuff costs money, right? You're doing me a huge favor, and I want to make sure we're taking care of you as well."

Olaf's eyes brightened. "Ah, yes. Your contact has already arranged for the payment. Please, let us not talk of money."

"Instead," Clive said, appearing next to Ben, "let us discuss the plan. You are here to examine the grounds of EKG Corporation, no?"

Ben nodded. "Yes, I'm — we're — hoping to find anything strange and document it. Anything that's out of the ordinary down to anything we deem suspect or criminal."

Clive and his uncle shared another knowing glance.

"You have information about EKG?" Ben asked.

"No," Olaf said. "Seems as though no one around here does. No one works for the company, and hardly anyone sees any vehicles heading to their headquarters. There is a rumor that all traffic to the corporation comes from the other side of the mountain range. As ridiculous as that sounds, I tend to believe it — I am not sure I have ever seen anyone on the highway that leads to the western entrance."

"I see," Ben said. "Well, that's what we're going to find out.

Anything that's strange, or weird, or just out of place. We'll document it all, then see if there's a pattern or any useful data. I'm not really sure what *exactly* we're looking for, but my, uh, client seems to think we'll know it when we see it."

He wasn't sure how much Mrs. E and Julie had shared with this man and his nephew, but he wanted to get going, anyway. He needed to check in with his team back in Alaska and with Eliza here in town. She would want to see that he was prepared, and meet Clive. In addition, Ben wanted to extract as much information as possible about EKG before they disembarked, and Eliza seemed like the one with the most knowledge about the company.

The more he traversed through the streets of Grindelwald, the more he believed that this tiny, beautiful mountain town would be entirely better off without the presence of a secretive company nearby. He had no proof of that yet, so there was little anyone could do to change it.

But if they were able to find *anything* that corroborated Eliza's claims — anything that even remotely suggested the images she'd shown him were true — he was going to do everything in his power to help her in her quest to take them down publicly.

He saw it as the CSO's mission to extricate this amazing little mountain oasis from the oppressive grasp of the corrupt corporation. If there was any truth at all to any of this, Ben was going to find it.

And he was going to do what was necessary afterward.

He shook hands with both men and gathered up his cases, made plans to meet up with Clive in a few hours at the pub, and then turned to leave.

Olaf and Clive saw him out, Clive following him out the door to flip the sign back over to the "OPEN" side.

No one was nearby, and Ben wondered if the town had given them this privacy on purpose — so far, everyone seemed to know exactly why he was here, and what his mission was. They were rooting for him, hoping he could save the prized daughter of Grindelwald and destroy the evil corporation.

It all seemed like a fairy tale to Ben — a modern-day damsel-in-distress story.

He hoped he was the hero in all of it, and he hoped the author of whatever story was playing out was firmly on his side.

CHAPTER 18
ALINA

SHE FELT NOTHING BUT FEAR. She couldn't sense it, though. Not truly. It was as if her brain were telling her to 'be afraid,' but it was not allowing her the actual emotional response of it. Her skin was crawling with a million pinpricks, yet she seemed simultaneously desensitized to them.

Like being paralyzed over her entire body, yet unable to even register the discomfort. She had a knowledge of her predicament, and that was it. Her involuntary reactions to that predicament had somehow been stifled.

Perhaps it was something in one of the myriad cocktails of medications they'd pumped into her, were still pumping into her. Alina's arms and neck had been punctured; a hundred little needles jammed into her flesh. Bags of intravenous liquids hung from metal stands above her head.

She stared upward, at the stark-white ceiling. Some of the panels above her eyes were lights, yet all of them blended together in a wash of white and hospital-grade brightness. It was a blurry, fluid, singular image of blinding white. It reminded her of the time she had been in the hospital for a few days after eating shellfish in high school. She hadn't even known she was allergic to shellfish until that moment, and it had nearly been too late. Her parents had waited with her there, her father even closing the inn and spending the night by her side.

But today — or tonight, or whatever time it was — there was no one next to her. She couldn't *see* that, of course, but she knew. Her parents weren't there. They *couldn't* be there. They had no idea where she was.

Now that she thought of it, *she* didn't know where she was.

She tried to think. *When was the last time I was outside? What was I doing then?*

She remembered walking down the pathway near the forest. She had been in a hurry, but then...

She couldn't get her mind to recall what had happened.

She remembered fear. A visceral, terrible fear. Something had been behind her, right?

There was a noise. A scratching sound, something from the forest. But then it had seemed to multiply as if it were coming from more than one place.

Now... she was somewhere else. *How much time had passed?* Alina wondered. *Where did they take me?*

She could feel the hundred needles pushing liquid into her veins. She felt the fiery concoctions coursing through her. Whatever it was, it was both relaxing and painful. It felt like a bath of scorching-hot water, just before her body got used to it, but it was *inside* her body instead of on the surface of her skin.

A noise.

Someone had entered the room.

"Hello, my dear," a voice called out. It was Swiss German, but it sounded as though they had a slight accent. Not French. Perhaps English was their natural tongue? Or Italian?

She couldn't respond, though she didn't try, either.

Footsteps, and a silhouette appeared over her head.

"I hope you are not in pain," the voice said. It was a man.

Small, beady-eyed, with black glasses. He wasn't balding or thinning, but she couldn't see clearly with the bright lights behind his head.

She tried moving her neck, but it felt as though it were fixed in place.

"Please," the man said. "Try not to move. The examination is nearly complete, and your body is still reacting to the chemicals. It won't be long now..."

She wondered what that meant. But again, it was a wonder that seemed out-of-body, as if she were wondering how a rag doll that had been run over by a car felt.

"I will have the staff bring you a pillow, although you will not need it in the next couple of days."

He paused and grunted under his breath, as if he were chuckling about something.

What does that mean? she wondered.

She forced her mouth to open. It stung, and her jaw immediately tensed up and froze. Still, she forced it open and closed. A few times, slowly.

He saw her and leaned in. "Are you okay, my dear? Do you need water?"

She tried to nod, but couldn't. Still, he seemed to understand. He pulled up a hand, and she could see a tray behind him. On it, a large cup with a handle and lid. And through the top of the lid, a straw. He grabbed it, then pulled it over to her.

She sipped, then coughed. She tried again.

"Slow, my dear," he said. "For the first surgery two days ago, we couldn't allow you to drink any water beforehand. Now it is okay. You are on an IV drip to keep your hydration levels, but a bit of water will not hurt, either."

She couldn't react, so she just kept drinking.

"Unfortunately, it will have to be the last ingested water you receive, as the next surgery is the big one. We have it scheduled, but we must ensure your strength is up for it. That's what I am here to do."

He didn't seem to mind having a one-way conversation, but Alina wasn't sure what she would have said to him if she could speak. He began humming to himself, his tiny eyes peering down at her naked body from behind his glasses.

She had just noticed that she was on the table, uncovered. Unclothed. As with the rest of the emotions she had been feeling, she could sense them but couldn't truly *feel* them. They were part of her, but in the way a favorite pair of socks was a part of her. Her hair was hers, but it wasn't like she could feel it.

The man — or doctor — examined her, taking in her body and marking notes down on a clipboard. He had a detached expression on his face as he hummed along as if he were simply examining the table itself. He worked for a few more minutes, then dropped the clipboard on the tray behind him, where he'd placed the water after taking the straw from her lips.

Finally, he took a step back, then clasped his hands together.

"Well, my dear. It has been long enough. I believe you are finally ready. My name is Dr. Canavero, and I will be with you until the very end."

She felt something new, something she hadn't felt yet. *Was she about to cry?* There were no tears, but there was the *feeling* of tears, something from deep within her that couldn't quite come out.

"I will alert the team and prepare the other patient. Thank you for your cooperation."

He made the grunting, weird laughing noise once again then turned and left the room.

She heard the door slam, but her eyes were still affixed to the ceiling above her.

The sense of crying was stronger now, and she began breathing in slighter, faster breaths.

CHAPTER 19
BEN

"I SEE you stopped by *Roth Toni*," the barman said with a chuckle. He was looking at Ben's new hunting coat that he'd picked up from the store earlier.

Ben had barely stepped over the threshold of the *Downtown Lodge* once again when the older man behind the bar had yelled to him. Three patrons, two sitting together at a table in the corner of the room and one sitting at the bar itself, glanced up as he walked in. None of them seemed to care, as they all focused back down at their drinks.

Ben grinned. "I did," he said. "Had a few errands to run this morning, but I had time to stop in this afternoon."

The man looked at his wrist for a watch that wasn't there. "It's half-past four," he said. "Seems like it's *still* afternoon."

Impressive, Ben thought. *A man who always knows what time it was.* His own father had been like that — a seeming perfect sense of time, no matter the hour of day or night.

"You saying it's too early for a drink?"

The man waved him over and gave him a distressed look. "Now that's not at all what I'm saying, friend. Here, first one's on me."

He slid a glass over. Beer, the same Ben had been drinking before, ice-cold as if it had been poured only seconds before.

"Wow," Ben said. "You know I was coming or something?"

The man just winked. He left to check on the three other customers in the bar, poured a few drinks, then returned to wiping down the bar top.

Ben took the time to think. He sipped at the beer and thought about Julie, about Alina and Eliza. About the newcomers Clive and his uncle Olaf. The Vanderstadts seemed like good people, and Ben would be happy to have Clive along with him tomorrow when they set off.

The trouble was that Ben still wasn't quite sure *where* they were setting off to. EKG's land was commonly used for hunting, through a deal between the canton and the company, but it was all highly regulated and — Ben assumed — highly scrutinized. He figured EKG at least would have solar cameras in the woods, at least on the property line. Would they allow trespassers like Ben and Clive?

There really wasn't any way around it. Eliza seemed to have a good plan, a route through the region toward their headquarters that she'd given Ben yesterday. It led to where she claimed the massive buildings and campus lay on the other side of a ridge, invisible to the town of Grindelwald.

But what sort of security EKG had out on patrol was information Eliza hadn't given him. She couldn't, as she didn't have any idea. She'd told Ben that the route would get them there unseen, but it was still unnerving for Ben to go in blind. He'd grown accustomed to Julie's and Mrs. E's tech capabilities, and Mr. E's connections in the communications sector.

On previous missions, Julie had guided Ben over and around the area behind their cabin using GPS and drone technology, and he'd even seen her tap into a satellite feed that Mr. E had somehow had repositioned over their area.

Out here, in the middle of the Swiss Alps, he would be flying blind. Cellular service out here was nonexistent, and Julie had warned him against even trying — if EKG was monitoring the right frequencies, or scraping data from any nearby cellular towers, it could easily ping his location directly to them.

So tomorrow, anything he could see with his own eyes would be the only 'intelligence' available to him. Clive was certainly an asset he was happy to have along, but he still missed having the heads-up GPS location constantly updating on his phone.

He took another sip as the bartender sidled over. "Everything okay, son?" the man asked.

Ben nodded, raising an eyebrow. "Just enjoying a bit of peace before the storm."

"Ah, the tempest sets in," the man said. "Sounds like you're leaving tomorrow."

Ben frowned.

"Good guess?"

"We — I mean, *I* am," Ben said. "Why? Have you heard something?"

"I hear everything here, son," the man said. "I even heard you spoke with Ringgenberg."

Ben nodded again. "I did. I'm hoping we'll come across Alina, but I'm afraid I'm not trained for that sort of thing. I'm not sure how much help I'll be."

"You'll be just fine. If she's out there, I know you will find her."

Ben was starting to grow slightly annoyed with this superhero treatment, but he kept his face blank and expressionless. "Yeah, well, I hope so."

The man seemed as though he might be about to leave, but then he leaned forward and glanced side to side. "Listen," he said, a bit of his French accent slipping out as he spoke. "I just... I want to make sure you know the danger you might be putting yourself in."

Ben wasn't sure how to take that. "What do you mean? I'm just going to poke around, check for Alina, and help Eliza find —"

"I know, I know. It's just... there's been some changes."

"*What* changes?" Ben asked. He was *definitely* growing annoyed with the fact that everyone in Grindelwald seemed to know more about his mission than he did. "If there's something I need to know, I'd appreciate it if —"

"I just heard that there's another group going out tomorrow as well. Three men. One looks like a military gentleman. The other two, I'm not sure."

"They were here?"

The barman nodded. "Came in late morning, maybe around lunchtime. Two of them ate. One of them, the military fellow, seemed to not want to be here."

"What did they say?"

He shrugged. "Nothing, really. Just overheard that they were 'heading out tomorrow,' out into the land you are off to."

"And I should be worried?"

"Well, that's just it — I don't think so. But I don't know. They didn't seem... hostile. But it also seems strange, you know. That they would be hunting the same land you're on, at the same time."

"Hunting?"

"I assume that's what they're planning. Seems like a hunting party. We get them from time to time, you know. A richer fellow, with an assistant or helping hand of sorts. And a professional, someone who actually knows what they're doing out there."

Ben took in this information. He, too, wasn't sure how to interpret it. It did seem strange. "But you seem to know everything about me," Ben said. "How come you don't know about these guys?"

The barman and innkeeper shrugged again. "Who knows? They have been relatively quiet, slipping in sometime a day before yesterday, I believe. Ringgenberg, the others, no one's seen where they're staying. They eat, drink, get coffee, that's it."

"I see."

The bartender held his hands up, palms facing Ben. "Look, son,

I'm just saying to watch your back. Seems it's a strange time in Grindelwald. Poor little Alina's lost, your friend Eliza seems to want a piece of that weird, mysterious company up there, and these gentlemen are in town for some reason no one knows about."

"And the deaths," Ben said.

The man stepped backward. "What do you know of 'deaths?'"

"The dog and the two others. They went missing, right?"

"No one said anything about *deaths*, son."

"Right," Ben said. "Sorry, really. I just meant —"

"I'm just saying to watch your back. That's it. No one wants this, and we all want to see Alina back."

"I get it," Ben said. "I didn't mean —"

But before he could say anything more, the door jingled and opened. A blast of cold evening air curled inward and hit Ben in the back of the neck. He stopped talking and turned around, looking to see who the newcomer was.

The bartender was suddenly there, leaning over the bar and whispering into Ben's ear.

"That's him," he said. "The military one. The one who's heading out there tomorrow."

CHAPTER 20
BEN

BEN STAYED INSIDE for another thirty minutes, drinking beer and texting with Julie. He checked his TownHall page; an account Julie had set up for him because 'all the other kids were using it.' He carried a general hatred for social media, but he had to admit it was nice to see some of his old grade school friends and what they were up to.

But after his second beer, he got tired of the mental decay of it and decided to get to bed early. He tried again to close his tab and was once again waved off by the old barman.

The 'military gentleman' the barman had pointed out had come in and sat three stools down from Ben, right in the center of the long bar. He hadn't looked at Ben, nor had he said anything at all to anyone.

Ben had sized him up. He was a massive, muscular thing, hairy and thick, but it did seem as though the man carried himself with a noticeable military swagger — a stiff, proud, assuredness that marked an ex-military or Marine from a mile away. Ben had seen it before in men and women. Mrs. E carried herself that way, even though Ben wasn't entirely sure she had military experience.

The barman passed the newcomer a beer, the same one as Ben's, and the man drank it in a single gulp. Another appeared in front of him, and this one he sipped slowly, calmly, savoring it. It was like he was trying to catch up to Ben.

As far as Ben could tell, the man hadn't returned the favor and sized Ben up. Perhaps it was part of his swagger, part of his demeanor. The man could have been like one of those 'ringdingers' back home who just enjoyed the feeling of superiority over their civilian 'normie' counterparts. Still, Ben thought it more likely the man was simply just an experienced soldier, used to being respected and not at all concerned about his well-being in a poorly attended local pub.

And there was no reason the man should have been worried about his well-being. Ben was the only person in the room younger than him, and the only one who seemed remotely capable of putting up a fight if the man were to get hostile. But there was also nothing about him that suggested hostility, just as the barman had mentioned. Extreme apathy, sure. But Ben got the sense that as long as everyone there left him alone, they'd all be fine.

So Ben stood and left, and waved at the barman. He wanted to get back and spend some time FaceTiming with Julie, and he wrapped up inside his coat and walked outside.

He hit the sidewalk and prepared to turn the corner when the jingling sound of the door reached his ears.

Weird, he thought. It hadn't made that noise when he'd left the first time, so that meant —

He turned, noticing that the door was still open.

And the massive silhouette standing in it told him what he needed to know.

Great, Ben thought. *He followed me out.*

Ben had had the sneaking suspicion that the man, for some reason, had been simply waiting for Ben to leave. He hadn't so much as turned his head in Ben's direction, but still... Ben had sensed it.

He clenched his fists. *Let's hope he just wants to talk.*

"I just want to talk," the man said, his German-stilted words clipping out.

Ben stood, silent on the sidewalk.

"Walk with me?"

Ben shrugged, then took a step forward. He was now two feet in front of the man, and —

The blow caught him off-guard. Ben grunted in pain, doubling over. His lungs constricted, and he felt his insides gasping for air.

He stumbled, his hands clasping at his gut.

The man hit him again, this time right in his spleen. Ben saw stars. "What — what the hell —"

"I heard you intend to hunt tomorrow," the man said.

"What? What the f —" Ben couldn't even curse properly. He sucked in air, still hunched over on the sidewalk.

"I know what you are looking for. You will not find it because you will not be there."

Ben gasped, then stood up straight. He was finally able to find his words. "Listen, asshole. If you think you're the first jackass who's tried to intimidate me —"

One, two. The punches landed in such quick succession that Ben wasn't sure they were even from the giant of a man. But his body reacted before his brain, and Ben fell to the hard concrete sidewalk. His vision spun. *Oh, my God. He hits hard.*

Ben had been in more than a few scrapes. He'd dodged bullets, caught some, and lived to tell about it. But this was something different. This man wasn't here to *kill* him. Ben had been in fights that had lasted for no time at all — it was kill or be killed, and if either of those failed the perpetrators ran and hid.

But this was more like a street fight, something Ben wasn't intimately familiar with. It was about intimidation, scare tactics.

And Ben was starting to feel scared.

"Wh — what do you want with me?"

"You?" the man snarled. "Nothing. I want you to stay here,

where it is safe for people like you. I want you to do *nothing*. Tomorrow I will be leaving. Walking out there to hunt for it, just like you intend to do."

"Wait, what are you —"

"But I am warning you now, and I have no more time to waste on warnings: if I see you out there, I will be forced to do more than just *warn* you."

Ben was shocked, confused. And in a lot of pain. He was resilient enough to know the blows would wear off, nothing but bruises to his body and his pride to remain. But still... what the hell was this guy talking about.

He crawled around and finally stood up. "All right, bub. You made your point."

The man stared at him. Orange cast from an overhead streetlight made his hairy, pockmarked face that much more rutted and weathered.

"You're saying you're hunting for something out there. Cool. But I'm *not*."

For a flash, a brief moment, Ben thought he saw the man's expression falter. He couldn't be sure, as the light and his spinning vision were playing tricks on him.

CHAPTER 21
ELIZA

ELIZA EARNHARDT PULLED the strap of her hiking pack up higher, cinching it down to her shoulder. She loved this pack — lightweight and water-resistant, it had doubled as an overnight camping bag for numerous camping trips. She had stuffed it with essentials, as far as she could assume what essentials she'd need. Below-zero sleeping bag, extra clothing and layers, and a thin backpacking blanket were the main items.

She knew Clive Vanderstadt would be packing food for the group of three, so she had only thrown in a few of her favorite protein and energy bars and a packet of dehydrated coffee. People around here usually doubled down on tea, so she wanted to be sure she was prepared for any chilly morning they might encounter during the expedition.

Plus, she knew Harvey Bennett was a coffee drinker, and she wanted to have coffee on hand as a sort of olive branch — she hadn't told him she'd be coming along.

She saw Clive and Harvey through the break in the trees just off the road, where Clive had parked, and when her eyes met Harvey's, she knew immediately that Clive hadn't told him, either.

"What are you doing here?" Harvey asked her, his voice doing little to hide his incredulousness. She didn't sense any hostility, but she also didn't know the man well.

"I am coming along," she said, matter-of-factly.

"I... wasn't aware you were planning on that."

There was a pause, a standoff, until Clive broke the tension. "Harvey — Ben — my apologies. I did not mention it yesterday because I was not sure how you felt about a woman coming along."

Ben flashed his eyes over to Clive. *Now* there appeared to be some hostility there. "You didn't think I thought a *woman* could handle herself? Is *that* what you mean?"

Clive backed up a step. "No, I —"

"My *wife* has plenty of experience in the outdoors," Ben said. "If I ever had the impression women weren't capable of this sort of thing, I've gotten over it."

Eliza put a hand over her mouth, holding back laughter. Clive had performed admirably. "Harvey — Ben —" she said, "please don't take it out on him. We are just messing around."

Ben took a breath. "Yeah, sorry. I'm just... on edge."

She noticed for the first time that Ben looked winded. Flustered. And if she wasn't mistaken, he seemed to have bags under his eyes. "Are you okay?"

He nodded. "Yeah, I'm fine. Just had a little thing happen last night. It's all good."

"Right," Clive said. "So we are good, then. Why don't we talk about the plan?"

"Walk that direction," Ben said, pointing. "And see how long it takes to get to EKG's headquarters."

Eliza squinted, but she was still smiling. "You seem like the kind of person who makes better plans than that."

Ben started walking, but spoke over his shoulder. "No," he said. "That's also Julie. She's the planner. I'm the doer."

Clive gave Eliza a look, but she just shrugged. *Whatever is both-*

ering him really has him on edge. She set off after Ben, trying to keep up with his long, wide strides.

Eliza knew Clive and his uncle, Olaf Vanderstadt, from years before, when she and her late husband had visited the area for a back-country ski trip. They'd met and become fast friends, and Clive had even ventured into the backcountry with them on more than one occasion. She knew he was a capable mountaineer, camper, and wilderness expert, and she knew he was confident behind a weapon, as well.

She had certainly noticed the three rifles Clive was packing — one of them was intended for her, of course. She hoped they wouldn't have to use them, but she also had to admit that this week had already turned up some strange and interesting situations. First the disappearance of Alina, a girl from Grindelwald who had been away at university, and then the appearance of the three-man team of hunters — or at least, that's what the town seemed to think they were. She didn't know the men, and it seemed as though no one in town did, either.

That alone was strange. While Eliza wasn't from Grindelwald, she knew these mountain towns well — typically everyone knew everyone else, including the visiting tourists and vacationers. The pub owners, innkeepers, grocers, and service industry professionals were the first line of defense, they knew who was coming, when they would arrive, and what to expect.

No one she'd spoken to had been aware that three strange men would appear in Grindelwald this week.

No one seemed to know what they wanted while they were here, other than that they were to disembark on a hunting trip at some point.

No one seemed to know how long they'd be here.

It all added up to something fishy, and Eliza didn't like it.

Even if the men proved to be completely harmless, she didn't like any unknown variables — she intended to search out and find the

EKG company's headquarters, and then take pictures of whatever she could find there. Having extra unknown people around made that job more difficult.

She tried to control her breathing; she knew her tendencies. Thinking about her husband and his death caused her to feel anxious. Anxiety led to panic attacks, and that would not be a helpful facet to this mission.

They're just hunting, she told herself. *They're just here for the Ibex, and that's it.*

She looked up the hill toward Ben, who was hiking about twenty paces in front of her. *He's just riled up because he's serious about the mission.*

She then looked over her shoulder at Clive. He offered an innocent smile in return. She smiled back. *And then there's Clive.*

It wasn't that she thought he was a simpleton, but Clive had always just been a constant to her — nothing more, nothing less than what he presented to the world. He liked the outdoors, knew his way around a weapon and any camping gear she could throw at him, and didn't like confrontation. He seemed to embody the mindset of many of the Grindelwald inhabitants, here for life and fun and freedom and enjoyment. Anything less than those things was unacceptable.

The hill began to rise to a steeper grade, and she saw that Ben had slowed a bit. She wanted to ask him what was bothering him but knew that he would probably deflect. The most predictable thing about men, she'd learned, was that they changed the subject quickly when there truly was something bothering them.

Whatever, she thought. *As long as he's here for the mission. As long as he's as focused as I am on figuring out what EKG is up to.*

CHAPTER 22
LARS

THE SMALL MACHINE BEEPED AGAIN. Three seconds later, another beep. Two other machines around the room beeped in a discordant rhythm, different pitches and different volumes, a song both random and yet somehow coherent.

Lars looked down at the bed. It was the same bed she'd always slept in, the one their aunt and uncle had bought her when she was five years old, after she had grown out of her twin bed. She was on that same bed now, surrounded by her favorite stuffed animals and toys, even though she didn't play with any of them anymore.

The rest of the room was just as it had been back in France, save for the medical equipment and beeping machines surrounding her. The pictures were taken from her wall at home, the one with the hyenas from her favorite movie and the other with a picture she had painted four or five years ago. The walls were the exact same ocean-blue she had chosen when she moved into the room at their house, and the carpet — though not the exact carpet from that room — was the same. Lars had made sure it matched the feel and style, and the color was an exact match.

It had taken him months to source and find the carpet, rug, and other small features of the room. These tiny characteristics would be invisible to the untrained eye, but he needed the room to be perfect.

For her.

He wished there was no need for the medical equipment to be in here, but even more, he wished his sister didn't have to be in this room at all. He wished this wasn't a *replica*, that she could be back home enjoying her young life with the aunt and uncle who had raised her.

Lars' and his sister's parents had died when Lars was twelve; his sister had only been a newborn. The age gap between the two of them had made it difficult for them to bond at first, but by the time Lars was in high school she had begun looking up to him almost as a stand-in for their late father. Their aunt and uncle were busy with their own careers and had already raised their own children, so Lars ended up being somewhat of a caretaker for his sister.

As he became more and more successful, eventually working his way into a position at his grandfather's company, Lars had taken control of their personal and family life altogether. His sister adored him, and he wanted nothing in the world more than to please her.

That was all up until the accident.

Lars had just begun working for EKG when he'd gotten the news. A spinal or brain injury — the doctors hadn't been sure at the time — had rendered his sister completely comatose. Unable to talk, unable to use motor functions, unable to do anything but lie in bed, eyes closed, waiting for death.

The prognosis was dire. Doctors from around the world had examined her, and each had come back with a slightly different version of the same message: barring a miracle, she will most likely not recover. Too much damage had been done to the basal ganglia and substantia nigra; she was too long gone. Best get her to a comfortable place to live out her remaining days.

The other advice given to Lars had been to make the decision as soon as possible. No one needed to explain to him what that *decision* was: it would be his job to 'pull the plug,' and because she was barely a young woman when the accident had happened, his sister had never drawn up a will or even discussed this type of worst-case scenario.

But Lars knew he could never bring himself to pull the plug. He couldn't bear the thought of being the reason his sister passed away.

As he stared down at his sleeping girl, he wondered what she was thinking right now.

It had been almost three full years since the accident, and while the months after the accident had been nightmarish for him, he also knew he could solve the problem.

He knew there was an answer that wouldn't require him to take his sister's life.

That answer had appeared to him shortly after earning his place as head of the new division, shortly after speaking with Dr. Canavero about his early trials on mice and small mammals. It was controversial technology and an even more controversial procedure, but the medical ramifications would be groundbreaking and nothing short of profound.

If they worked.

Lars' entire existence had then transformed from one of a curious young man, working toward leveling up his career, to driven entrepreneur interested in pushing this new treatment to market as fast as possible. He wanted the recognition and fortune that would come with it, but his underlying goal was simple: save his sister's life.

As he watched her sleep, he noticed her eyes flickering behind her closed eyelids. She was dreaming, or thinking about something. Was she trying to communicate? As an ex-Army doctor, he knew enough about coma patients to know that they sometimes tried to interact with the outside world via means of tapping a finger or winking an eye open and shut. So far, his sister had done no such thing, but every day brought Lars new hope that she might begin to return back to normal.

He reached down and put her hand in his. It was small, cold. Not dead, but not quite alive, either.

"Are you warm?" he asked. "Do you need more blankets?"

A 24/7 nursing staff attended to his sister's every need, changing out sheets and dressing her in new clothing daily. She had a catheter to handle bodily functions, and a host of intravenous drips continuously regulating and monitoring her internal systems.

No expense had been spared, and nothing was out of reach for Lars. If a doctor recommended it, Lars would pay for it.

As he stood over her, Lars thought about his weakening relationship with Dietrich. The man was brilliant — truly intelligent beyond recognition — the trait that had attracted Lars to him in the first place so long ago. But where Dietrich's intelligence ended, cold, calculating rationality began. There *was* emotion in the man, but Lars had discovered that it took too much effort and energy to dig it up. He had penetrated the man's exterior chill before and found a warm, comforting companionship, but the cost was too great.

Lars' love had been pulled in two different directions, and there was no question in his mind which side was winning.

It was unfortunate for Dietrich, but Lars was doing his best to postpone the inevitable. With any luck, Dietrich wouldn't suspect that Lars was purposefully distancing himself from the relationship. The man had his spreadsheets and budget projections, and he had thrown himself into his work long before Lars' sister had slipped away, so there was nothing more Lars felt he could do to keep the relationship alive. Dietrich had committed to the company — to him and his grandfather — and there was nothing else Lars needed from him right now.

He let his sister's hand fall back to the bedside and turned a slow circle around the room. He had spent tens of thousands of dollars on two built-in lighting systems that emulated perfectly the changing daylight outside and cast it throughout the room through a fake window, complete with the original curtains and rod his sister had had in her actual room.

The ceiling above them had been reimagined from the standard drop ceiling office building-style into a plastered and finished drywall ceiling, complete with the crown molding their uncle had installed throughout his house.

It was, in every way, a perfect replica of the room. Even the square footage was the same, including the small closet near the bed, which Lars had filled with her childhood board games, wardrobe, and a few boxes full of stuffed bears she had been collecting that sat alongside the sheets and clothing the nurses used each morning.

He sighed. He knew the stakes were high — if Dr. Canavero couldn't figure out the third phase of the transference trial, everything they had worked for so far would be lost. Every purpose — his personal goal, his professional success, and his long-term fortune — would vanish overnight.

Dietrich had assured Lars that the progress they had made so far was *already* world-changing, but the man's pleas had fallen on deaf ears. Lars wanted none of it unless he could have all of it. He needed his sister back, or it was all for naught.

He took another deep breath, glanced down at his young sister breathing slowly on the bed, longing to hear her voice once again. It was heartbreaking, but he was going to find the answer. He was going to solve the problem no one in history had yet been able to solve.

His team was the best in the world, his resources were virtually unlimited, and there was nothing standing in the way of their success....

Except for time and fate itself.

CHAPTER 23
BEN

BEN and the team planned to camp the first night at about the three-quarters mark from where they believe the edge of the company's headquarters to be. They'd climbed for most of the day over gently sloping terrain, their boots crunching through hard-packed snow and over fallen pine branches.

It was beautiful country, and during the moments the trees opened up and allowed for a view back down the ridge, Ben could see the quaint and precious town of Grindelwald off in the distance. Small farmhouses and dwellings pumped smoke into the air from their chimneys, and he could see cars and bicycles milling about as the small city went on in its business.

He made a mental note for the fifth time that trip that he'd have to bring Julie back here.

The walk also made Ben feel a bit better about his encounter with the huge hunter from the inn. His back was still a bit sore, but the rest of the pummeling had worn off. He was still perturbed that he'd allowed the man to get the jump on him, but the fresh air and picturesque scenery had pushed his worries aside.

He was going to stop whatever it was EKG was doing to torment this place. He'd made the promise to Eliza, and he had made it to himself.

He wasn't afraid of some macho hunter, and he wasn't afraid of confrontation. If that idiot wanted to mess with him and play tough guy, Ben had gone a few rounds with people just like that before.

Besides, what was he going to do? Shoot at them?

They made camp beneath another open sky, this one ringed by a perfect circle of trees that formed a protective border around them. Clive and Eliza rolled a few larger rocks and small boulders into a smaller ring and cleared the snow and debris inside to prepare a fire. Ben collected fallen timber for firewood.

Within minutes of stopping they had a fire lit, and all were clearing snowy ground down to the dirt to use as seats. They would sleep under the stars, cowboy style, bundled up and protected from the elements by laying their bags on tarps and rolling in the edges. It wasn't going to keep rain or snow away, but there was none in the forecast.

They weren't worried about predators, either. In this area of the country there really were none. The few bear sightings over the past fifteen years hadn't given any of them cause for concern, and besides, they were all armed.

They did need a bit more wood, however, so Ben told them he was going to make a few concentric circles around their campsite looking for downed logs and trees. He took Clive's hatchet with him and a flashlight and began his search.

The sun had set, and the temperature was dropping quickly. There was hardly any humidity, so the air held no moisture to maintain the warmer temperature. He shivered, trying to force out the cold. He was large, wide, and typically ran hot, but he was having a difficult time staying warm today. He longed for his sleeping bag next to the fire — there was something pure and satisfying about sleeping out under the stars with a bag and the heat from the fire to keep him warm.

He shivered again, then tucked his neck and head down into the open flap of his jacket. He had a scarf, but it was tied to the outside of his pack back at camp. He'd only walked a few feet into the tree line, about twenty paces away from the others, but it was already dark and nearly impossible to see in the forest.

He shined his light downward at the ground in front of him as he walked, careful to step only on the packed areas of snowfall. He didn't want to have to brush off the snow from landing a foot in one of the deeper, fluffier snowbanks that rose up the trunks of the nearby trees.

A few motions caught his eye. He stopped, expecting a rabbit or bird to fly out from a hiding spot that he'd disturbed, but nothing came. He realized then that it had been a shadow, one cast either from his own flashlight or from the distant blaze of the fire. He stared at the spot for another few seconds, just in case it wasn't actually —

There.

Movement again. *No.* It wasn't *movement*, but his eyes were still playing tricks on him. It wasn't movement he'd seen, but something out of place. His subconscious had alerted him to the strange, out of place item his eyes had fallen upon and processed, but it had taken conscious effort and study to realize that he was looking at something that didn't belong.

Ben stepped toward it. It was off in a snowbank, but he didn't care. He fell through the snow, happy to find that it was only a few inches deeper. It had been some time since Grindelwald and the surrounding area had gotten any major snowfall. He crunched the snow beneath his feet and walked toward the object.

It came into view as his flashlight danced over the figure. It was larger than he thought. Or, rather, the object he'd seen was *part* of something much larger than what he'd initially thought.

He stared down, not believing what his eyes were seeing. Ben squinted as his light traveled over the thing.

What the...

He crouched a bit, letting his flashlight hand rest on his bent knee. He shone the light directly at the base of the large pine, then let it travel down over...

He stumbled, falling backward in the snow. His butt landed in the soft powder, but he shuffled backward even more, faster.

He tried to yell, but only a grunt came up. He dropped the flash-light in the snow, and he was immediately sorry for it. The light glanced off the object, now fully revealed, now fully extended and shadow, its tendril-like fragments jutting up and arching onto the tree trunk.

It seemed to be alive, but Ben knew it was still his mind playing tricks. His eyes adjusted, realizing that it was the light and the shadows that were putting on a show for him. He swallowed, then tried yelling again.

"H — hey! Clive, Eliza — get over here!"

One of them called back.

"Now!" he shouted. "Come quick. I found something."

He heard their footsteps landing heavily over the packed earth and snow as they ran. He reached for the flashlight with his right hand once again, lifting it up and pointing it back at the thing at the base of the tree. He couldn't focus, as there was too much to focus on. Too many pieces...

Eliza was there. "What'd you —"

Her breath caught in her throat. She stepped up next to Ben, and he tried to stop the shaking of the light so they both could see better.

"Oh my God," Clive's voice said from directly behind Ben and Eliza. "Is that..."

"Yeah," Ben said. "It is. I think."

CHAPTER 24
ELIAS

ELIAS ZIEGLER WAS TIRED. He wasn't exhausted, nor was he physically in need of sleep, but he was mentally drained. He had been trying to solve the puzzle for over a week, every day since he had come to this small village in Switzerland. He had been to the country before, but it had been years since he'd spent any amount of time here.

A native of Germany, he had grown up with a Nazi sympathizer for a grandfather and a father conflicted by his own political beliefs: he hated everything the Nazi party stood for and had wanted to completely sever himself and his family from the German elite. Thankfully it was two decades after the war, so his father had had no trouble cutting ties with their past and moving their family to Poland.

Elias and his brother grew up in Poland, but bounced around the European continent as his father, a mechanic by trade, looked for work. Elias Ziegler had become somewhat of an apprentice to his father, learning the craft and skill individually growing fond of anything related to machines.

Elias eventually traded his own freedom for service in the

German army, spending eight years there as an aircraft mechanic, and eventually becoming a GSG-9 operative.

He was trained not only in deconstructing and rebuilding machines but also in deconstructing the inner workings of human beings. It had been his specialty as an operative, and he had been tapped on more than one occasion to study and infiltrate an enemy compound in order to remove a specific person of interest from the playing field.

In other words, he was a hunter, plain and simple.

And he was very good at his job.

But he was tired now. Tired of trying to figure out what the hell these men wanted him to hunt. Tired of trying to interpret their coded speech they used when they thought he wasn't listening. Tired of receiving new information late in the game — namely hearing that there was now a new party involved in the hunt.

He had spoken with one of the members of this new party last night. The man was large, strong and resilient. But Elias was not surprised to find out that the man was no fighter — he had hardly tried to hit back when Elias punched him in the gut. Elias had had no trouble at all taking the man to the ground, and he knew he could have done much worse if the situation had called for it.

But he only wanted to send a message. His entire purpose was scaring the man, proving to the man that whatever they thought they were looking for out here was not something that should be bothered with.

He wasn't above jobs like this; he had warned off plenty of other people from similar hunts. But he was absolutely tired of having his plans changed every step of the way, of discovering new information and then being forced to act on it.

He looked over the small, flickering fire at the two men that were accompanying him. He despised one of them and simply couldn't stand the other. The trouble was, he wasn't sure which was which half of the time. He went from being annoyed to downright hating each of the men back and forth over the course of the day. They were weak, inexperienced.

Sure, the younger man named Lars — the assistant to the older man named Roger Dietrich — claimed to have training and experience and could start a decent fire, but Elias could see through his practiced exterior. He saw the man's perfectly manicured fingernails, his soft hands, and his porcelain skin that had barely touched the elements. He saw it in the way the man carried his pack, and in the way he stepped daintily over stones and logs across their path.

The man was an imposter, Elias was sure of it. He may have been the assistant to the banker-type man, but he was no true outdoorsman.

Which meant that Elias now had to babysit both of them. He had no illusion that his contract did not include keeping both of the men alive, but he did feel that collecting on the contract would be much more difficult if he returned without both of his companions.

So, he was tired. Tired of dealing with all of this. He wondered if he were just growing old, becoming the curmudgeon he remembered his grandfather had become. There was a time in Elias's life when he would have done just about anything to sleep out here, in the open under the stars, but now he longed for the comfort of a soft bed and a fresh cup of coffee prepared for him the next morning.

"Deep in thought, I presume?" the man across the fire from him, Dietrich, asked.

Elias answered with a simple raise of a single eyebrow. Dietrich would have to lean nearly over the fire in order to see it, Elias wasn't interested in starting a conversation anyway.

"May I ask what it is exactly you *are* thinking of?"

Elias considered responding with, *no, you may not*, but instead just grunted.

"He is upset we still have not told him what it is we are searching for," Lars said from Elias's right side. "I think perhaps it is time we —
"

"He misses home," Dietrich said. "Poland? Is that right? Or do you still claim Germany as your homeland?"

Elias wanted to pick up a handful of coals and toss it into the man's face, but he restrained himself. "I am German, from Poland."

He didn't care how confusing the statement might sound to the other Europeans.

"And there is no one waiting for you back at home, is there not?"

Elias grunted in response. He stood up. "I need to pee."

He walked to the spot almost out of sight of the fire they had started and relieved himself. He gazed off into the darkness of the woods, allowing his eyes and his mind to focus. As he unzipped his pants, he noticed a flicker, a tiny orange light.

He knew where they were; he had studied the area and had been climbing around it for the past week. He knew there was nothing out here; no buildings, no houses, nothing that would be able to create a light.

Which meant it was a fire. Which meant the man he had met last night had not heeded his warning.

Elias let out a breath, a long, deep sigh. He was going to have to warn this man once more, and this time he was going to have to ensure that the warning stuck.

CHAPTER 25
BEN

THE TRUTH WAS it was hard to see precisely *what* the thing was. Ben's light was quickly joined by one Clive pulled out of a pocket, and together the two men shone their lights on the object at the base of the tree trunk. Eliza stepped over to it, then began pushing around with a stick she'd found.

A piece of hard, crusted fabric fell off a protrusion on the object and Eliza jumped back. "It's a... it's a..."

"It's a body," Ben said.

"It *was* a body."

He nodded. Ben had seen dead bodies before, even fresh ones, but this was something else entirely. He had no doubt it was the body of a fully grown human, but it had been completely and utterly shredded. The head was barely recognizable — the skull had been seemingly split in half by some incredible force against the tree itself, and the rest of the body was equally mangled.

Half-buried in snow that had once been white, the entire mess was barely noticeable in the darkness. The blood-stained body and snow around it had simply melted into the background setting, causing the whole terrifying thing to be nearly indistinguishable from the forest around it.

Until they had light on it.

Then the body became real. Ben stared down at it after being helped back to his feet by Eliza.

"It looks like it's been... eaten."

"Or just decimated. Doesn't seem like the animal bit into it at all."

Ben looked at Clive as he spoke, hoping the professional hunter would have something to offer. But what Clive had said didn't make sense. "I don't get it," Ben said. "What animal? What could do this?"

Clive shrugged. "That is what I am trying to piece together as well," he said. "I don't know of any animals in this area that could do such a thing."

"What animal could do this in general?" Eliza asked.

"The corpse is uneaten," Clive said. "The flesh is still there. Completely ripped to shreds, but it is there nonetheless."

Ben held a forearm over his mouth. He'd been hunting before, and he'd had plenty of run-ins with creatures large enough to kill a grown man, but he wasn't seeing anything here that made sense to him.

It looked like a senseless murder.

The arms of the man were each resting at an angle to either side of the torso, still attached but mostly buried beneath the snow. They formed a straight line from hand to hand, as if the man had died falling backward and trying to catch himself.

But that's where Ben's assumptions ended. He couldn't figure out the rest.

The man's chest cavity had been split open, the ribs wrenched backward and stretched apart, as if the animal had been trying to open it up and climb inside. It was one of these ribs — broken and jagged and pointing straight up at the tree — that Ben had seen first. It had looked like a stick in the darkness, but one that had an unnaturally smooth exterior.

Most of the ribs still had clothing and pieces of skin and flesh attached, and it was one of these small ribbons of clothing that had fallen off when Eliza had moved it. Everything was half-frozen, half-buried. Dried blood was everywhere.

"Clive," Ben asked again. "What predators could do this to a man?"

Clive looked at them with large eyes. "A bear? Wolves, maybe? But I do not think they could stretch the ribs apart like that and..." he trailed off.

Eliza picked up the thread. "Not a wolf, and there aren't bears around here. And I don't think a bear could rip open a man's chest. I mean, you'd have to have hands that could grip like that, and I don't see claw marks."

Ben shuddered, shivering again. This time it wasn't due to the cold.

Whatever was out here, whatever had done this...

He didn't want to think about the rest.

"It's still out here," Clive said. "It didn't do this to eat the guy. This was something different. Purposeful, even."

Ben glanced at Eliza. She met his eyes for a brief moment, then looked away. She took a few steps to the side, distancing herself from the two men. Ben stood there, watching, wondering what in the world he could say or ask that would help make sense of the situation.

Instead, his eyes caught something swinging from one of the tree branches higher up. He reached for it but found that it was just beyond his fingertips.

"Find something?" Clive asked.

"I don't know. Here," he said, handing his flashlight to Clive. Ben jumped, grabbing the tiny rectangular thing with an outstretched hand and yanking it down off the branch. It fell with a snap, followed by a piece of the branch, which landed just next to the corpse.

"What is it?" Eliza asked.

Ben turned it over a few times in his hands. It had been attached to a lanyard, which had been strewn up into the branch. The lanyard piece had pulled completely off, but Ben was holding what the lanyard had been intended for. Plastic, rectangular, with rounded corners. One side was blank except for a thin black stripe that ran the length of the card.

"It's an ID badge," Ben said. Clive moved closer and pointed one of his flashlights down at the face of the badge. "Grigor something. I can't read the last name. It's been scratched off. But it also says —"

"Grayson, GmbH," Eliza said. "*Gesellschaft mit beschränkter Haftung*. The equivalent of an American *LLC*. Looks like this guy, Grigor, worked for some German company."

Besides the magnetic stripe, there was nothing on the back of the identification badge. Ben was careful to check for small, hard to read print or anything that might give them more clues. Satisfied there were none, Ben shoved the ID into his back pocket.

He looked up at his traveling partners. "What now?"

He didn't want to voice his concern. He didn't want to say aloud what he was worried about. Unfortunately, he had a feeling the others were worried about the exact same thing.

"EKG had something to do with this," Clive said, matter-of-factly. He stared into Ben's eyes. "It seems as though there may be more to this story than you have told us."

Ben's mouth dropped open, and his eyes widened. "*Me*? She's the one who brought me into this whole mess. If you think I'm holding out on you, feel free to march back into town and —"

"Enough, enough," Eliza said. She placed her hand on Ben's arm and mirrored the motion with Clive. "Listen to me, right now."

Ben and Clive looked at her.

"I told you. I warned you both before you ever started this mission that EKG is involved with some things they have no business being involved with."

"But if you knew —" Ben started to protest.

"I assure you," Eliza said, "this is new to me. Whatever this is — whatever killed this man — I had no idea it had gotten to this point. Besides that, we have no proof that EKG is involved here, with this man's death. Grayson, GmbH could be some sort of security firm, or it could be just a company they hired to keep their grounds. We don't know. But I do know this: I brought you out here because I believe EKG is doing something the world will want to know about, something that we might be able to stop. I still think that's true."

"So, you're going to keep going?" Ben asked.

Eliza looked at him, long and hard. He felt her eyes boring into him, questioning him silently. He knew what she was thinking, and he knew what she was going to ask.

"You know damn well that I'm going to keep going, then," she said, finally. "Are you going to help me?"

CHAPTER 26
ELIZA

THE REST of the evening resumed uneventfully, although Eliza knew the two men, just like her, were replaying the events that had transpired over and over in their minds. In truth, it terrified her. Whatever was out there, whatever had killed that man, was still around.

Clive seemed to think the man had been killed only days ago, judging by the lack of deterioration and decomposition of the body. She had to admit it seemed plausible, as she couldn't find any decay on the parts of the body that remained intact.

But that was just it: the entire upper half of the body had been destroyed, decimated. Besides the man's arms, which were stretched out into that strange, perfectly straight diagonal line, his chest and head had been worked through by some unknown force, one greater than what any of the three of them could have ever imagined. At the same time, it didn't seem like a machine had done the job. Whatever it was had been alive, organic. It had been some kind of animal.

Some kind of creature.

Eliza thought about the images on her phone, the ones she had shown Ben. *Could EKG really have created something so sadistic? Could they have performed some sort of strange, macabre surgery?* It seemed implausible, unnatural. But the results seemed to speak for themselves.

Eliza shook off the thoughts. They needed to focus now on the task at hand and not dwell on the terrors of the past. She thought of her husband, the reason she was doing all of this.

No, that wasn't true.

She was doing it for him, sure. But now, after years of working toward their ultimate shared goal, she had changed. She was no longer a tagalong, no longer working toward his dream.

Her husband's dream had become her own. It had become hers. She felt it, deep inside herself. The truth of it all that she needed to find. She understood now what had driven him. When once she had been satisfied to be driven by his goals and dreams, she now felt them for herself, adopted them as her own.

She was a zealot for her cause, just as her husband had been. She hoped now that she could persuade the others, Ben and Clive, to take up her cause as well.

They'd stayed up for another few hours around the warmth of the fire, until it began to die down. They spoke of the past, of her late husband and Ben's wife, Julie. It had taken some egging, but she and Clive had been able to extract a bit about how Ben and Julie had met. An incident at Yellowstone National Park back in the United States a few years ago had brought them together, Ben a ranger at the park and Julie working for the CDC in a new program called the Biological Threat Research Division.

Eliza had gotten the sense that Ben was a bit reclusive, the type of man who didn't want to open up freely. Her instincts had proven correct when she had asked about Ben's family. When she'd asked about his parents, he just shrugged and said they had passed years ago.

He mentioned he had a younger brother but didn't offer any more details when pressed on it.

For their part, Eliza and Clive had shared freely, even laughing over stories of camping trips with their families that had gone awry. All in all, the night had proceeded well enough, and by the time they went to sleep, Eliza felt satisfied that the terrors of hours ago had been safely locked away in the recesses of their memories.

She'd slept soundly, surprisingly. Something about the warmth of her body with the cool air on her exposed face always made her feel cozy when sleeping outdoors. It also didn't hurt that they had passed around a flask of some sort of whiskey that Clive had snuck into his backpack.

When the light of the morning poked into Eliza's eyelids and forced them open, she was rested and ready to get up. She stretched in her bag, her arms above her head, then rolled to her left side. She blinked a few times, looking at Ben, in his own sleeping bag.

His eyes were open, staring at her.

It was startling, abrupt. She immediately sat up.

"Sorry," Ben said, smiling. "You seemed like you were sleeping so peacefully; I didn't want to wake you. I just woke up myself. Have to pee, but it's really nice and warm in here."

She laughed at that, then rolled over to check on the other member of their party.

She saw Clive's sleeping bag, but it was flat and empty.

"He left about 15 minutes ago," Ben said. "He has some stuff for breakfast that will go bad by tomorrow, so we thought we would cook it up and then head out in about an hour. He went to go find a few more sticks to get the fire going."

She nodded, pulling herself up into a sitting position and brushing the leaves off the back of her head. "Okay," she said. "As long as there's bacon, I'm sure we can take an extra hour."

She noticed Ben arching his eyebrows at her, a playful expression on his face.

"What?" She asked.

"Nothing," Ben shrugged. "And here I had you pegged as one of those vegetarians or vegans or whatever."

"'*Vegetarians or vegans or whatever*?' Those aren't the same thing, you know."

Ben feigned a look of being hurt, holding his palms up. "Easy now," he said. "Any friend of bacon is a friend of mine."

She smiled back at him just as he turned and exited his sleeping bag. He stepped out, completely naked but for a pair of boxer shorts. He rummaged around on the ground, looking for his jeans and plaid long-sleeved shirt. When he found them, he began hopping around, trying to slide his leg into the pants.

Eliza arched an eyebrow. For as large a man as he was, Eliza hadn't expected him to be so... fit. His back had a perfect V-shape to it, his shoulders wide and muscular. His waist wasn't narrow, but it also wasn't overweight, either. His thighs and legs were lean and strong, and she wondered how many of these "missions" he and the CSO had been on.

She had interacted with career soldiers before on occasion, and Ben would have fit in with any of them.

Ben turned and saw her examining him. He didn't blush, but it did seem like he began putting his shirt on much quicker.

She was about to apologize and try to pretend as though she wasn't just checking out a married man, when she heard a noise off to her right in the woods.

Footsteps. Running.

CHAPTER 27
ELIZA

"HEY!"

It was Clive's voice, and he sounded breathless, in a hurry.

He yelled again, and Eliza was on her feet a moment later. She had slept fully clothed, so she threw her hiking boots on over her socks and began tying them as Clive burst out of the tree line and into their camp.

"Whoa, buddy," Ben said. "What's going on? You okay?"

Clive was alternating between shaking his head and nodding, trying to catch his breath. He dropped a handful of large sticks toward the fire pit, then placed his hands on his knees and breathed a few deep breaths.

"An - another one," he said, his voice barely above a whisper. "Another one. Back there. Up the hill a bit."

Eliza noticed that his words had reverted to his native German, so she translated for Ben. "Where?" She asked. "Point to it."

Clive didn't turn around, but he pointed over his shoulder up the hill.

"Another... *body*?" Ben asked. "Like the one we saw last night?"

Clive nodded, slowly at first but then more rapidly as he grew more fearful once again. "Yes, yes. Just like the one from last night. I saw it; this time, it wasn't buried under snow. This time..."

Eliza glanced at Ben, who was looking straight at Clive. He finished Clive's sentence for him. "This time, it was fresh. Is that what you mean?"

Clive looked at Eliza, and she immediately saw the pure, sheer terror in his eyes. The younger man seemed one wrong word away from breaking in half. She stared at him, waiting.

Finally, he spoke again. "Yes," he said, whispering once again. His eyes glistened. "He - or she, it's impossible to tell - is even less recognizable. But they died the same way: their upper body, their torso. Ripped apart, opened up, like... like..." he fell to his knees and Ben was there immediately, holding him by his elbow and shoulder.

Eliza walked toward him. "Clive, we need to see him. The body. We need to know if it had anything to do with EKG, or that Grayson company. Can you take us there?"

Clive was shaking now, his face a contorted mask of pain and fury and confusion. He looked possessed, intensely demonized.

"It's okay," Ben said, helping Clive to his feet. "Eliza and I can go. We don't all need to. If you want to just wait here at camp, you can point us in the direction of —"

"No!" Clive yelled. He looked around frantically; then his eyes landed back on Eliza and Ben. He calmed himself down, taking a few seconds to breathe. "No," he said again, softer. "I don't — if it's all right with you two, I mean, I'd rather not be out here alone."

Ben nodded, and Eliza understood. This man was a trained and professional hunter, someone who had spent countless nights in the dark, hiking and waiting and sleeping in a land that was not his own. He had seen and done things most people never would, and yet here he was, in broad daylight, whimpering.

She understood, and she didn't fault him for it. Truth be told, a part of her believed that last night's encounter was just a fluke, something random and strange, and yet something unrelated to their mission. She *wanted* it to be an accident, just a strange and terrible coincidence.

But now she knew the truth.

Now she knew that what they were up against was not just a corporation and its inhumane experimentations.

Now she knew that they were up against something very real, something that had been set loose for one singular purpose: to kill.

The creature was not eating its prey, nor did the deaths seem accidental. Eliza knew better than to buy into wishful thinking. They had stepped behind enemy lines, and they now had gone from being the hunters to being the hunted.

She vowed not to leave either Clive or Ben behind, anywhere. As long as these men were committed to the mission that she had assigned them, she committed to pushing forward as a team.

This beast, this creature, killed what appeared to be people who had been alone. If they stuck together, remained as a unit, they might be able to overwhelm it. Better, it might feel as though it wasn't worth the effort.

The hairs on the back of her neck rose as she thought about the implications.

It killed again, and recently, she thought. *That means it is definitely still out there. It means it is still hunting, still searching for whatever it is it wants to find.*

She shuddered.

It means it could be watching us right now.

"Let's head out," Ben said. "We can use the extra time to check out the crime scene and see if there's anything to gain from it."

Eliza nodded. "I agree," she said. "If there's any chance we can figure out something in common between the two incidents, we might be able to prevent it from happening again."

She didn't feel comfortable adding the line, *happening to us.*

Ben was already rolling up his sleeping bag and stuffing it into his small pack. "So much for the bacon," he said. He tried to put on a smile, but Eliza could tell it wasn't worn genuinely.

"Let's just figure this out and get going," she said. "Chances are we find a place to stop early tonight, since headquarters is probably just over that ridge. The bacon should still be good by then since the weather is supposed to hold and be pretty cold most of the day."

Clive seemed satisfied by this plan, and he hiked up his pack and turned toward the forest, inhaling a deep, long breath. She noticed that he was also clutching the rifle he had mounted to the side of his pack. If she had to guess, she thought the rifle would be in his hands, loaded and at the ready, before too long.

She and Ben were also armed, and she wondered if it might be a smart idea to be prepared for anything.

She opened her mouth to voice that concern when a sharp *crack* sounded in the distance. If she wasn't mistaken, it sounded like —

"Run!" Ben shouted. "That was a gun, and it's shooting in our direction!"

She and Clive didn't need to be told twice. Both of them, followed closely behind by Ben, began running toward the tree line.

Great, she thought. *Now there are two things out here trying to kill us.*

CHAPTER 28
BEN

THEY RAN AS THOUGH their lives depended on it. For all Ben knew, their lives *did* depend on it. He felt as though they had jumped out of the proverbial fire pan, and they were now racing for their lives against not one but two unknown and unseen forces.

He wasn't sure the shot was directed toward them, but he knew the sound of a gunshot better than most. He'd heard the round zinging through the trees, slapping into the trunk of one just past their campsite. It didn't take a genius to figure out where the shot had come from and where it had landed — and, thus, that they were standing directly in the line of fire.

Either the other hunters, including the one that had decided to make a very physical point to Ben two nights ago, had found this creature or something else worth shooting at...

...or they were shooting at him.

Their route twisted through and around trees, over fallen timber and boulders, and higher up the ridge. There was more snow here, and Ben's feet soon began to fall more heavily, deeper into the lightly packed snow that had fallen at some point in the past few months. They were still well below the tree line, but it would only be a matter of time before their cover was blown and they were slowed to a crawl.

He hoped it wouldn't come to that. He hoped they would be able to continue toward the EKG headquarters and keep their attackers to the left, to the north. He hoped they had been shooting at movement, thinking them some sort of game or wild animal or the creature that had attacked the other men itself.

He could hope, but he also had a pretty well-developed gut instinct about this sort of thing. He was no soldier, had no military experience other than what his best friend Reggie had taught him. But real-life experience often paid more significant dividends than its video game or textbook counterparts, and he had plenty of that. Ben was no stranger to being targeted and shot at, and even though he didn't like the feeling, he knew how to defend himself.

They needed shelter.

A crack shot through a bunch of trees more than 200 yards out would require intense concentration, plenty of skill, and no shortage of luck unless the shooter were a trained sniper. The man he'd met at the bar two nights ago seemed as though he might fit that description, but there was no way to tell. There was just as good a chance the man was simply a grunt, someone with a grudge, a gun, and a reason to use it.

He wasn't surprised that the man's shot had missed, but he was surprised the man hadn't taken a second or third shot. If his team were in fact the target, surely the shooter would have taken three or four potshots, just in case one of them landed.

Was it a warning, then? Ben considered this. It could very well be that whoever had shot in their direction just wanted to warn them off, similar to what the man had done two nights ago. He certainly had come on strong, not hesitating to lean into his point and give it the physical backing he thought it deserved. This, like that night, could have been a similar show of strength.

And now that they had seen and heard of at least two instances of brutal murder out here on EKG land, Ben was coming around to the man's side: it seemed as though there was something to warn them away from. Perhaps the man had been correct after all. Coming out here was not a good idea.

But then why wouldn't they just fire their weapon in another direction, or at least diagonally, off to their side, so there was no chance a stray bullet would strike one of them? A warning shot from a rifle was no laughing matter, no matter the direction the shooter initially intended.

These unanswered questions plagued Ben's mind as they ran. He was thankful the other two were in shape and could handle the slog through the deeper snow, and he was grateful he was in shape enough not to need to stop and rest after five minutes of travel. He was large, well over 200 pounds, but he carried his weight well. He had trained with his wife and his friends in climates much like this one, with thin air and plenty of ground resistance.

They did eventually slow, but it was after about half an hour of jogging. Eliza, in the lead, held up a hand and began walking as they entered a large, wide clearing.

"It will take too long to go around," she said. Pointing downhill to the north. "And my best guess is that the shooter was down there anyway, so I have no interest in getting closer to them."

“Agreed,” Ben said. “I have a hunch I know who it is, and if it’s true, they might be heading the same direction we are.”

Eliza looked at him as if he had just revealed a secret that completely changed the trajectory of their mission. In truth, it was a secret that Ben had held close to his chest, but it didn’t change anything. If the man who had confronted him outside the pub was the same man who was firing upon them, it didn’t make Ben want to curl up and hide.

It made Ben want to push faster, to figure out what it was, exactly, the huge, hairy man was hoping to keep from them.

Ben waved off her glance. “We can talk about it later,” he said. “We need to get somewhere safe, somewhere defensible.”

“I agree with that,” Clive said, speaking for the first time in the past half-hour. "Get me somewhere I can set up and not worry about my six. They won't be able to come near us."

Ben had to hand it to him. The man was understandably shaken up by the two brutal deaths he had seen out here, but he still had the poise and demeanor of someone who did not appreciate being attacked in broad daylight.

"The ridge rises to some cliffs up ahead," Eliza said. "My husband and I used to practice on these boulders long ago. I think those were even on the route we took when he..."

She didn't finish her sentence, but Ben gazed in the direction she was looking. He saw the cliffs, poking out from just above the trees. They were still a half-mile or three-quarters of a mile away, but they could reach that quickly.

He knew she was probably not excited about traversing the same ground she had traversed with her now-dead husband, but he also knew there was no choice. Large rocks and boulders would be a perfect place to set up and defend their position if they were to be attacked once again.

Ben tightened the straps of his pack and began marching forward toward the cliffs. Eliza continued as well, maintaining the lead, while Clive drifted back behind Ben. They formed a line as they tromped through the woods and over the snow-covered ground.

Getting to the cliffs would put them within half-day of the headquarters, according to Eliza's estimates. It would also give them the opportunity to rest, to talk through what they had seen and heard, and get them prepared for whatever might be confronting them tonight.

And, Ben couldn't ignore the fact that it might get them some of that bacon Clive claimed to be holding somewhere on his person.

CHAPTER 29
BEN

THEY REACHED a shallow cave nestled at the base of the cliffs without anyone shooting at them again. Ben was growing weary, his legs on fire and his lungs aching with the exertion. A hike, even one through terrain such as this, would hardly be enough for him to feel the exhaustion, but the added pressure of knowing someone was out there hunting for them made all the difference.

He could tell the others were tired as well. They reached the cave and simply collapsed on the ground. They removed their packs, and Clive began handing out strips of homemade jerky. Ben washed his down with a long sip of water from a canteen, and only after 15 minutes of rest and catching their breath did they begin to look around.

“It looks shallow, not much here,” Eliza said.

"Yes," Clive said with a mouthful of jerky. "I noticed an offshoot about 15 yards back. Could be a smaller room off of that, but otherwise, it seems like it shrinks down and closes about twenty paces behind us."

Ben shined his flashlight down into the mouth of the cave and saw what Clive was referring to. They would have to examine everything before hunkering down for the night, but Ben felt confident they were alone in the cave.

If they were going to be ambushed and attacked, it would have happened already.

Still, he didn't complain when Clive began setting up a small perch behind a boulder near the mouth of the cave. Clive retrieved one of the assault rifles and set it, loaded, next to the boulder, pointing outward. He placed two additional magazines next to the gun and then sat against the wall of the cave next to his weapon.

It was a simple but effective defensive position. Ben knew it took some times up to dozens of seconds to get a weapon prepped and ready for an attack. More if the one being attacked was surprised or scared. Ben himself had been in numerous firefights and knew how long it could take to mount a counterattack, even when his weapons were already loaded and ready to go. By setting the weapon out and at the ready, Clive was ensuring he would have as little work as possible to begin firing back if someone decided to take potshots at them in the cave.

Ben decided it was probably smart to check out the rear portion of the cave as well, just in case someone was lying in wait for them. He stood and walked toward the offshoot section, holding his flashlight with one hand and his sidearm with the other. He had checked and rechecked the Heckler & Koch pistol and tested its weight in his hand. He was no expert, but he had held enough of them to know his preferences and his limitations. The heavier pistols tended to fly high, while anything smaller than a .357 in his hands typically was simply hard to aim at all.

This one felt right, but more importantly, this was the one he was carrying now. It would have to do.

He wished his friend Reggie were here. He wondered what the man was doing — he assumed Reggie was cavorting around with Dr. Sarah Lindgren, his on-again, off-again fling who had worked with

CSO a year ago. They were both good people, and Ben would have been more than happy to have either of them along now.

Most of all, he missed Julie. She was back in their cabin outside of Anchorage, hopefully looking down on him right now. He didn't have any cell service, but he knew she and Mr. E were capable of all sorts of technological wizardry.

Eliza had stayed near the mouth of the cave with Clive, working on building a small nest in which they could put their fire later. Alone, Ben stepped cautiously around the corner of the cave, entering the smaller room.

His breath caught in his throat when he saw what was waiting for him.

He forced himself to breathe. *Take a step back,* he told himself. *You expected this.*

The truth was, he *should* have expected this, but he didn't. They had already found two dead bodies, part of him figured there would be no more to discover out here.

The other part of him knew the truth: they had already discovered two bodies; they would probably discover many more.

This body, the third, was similar to the first he had seen. One of its arms was splayed outward, nearly horizontally in proportion to its body. The other was... not attached.

Ben drew his breath and stepped into the room, intent on getting a closer look. He wanted to turn around and run back to the mouth of the cave, ignoring all of this and pretending like it didn't exist, but he knew Clive and Eliza were counting on him.

He steadied himself and pointed his flashlight down at the scene. This one's face was still mostly intact, and he could tell that it, too, was that of a man. His feet were still straight, lying calmly on the stone floor as if the man had died in his sleep.

But Ben could quickly see that he had not died in his sleep. Or if he had, the man had not died peacefully.

His chest had been split from the neck to the belly, and intestines and organs spilled outward onto the rock. The ribs were mostly intact, but they had been spread apart and looked like wings rising from the man's torso. A slick of blood covered everything, making it difficult to make out more details.

Ben forced himself to step over the man's outstretched legs and toward the far wall, where the corpse's arm was pointing. He flicked the flashlight around near the base of the wall and then found it.

The other arm.

The man's arm had been completely severed at the shoulder, ripped from its mount and tossed over here into the corner of the room. It looked as though it had hit the wall and splattered to the floor as if it were reaching back for its still-attached counterpart.

Ben was disgusted, unsure of what to do or say. He would have to tell Eliza and Clive, but he wasn't sure how the younger man would react.

He was about to turn around and head out of the room when he noticed one final detail he'd missed before. He stepped over closer to the arm and reached down to pick up the object.

It was a rifle, single action. Not like one of the select-fire assault rifles his team was carrying, but a simpler, older model. He examined the gun, looking for any signs of wear or damage. As far as he could tell, there was none.

Had this person even tried to fire back? Had they tried to defend themselves? It was impossible to tell, but it did seem as though the rifle had been simply discarded to the side, tossed aside by either the man or his attacker. *But why? Had the attack been so swift and sudden it had been impossible to prepare?*

These were questions Ben couldn't answer; questions he didn't *want* to answer.

He looked around for more evidence, specifically anything that might point to this man's involvement with either EKG or Grayson. He found nothing useful; the man hadn't been carrying a wallet or identification of any kind.

Ben backpedaled out of the room and began to turn around when he nearly bumped into Eliza.

"What is it?" Eliza asked, clearly reading the concerned expression on Ben's face.

Ben swallowed.

"Another body?"

He nodded.

CHAPTER 30
BEN

"I AM NOT SLEEPING HERE," Clive said, looking up at them.

Ben had walked with Eliza back to the mouth of the cave where Clive was waiting, playing defense. He looked down at the younger man and explained what was going on; what he had found. Unsurprisingly, Clive had not been terribly excited to hear the news.

"Clive," Eliza said, "he is dead. He can't hurt us now."

"Trust me, I am not worried about *him* hurting us. I am worried about what did that to him."

Yeah, Ben thought. *You and me both*. "We are as prepared here as anywhere. There's only one way in and out of the cave and if all three of us are defending it there's no way anyone gets in."

He didn't say what he knew was on all of their minds: whatever had done this to three bodies was most likely not human. Therefore it was impossible to actually know whether or not the three of them *could* defend their position against the thing.

"Does not matter," Clive said. "I am not sleeping here. Not next to a dead man."

"Clive, if you leave the cave now, alone, you might *become* a dead man."

Ben looked around at his team. Clive was huddled on the floor of the cave, looking up at the rest of them. Ben knew how he felt. The man was young, inexperienced. He had probably never seen a dead body before, and now he had seen three in fewer than 24 hours.

And not just any dead body. Bodies that had been absolutely massacred. Bodies that had been ripped to shreds, their insides now lying in heaps next to their remains.

He would have to talk to Clive separately, later. Ben wasn't much for making speeches, nor was he great at pep talks, but he also remembered back to the first time he had seen something devastating.

His mind flashed back to that fateful camping trip over a decade ago. His brother, his father.

The bear.

His father hadn't made it out alive. His brother had been hospitalized.

It was a memory Ben did not like returning to, but like all memories, it was something that had become a part of him now. Something that had strengthened him, however high the cost.

Ben also knew, deep down, that Clive was fine. He was stronger than he looked, and while the kid had never seen something like this, he had spent enough time out in the woods, around dead animals and the horrors of nature, that Ben knew he would bounce back. Ben would talk to him later and remind him of that. It wouldn't make everything okay, but it would be a start.

Better, it would bring him back to the team.

He also glanced toward Eliza, trying to read her expressions in the dim light of the cave. It was growing dark outside, and Ben wasn't sure how much time was remaining in the day. Eliza gazed back at him, her eyes boring through Ben's body, looking at him and looking at nothing all at the same time. He wondered how she was holding up. *Had she ever been through anything like this*? He wondered. *Had she seen death, stared it down, face-to-face?*

He couldn't tell just based on her expression, but he knew that there was no sane human who could experience something like this and not be affected, at least a little.

Hell, he knew even *he* would be having nightmares about this one for a long time.

"Are you okay?" He asked Eliza. "What are you thinking about?"

Her eyes flickered up toward the ceiling for a second, then settled back onto Ben. It was clear she had been thinking about something very intently, though he couldn't imagine what. "Nothing," she said.

"Bullshit," Ben said. "If there's something you know about what's going on here, it's time you —"

"*I said* it's nothing," Eliza said. "I don't even think it's related. I don't know how it could be related."

"Well," Ben said, looking down at his watch, "seems like we've got all night to discuss it. We are not going back out there now, and it's going to be dark in thirty minutes. We've got a dead body in another room, and all three of us are worn and ragged. Besides that, we've got people tailing us, possibly trying to kill us. I'd suggest that whatever it is you're hiding, you let us know."

Eliza's gaze turned to one of pure indignation. "*Hiding*? I'm not *hiding* anything. I was just thinking about something that happened a long time ago."

"Well, you obviously think it's somehow related to this," Ben said. "And we can help you figure it out." Ben wanted to know what she knew — he *needed* to know. It was the only way they were going to figure this situation out and stay one step ahead of all of it. He also knew it could be helpful for Clive to have something to think about, a puzzle to solve.

"Come on," he said, stepping toward her. "Let us help you. Tell us what you know, and we'll see how it all fits together."

CHAPTER 31
BEN

"OKAY," Eliza said, shakily at first. "Okay. It was five, maybe six years ago. My husband was still alive. I was working for EKG and finishing school as well. I had published a few papers, and a few of them were getting popular in the typical circulation."

"Typical?" Ben asked. "What do you consider typical?"

"The usual — philanthropy organizations, universities, peer reviews," she said. "I wasn't writing anything groundbreaking — at least I didn't think I was at the time. But I was speaking at a university one evening when I got canceled. Literally escorted off the stage and told there was an emergency, and they needed to close it down."

"I'm guessing there was no emergency?" Ben asked.

"Not that I was ever aware of," Eliza said. "If so, they kept it hush-hush."

"You mentioned that before," Ben said. "You said your talk had been canceled midstream, and that you thought it was EKG who had done it. What was the talk about?"

"Honestly? I don't even remember," Eliza said. "It would have been something based on my paper that I had been working on at the time, something about electronic vibrations and relational spinal activity in chimpanzees."

Ben looked at her, cocking an eyebrow. “Sounds like it was pretty close to the research you showed me a few days ago,” Ben said. That stuff they were doing on that table, to that ape. Your research might have actually *helped* them —“

She held up a hand. "I'm going to stop you right there, Ben" Her voice was no longer shaky. It had risen in pitch and timbre and returned to the confident tone he was used to. She took a step toward Ben. "I quit shortly after that. I knew that my research was useful to them, to what they were doing there. That's why we are *here*, Ben.”

“What was it you remembered?” Ben asked. “We’ve been through all of this before; it was one of the first things you said when we met two days ago. So what changed? When you saw that man in there, and the first one, by the tree. What is it about these deaths that has you looking off into the distance, reminiscing?”

There was still poison in her eyes, but her voice softened a bit. “Well,” she said. “It was... I guess it was the *way* they did it. They had a university security officer escort me off campus, but he handed me over to two other men. That night. They were, I’m not sure what to call them — professional security?”

“Rent-a-cops?” Ben asked.

"No," Eliza said, shaking her head. "Definitely more than that. They didn't look like police officers, but they also weren't just civilians. They told me they were going to give me a ride back to the hotel where I was staying."

“Did they?” Ben asked.

She nodded. “Yes, eventually. But they took forever about it. They drove slow, meandered around town a bit. I thought they were lost, trying to figure out where my hotel was. I chalked it up to their being from out of town as well, like me.”

Ben squeezed his eyes shut and thought about it. “Could be, they were trying to bide time for whatever reason. If there was no emergency at the university — no real reason to pull you off the stage — then those men could have been from EKG and were trying to prevent you from walking into your hotel room while more of their friends bugged the room."

"I thought of that. I even called my husband and told him about it afterward, and that was his first thought as well. But they weren't from EKG," she said.

"How do you know?" Ben asked. "Are you sure?"

"Well, I remember looking for their company name. Logos, or decals, or something that would tell me anything about who these men were. They weren't mean or hostile or anything, quite the contrary; one of them was actually nice. He offered to stop for coffee if I recall. But I was still shaken up from what had happened at the university and why I had been shuffled into a car with these two men. I was still under the impression that there was some emergency; a bomb threat or something like that, and they were just trying to keep me safe."

"Makes sense," Ben said.

"But I never did see any logos, at least I didn't think I did at the time. But now..."

Ben knew where she was going with this. He understood now why she had been hesitant after seeing the third massacred man in the other room of the cave. "Did you recognize that man in there?" Ben asked.

She shook her head. "No," she said. "But I did see a piece of his clothing. Just for a second, and it didn't hit me until right now."

"The *Grayson* logo," Ben said, pulling out the ID card he had pulled off of the first dead man. "Like this one?"

"Yes. That's it. It's on a piece of his shirt. It was ripped off of him and left on the floor."

"And it's the same one you saw on these two men who escorted you off-campus?" Ben asked.

"It wasn't on their clothes. I didn't even see it until I got out of the car, and I didn't think that it would be associated with them because of where it was. It was above the rear bumper, like where you would put the name and logo of the car dealership."

Ben knew exactly what she was talking about. Tiny placards that were affixed to the area above and around the license plates on some vehicles as a marketing tool. He understood now why it would not have registered in her mind before.

"I swear it was the exact same thing. It said, 'Grayson,' in the same font and style. Monochrome, looking just like it belonged there on the car. It hit me when I saw that piece of the shirt. I knew immediately where I had seen it before."

"Well," Clive said, "I guess that settles it."

They both looked down at the younger man, still crouched and huddled on the floor of the cave.

"This is EKG. It has to be. They hired people then, and they hired them again to clean up their mess now. Whatever this is, they don't want it getting out. They tried to scare you before, to silence you and your husband."

Eliza had calmed down now, but he still saw the boiling fear in her eyes, quickly turning to anger. He didn't know what they were truly up against out here, but he knew for a fact that it was bigger than they'd imagined.

It — something related to EKG — had killed three men so far.

And we're walking right toward it, Ben thought.

CHAPTER 32
BEN

BEN AWOKE to the sound of a squirrel chittering near his head. He moved his hand a quarter of a millimeter, which sent the squirrel fleeing to safety elsewhere. He had slept fitfully, unable to erase the visions of the two dead *Grayson* men and the one Clive had seen.

In Ben's dreams, his mind had created a vision of the second dead person, the one Ben had not seen with his own eyes. He, like the other two, had had their hearts ripped from their chest and had died a bloody, terrifying death.

What was worse, his subconscious had allowed him to interact with each of the dead men. They had been alive in his dream, wide-eyed and shaking with fear, while their chests had been ripped open, then bloodied and desecrated.

Unfortunately, Ben recalled the dream vividly. He remembered interacting with each of the men, asking them questions about their death, even in his subconscious trying to piece together the puzzle.

Why had they been killed? Why had they been killed in such a way? What were they trying to tell him?

Each of the men had answered, and each answer was the same.

It came for us in the night.

And yet, Ben had made it through this night, just as he'd made it through the previous one. The past night he had spent in a cave, semi-protected from the elements and whatever might attack them, but the night before last he had spent out in the open, on EKG property, vulnerable and defenseless.

So, then, why had "it" come in the night for these men and not for him? If he believed what his subconscious was trying to tell him, the creature only attacked when it was dark. Why? Was this just a trick his mind was playing on him? Or was there something more to it?

He wondered if there might be anything lodged deep within his brain that would give him a clue. He thought he'd explored the expanses of his mind, trying to figure out any pieces of the puzzle he might have forgotten without realizing it, but he could find none. He rolled onto his side, noticing that the tiny ground squirrel was still poking its head into the cave, peeking at Ben and the new visitors. Ben figured this was the squirrel's home, and that he — the human — was the invader.

"Sorry, little guy," he muttered. He had always had an affinity for nature and its inhabitants. Ever since he had started down the path of becoming a park ranger many years ago, he had realized that he often felt more at home with the animal kingdom than his own.

Ben rolled over again, this time ending up on his left side. He must have slept on this one, as it was growing sore. It was still dark in the cave, even though he could see a few orange embers from the tiny fire that had refused to go down without a fight. It was still smoking, and he knew there would be hot coals underneath the ash they could use to start up the fire this morning.

It was chilly as well, the cold from the outside somehow seeping into their layers overnight. He longed for some of Clive's bacon, wondering how long they had before it all went bad. On camping trips with Julie, they were able to keep cold food in their packs for up to a week sometimes, depending on the temperature during the day.

He pressed his fingers through his hair, hoping it didn't look completely disheveled. He felt as though he'd slept on a concrete slab. The rock he had slept on was only marginally better, and he knew he would be aching for a bit after they got going this morning.

He sat up, pulling the sleeping bag down to his waist, and got a better look around.

He reached for his flashlight and turned it on, hoping the light wouldn't wake the other two members of his team. He saw the lump to his left which represented Eliza in her sleeping bag, but when he slung it around to where Clive had been, he found...

Nothing.

"He's gone," Eliza said.

He swung the flashlight around quickly, and she winced when it hit her eyes. "Sorry," he said, moving the light to a spot just above her head. "What do you mean, he's *gone*?"

"I mean he's not here. He left. He took off sometime last night or early this morning."

Ben was stunned. "Are — are you sure? How do you know? Didn't he say anything to you? You didn't try to stop him?"

"He didn't say anything, Ben. I didn't see him leave, nor did I hear him. I woke up about fifteen minutes ago and saw that he was gone. I thought it would be better for you to sleep rather than wake you up and startle you."

"But — but we could be looking for him," Ben said, growing frantic. "We could be out there right now, trying to find him. Surely he didn't just get up on his own to try and..."

The truth was, Ben had no idea *what* the younger man would be trying to do. He had even said as much last night, telling them there was no way he was going back out there.

Ben stood up now, stretching and rubbing his eyes. He had not slept well, and he knew the results would manifest themselves physically throughout the day. He longed for another two hours of rest, but he knew he wasn't going to get it anytime soon.

"Ben," Eliza said, "he's probably just looking for firewood. He did that yesterday, remember? He went out to find —"

"And he found a dead body, Eliza," Ben said. "He found something absolutely horrifying, and you saw what had happened to him. He wasn't himself yesterday, and I know he hasn't all of a sudden snapped out of it."

"Yes, but it doesn't mean I'm wrong."

Ben looked at her sidelong, wondering if she was still hiding something from him. He didn't believe she was, but he also didn't know her very well. The truth was, he was unsure of just about everything at the moment. He stepped to the front of the cave, looking outward at the forest to the north. A thin layer of frost had covered everything, giving the woods a sparkling gleam that he had to admit made the scene even more beautiful.

He turned back to Eliza. "We have to go after him," he said. "I'm not asking permission. I'm telling you. We need to —"

"Ben," Eliza said. "Calm down. Please. Clive may be spooked, but he is not insane. He just went out to pee or to look for firewood."

"He would have said something," Ben said. "Or he would have been back by now if it was a quick bathroom trip."

She shrugged. "I don't know what to tell you, Ben. But you seem to me to be a smart man. We can't afford to have one of us go look for him. One of us has to stay here to watch our stuff and our weapons. If one of us goes out there, then we're split up. I don't think that's what you want, either."

Ben had to hand it to her. That was precisely the dilemma he was facing right now: how to look for the youngest member of their party without splitting up their team.

CHAPTER 33
DIETRICH

DIETRICH STEPPED out of his tent, yawned, and stretched his arms out wide. He had the cell phone in his left hand and a small device that would activate a satellite uplink with the phone in his right. He was amazed at the size of the thing; when he had first started down this career path many years ago, these things had been about ten times this size.

There was a slight sacrifice in quality going with a much smaller footprint. Still, it was necessary — with the advent of modern cellular technology, he didn't actually need to connect with a satellite directly. Instead, he just needed to connect to one of the myriad cell towers in the distance back in the city of Grindelwald.

He walked a few paces away from the tent and turned around. The three tents had been set up in a semicircle around their fire. It was still smoking, as they'd decided to keep it burning through the night, which he thought was imprudent and unnecessary. Now, the fire could hardly be called a fire; it was barely a flicker of coals. Mr. Ziegler and Lars had decided it would be best to keep it small, and he hadn't argued.

Dietrich turned back around and walked toward a small outcropping which he knew hid a small opening just beyond it. This was where he would make the call.

There was nothing special about the cell phone, but he needed to get out of earshot from the others, and he needed to get to a place open enough that would allow him to connect with a cell tower back down the mountain. He plugged the device into the phone through its charging port, then opened the specialized app that doubled as a simple GPS location unit, urging him in the right direction until the signal was strong enough for the phone's screen to show a solid green light. He marched until he found a decent spot at the far edge of the clearing, with a heading of north-northeast. He set the phone and the device down on the ground and crouched to one knee to make the call.

He had learned the hard way that holding the phone and the device up to his ear caused enough interference that most of the calls would be dropped. So now he used a small Bluetooth headset that simply connected with the phone once a strong enough signal was present. He placed the Bluetooth device over his ear and adjusted the microphone, then double-tapped the side of it to initiate the call.

It only took one ring to answer.

"Line?"

"Secure," he said. The man on the other end of the phone was just barely competent enough to know that a secure line was necessary, though he knew they had no idea how to achieve it or what underlying technology made it all happen. He was old-school, from a different time.

Dietrich, on the other hand, was a trained professional through and through, and like a true professional, he had spent ample time learning the tools and tricks of the trade.

He not only knew how this satellite relay worked, he knew the devices would have checked for the most secure transmission possible, opting to relay from a single cell tower rather than spread the message around an array. He knew the device also emitted a reverse scrambler frequency that would prevent anyone from eavesdropping on this call, even if they were somehow able to hack into it.

And, most important of all, he knew how to have a conversation over a secure line: you didn't just start talking as if you were face-to-face inside of a secure room. You had to maneuver the conversation using semi-coded words that gave the opposite party an *idea* of what you are talking about without giving out exact details.

This is the approach he opted for on this call. "We are about three klicks north of their position. They are higher up the ridge, holed up inside a cave. We believe they will be on the move within the hour, but we are watching to be sure."

"We discussed this already," the voice on the other line said. *"You were to neutralize the targets, and ensure — "*

"I understand the mission parameters, and they will be followed to the letter. I can assure you of that, though I cannot inform you of the exact time and location the neutralization will occur." He hoped his annoyance was heard on the other end, as he did not like being scolded for doing his job.

"I understand, I was just trying to make sure that the — "

"The job will get done; I give you my word. These things are delicate situations, and it is not just a hostile party we are up against."

"Yes, you mean the..."

Dietrich shook his head. "No," he said. "While that is still a variable, it is not one I am concerned with. We planned for that — that is why we've brought the hunter on. I'm talking about the party I am with now. There is no cohesion as a unit. I know that was never the intent, but it makes any movement challenging, and when there are mission parameters that are not shared amongst the — "

Now the man on the other end cut him off. *"The job is difficult. But it must be done."*

The man sighed, not caring if it was heard on the other side of the call. "Yes, I understand. As I said, it will be done."

There was a pause, and then, *"Very well. Make a call when it is done. I want this all wrapped up by the end of the week."*

Dietrich disconnected the call, and then flicked around the phone's screen to check for the recording he had made. All of his calls, incoming and outgoing, were recorded by another app on his phone. One could never be too careful with this sort of thing, and while he had the secure uplink initiated, he thought it prudent to upload his previous two communications to his cloud server.

He heard stopping and shuffling behind him. He grabbed the phone and uplink and held it close to his body while he unzipped his pants.

"Morning," Lars yelled from behind him. "Taking a walk?"

"Grabbing a piss," he said gruffly, not interested in engaging yet. "I'll be back in a few minutes. Are we eating breakfast?"

He could almost hear Lars shaking his head. "No, we need to get moving. And we don't want to attract attention."

He finished, then zipped up his pants and turned around, sliding the phone and satellite uplink into his pocket. There would be a time to reveal all of this, but it was not yet. They still had the other group to worry about.

CHAPTER 34
BEN

BEN AND ELIZA decided to look for Clive together. It was the only way to ensure neither of them could be ambushed without the other around, and while they would give up any protection the cave might offer, being out in the woods would also give them more possible chances of escape.

Ben didn't love the plan; it slowed things down, and it made their ultimate goal — getting to EKG headquarters and figuring out how to get inside — more difficult. But Clive was part of their team, and it had been half an hour since Ben had been awake, and Clive was still gone. He still felt as though Eliza was right, that Clive had left to go hunt for food, but Ben still held reservations about that idea.

First, Clive had been terrified last night after discovering the third dead body. Second, Ben knew they had enough food, sparse and bland as it might be, to get them through another three days out here without needing to head back into the village. There simply was no reason to hunt for any game out here, even for something as small as a rabbit or squirrel.

Eliza had nodded along when he'd explained this to her, and she said it made sense, but he could tell she still had some hangups.

Which meant her concerns were likely the same as Ben's: that both of them were actually worried about Clive because they were worried about *everything*. They were worried that something had gotten in Clive's head, and he had lost some of his sanity and was now traipsing around the woods in semi-madness. Or, that Clive was fine but somehow determined to find and kill whatever it was that had killed these men. Neither option was good, and both options meant that they would need to go after Clive.

"Your turn," he heard Eliza say.

Ben whirled around to see her standing a few feet away; her backpack slung over one shoulder. A strand of red hair trickled down over her forehead and into her eyes, and she blew it to the side with a puff from her lips.

"What are you talking about?" Ben asked.

"I said it's your turn," she said again, placing her hand on her hip. "I told you what was going on with *me*; now I want to know what's going on with *you*."

Ben opened his mouth to respond, then closed it again. He repeated this motion a few times, feeling like an idiot. *What is she talking about? How can she know that there's something going on? How do I even know that there's something going on?*

"There is nothing —"

She moved her hand from her hip and held it up outward to Ben. "Save it, Ben. I know you are just as concerned about all of this — about Clive — as I am. But I can also see beneath the surface. My husband was like you; he was calm, reserved. But that didn't mean he was emotionless. He had his moments, Ben. At first, early on in our marriage, I thought he was just stoic. But I came to learn that it was all bubbling up just beneath the surface, and if I didn't pry it out of him, it would stay there, festering like a wound."

"That's..." Ben said. "That's a very colorful way to describe it."

She shrugged. "Tell me it's not true."

Ben smirked, then blew out a breath. "Okay," he said. "You win.

I haven't lied to you, Eliza. And I won't. But I also haven't been very open with either of you."

She nodded. "You're talking about two nights ago. What happened?"

"How can you — how do you know anything about — ?"

"This city talks, Ben. You know as well as I do. Nothing said in a public space goes without being repeated. I would call it gossip, but it's a bit more like everyone looking out for each other."

"Yeah, I get that." Ben knew exactly what she was talking about; he had experienced exactly that. He even sort of liked it; it gave him the sense that everyone in town was on the same team, rooting for one another. "So then you heard I was attacked?"

Eliza's eyes widened in surprise, and her mouth dropped open. "*What?* What are you talking about? No, Ben. I had no idea you were attacked."

"Then what did you hear?" Ben asked.

"I was told by someone I ran into at the store that there was a big, intimidating man in town."

Ben stared at her. "So I am a 'big, intimidating man?'"

She giggled. "No, I never said *you* were the big intimidating man. That's what I thought, too, at first. Instead, they said there was a big intimidating man in town who was *talking to* the American."

"That makes sense. I'm the American."

"Which means someone was talking to you two nights ago, then. And while I have no idea what 'talking' is supposed to mean in this case, it seems as though it was noteworthy enough for some locals to comment on it." She paused, waiting for Ben to interject. "So, who was he? Did you know him?"

Ben shook his head. "No, and I still don't. But he followed me out of the bar and punched me in the gut, then in the kidney. It was... He hit pretty hard, and I went down to the ground."

Eliza seemed impressed, but she also had a look of concern in her eyes.

“I’m fine,” Ben said, “even though I was a little sore yesterday morning.”

"But, I'm guessing that it wasn't your kidney that made you all brooding yesterday, either?"

He took a breath. “No, you’re right. It was what he said to me. He told me this — punching me — was a warning, that if he saw me out here, he was going to have to make the warning more intense or something. I don’t really know what he was talking about other than, ‘don’t go out on EKG land.’”

“You think he was EKG?” she asked.

He shook his head. “No. I don’t know. Could be, but I doubt it for some reason. I don’t think he was *Grayson* either, because he just had a sort of independent look to him, like he was rough around the edges and didn’t play well with others or something.”

“Definitely seems like he didn’t play well with *you*, Ben.”

"You got that right," Ben said. "And I don't plan on going down as easily if we see each other again. That said, I'd sure like to not have to see him again. The sooner we get to EKG and figure out what the hell is going on around here, the better."

"We still need to find Clive first," Eliza said. "But I agree with you. We need to figure this out, and this incident seems to be beyond coincidence."

Ben hesitated, considering walking outside and beginning their hunt for Clive when he looked back at Eliza. "There's more," he said. "He didn't just warn me away from this place. He seemed to think we were hunting for something; that we were out here looking for the same thing he was going to be looking for."

“You mean he is trying to find whatever this thing is that killed these men?”

“It seems so, yes. Whatever this creature is that’s running around, ripping people’s hearts out, is the same one that this dude is looking for. And he doesn’t want competition, either.”

Ben could see Eliza working this over in her mind. She looked up at the ceiling of the cave, then slung the other shoulder strap of the backpack over her arm. She cinched them tight and stepped up closer to Ben. "I think it's another piece of this puzzle, Ben," she said. "And I think it's important to keep all of it in mind. But it doesn't change our mission. Clive, then the EKG. That's it. Whatever this thing is, even if it's related, we need to get to Clive first — then EKG — to figure it out."

"I agree," Ben said. "And I think we need to get moving. Whoever is out there taking potshots at us, maybe this hunter guy, is probably —"

Crack!

At that moment, the sound of rifle fire made Ben jump. He heard the round hit the dirt near his feet, and he dove to the side, wrapping his arms around Eliza as he fell.

She screamed in surprise, but flew with him, immediately adjusting to the tackle. He felt her lithe, athletic body spinning to regain control of her fall.

He landed on his face in the dirt at the front of the cave while Eliza landed in a practiced crouch. His arms were still wrapped around her hips, and he extracted them while pushing himself up and to the side.

"Yeah," he said. "I definitely think it's time to get going."

CHAPTER 35
BEN

"GET DOWN!" Eliza yelled as another shot rang through their ears, echoing in the cave. Ben was still on the ground, and Eliza suddenly broke her crouch and launched herself over Ben's prone body, landing on top of him.

Her cheek pressed tightly against his face, and he felt her breasts pushing into his back...

They lay there for a moment, still. Ben was growing more uncomfortable by the second, and yet he knew his comfort was probably less important than not getting shot.

Still, the way Eliza had thrown herself over him... Was he reading too far into this? *Is she hitting on me?*

He shook his head, feeling the heat of her hair beginning to choke him. He hadn't been this close to any woman besides Julie for as long as he could remember.

Julie.

He needed to move, even if it was just to shift over to the side so they could both share the cave floor as cover. Besides, he didn't want to have to explain to Julie how a woman was shot and killed while lying on top of him.

"We need to get out of the cave," Ben said, his voice barely above a whisper. There was no need to talk loudly, with her literally lying on top of him and her face smashed against his.

"Okay, right."

The voice was soft, barely audible. Gentle, too. Almost like...

He pushed away and heard her grunt in disapproval. He crawled to the side of the cave opening, where there was a large boulder over the right side of the opening. She followed behind him with her hand on his arm. He could feel it there, warm, hot even. *Was it getting hotter?*

Shake it off, man. This is ridiculous. You're fighting a war against a bunch of unknown enemies, and you're thinking about this?

"I think I see something," Eliza said. "Over there, just down the hill and to the —"

Crack!

The sound of the rifle shot again made Ben jump. It was louder here, where they were closer to the source of the gunshot, without some of the rocks getting in the way. He quickly flicked his eyes that direction, following Eliza's finger as she pointed. He grabbed for his rifle, then set the end of it on top of the boulder that Clive had been using the night before for the same defensive position.

"You think you can hit them from here?" Eliza asked.

Ben shook his head. "Maybe, but I'm not going to try. I don't shoot things I can't see."

He waited for her to respond. It seems like hours passed. "Even if they're shooting at you?"

"Yes, even if they're shooting at me. Unless I know *exactly* what is behind that gun, I ain't taking any shots. It could be Clive, gone crazy, or something like that."

It was something his father had taught him and his younger brother, Zach, long ago. *You absolutely never shoot without knowing what you are shooting at.* Bonus points if you knew what was behind the thing you were shooting at.

Ben had, unfortunately, been in a few scrapes that involved

exchanging gunfire between two sides. He had more experience than any civilian he knew, and more combat experience than most military men and women he knew, and more experience then most people *wanted* to know.

He had been trained over time, both by his friend Reggie and through different programs the CSO put them through, but nothing could prepare someone for battle like actually being in a battle. Still, *prepared* was potentially the wrong word. He had come to learn that there was no such thing as being truly prepared to fire a weapon at another human being.

There was nothing that could prepare someone's mind enough to take a life.

At least not that he knew about.

He felt Eliza's hand move slowly up his arm to his shoulder. Or was it just that he *thought* it was moving slowly? He couldn't be sure. He knew for a fact this woman had never been in a situation like this, and he knew everyone reacted differently. Maybe Eliza's instinctual reaction was to get more flirtatious.

He shook his head. *No, that's absolutely ridiculous.* Her hand was on his shoulder, squeezing, and it was not because she wanted to sleep with him.

She was trying to tell him something. He waited, feeling her hand squeeze once more than lift up and point in another direction.

Then, almost faintly enough that he couldn't hear, she spoke. "Over there, Ben. If we can cut across this small opening and get there, the trees are denser and there are a lot of boulders that might protect us enough to get away.

Ben saw what she was talking about. The ridge they were on — the one their cave was in — stretched mostly up and to the southeast, but there was a small offshoot of it that was set apart from the larger mass of rocks and cliffs that stretched northeast. It was about twenty yards away, certainly easy enough to sprint toward without getting hit, especially if they laid down covering fire before they ran.

He explained this to Eliza, telling her exactly what to do and when to do it. She nodded quickly, frantically. "Okay, she said. I — I got this."

Ben looked her up and down, trying to gauge her ability to knowingly insert herself into a firefight. She was shaking, but he wasn't sure if it was just adrenaline or fear or both. If he were lucky, it would be mostly adrenaline and dopamine and a bit of fear. A healthy bit of fear is what kept humans alive, he knew.

"On my count," he said. "One, two —"

Eliza ripped her rifle open, firing three burst rounds before Ben could finish the count. She hadn't run to the opposite side of the cave, either, before firing. Ben's ears immediately went silent; then, a second later were filled with the ringing sound of temporary deafness. He roared in pain but forced himself to hold his own rifle forward.

He pushed her sideways with his hips, still crouching so as not to be hit in the back by one of her wildly aimed bullets. She seemed to get the hint and stopped firing long enough to run over to the left side of the cave.

Ben didn't wait for an invitation. He jumped up and forward, keeping his assault rifle aimed downhill at the ready, his finger over the trigger guard. He ran in the opposite direction, however, making a diagonal the other way toward the smaller ridge to his right. He reached it in a handful of seconds, then jumped and slid, baseball style, feet-first into a small snowbank, where he came to a cushioned yet abrupt stop. He immediately checked his sites and aimed toward where the shooter had been perched.

Eliza was still firing wild bursts in every direction, seemingly not getting any more controlled the longer she shot. He dropped his weapon for a second and cupped his hands over his mouth. He yelled. "Eliza! *Now*!"

She fired once more, then looked in his direction. He waved at her to follow, and he thought he saw her nod before charging out of the mouth of the cave and down the hill.

Satisfied for the moment, Ben brought his rifle back up and gazed down the sight toward the forest where their attacker waited. He saw no movement that looked human, but he kept his gun up and ready while he listened for Eliza's footsteps.

They were too fast, too wild. He had misread her earlier — she hadn't been *flirting*. She was absolutely terrified, frantic and running on adrenaline and fumes, totally unprepared for a situation like this.

He had let his own ego get in the way. He owed her an apology, but that apology would have to wait until they were safely out of harm's way.

Her footsteps were arrhythmic, almost random, and she plodded along over cracked, hard-packed ice and snow and smaller gravel and wisps of grass that had fought through the cold. When she was only about five yards away, he saw her right leg extend as it caught on a small patch of pebbles.

She slid for a brief moment, the jolt startling her and causing her to stumble and fall forward. He dropped the rifle and reached up involuntarily, catching her before she hit the ground. He quickly set her back down on her butt and gently nudged her leg straight.

"Ouch," she said, sucking through her teeth. "Oh my God, I think I broke my knee."

CHAPTER 36
BEN

"IT'S DEFINITELY NOT BROKEN," Ben said, trying to reassure her with his voice. He squeezed gently above and below the knee, then worked his hands toward the kneecap, trying to feel for anything out of place. "Yeah, just a bad sprain. Maybe a small tear, but you're going to live."

He glanced up at her eyes only to find them piercing through him. "I did good though, didn't I?" She asked. "I did what you said, right?"

Ben smiled. "You did... You did fine. We are alive, and we're going to live at least for another few minutes."

She laughed at that. A deep, guttural belly laugh that was more than a bit out of place. It took Ben by surprise, but then he remembered what she was going through. *This is completely unlike any of her previous jobs,* he thought. This was something wholly foreign to her, completely out of left field.

"Can you bend it just a little?" Ben asked.

She stopped laughing and nodded, bending it about an inch and then wincing in pain.

"Just leave it there for a minute," Ben said. "We are not in any rush. Our backs are up against the rocks, and whoever was attacking us will come from this direction, so we will see them before they get here."

She nodded, then pulled out her water bottle from her pack and took a long sip. He noticed that she had about half a bottle left. His was a little lower, and they didn't have any extra. If they got stranded out here, they could melt snow for drinking water so that they wouldn't die of thirst.

But he also knew the only way they would be stranded out here is if something terrible happened. If they were all severely injured, for example. He tightened his grip on his gun.

"Was it him?" Eliza asked suddenly. "Was it the guy you talked to? The one who beat you up?"

"First of all, he didn't 'beat me up,'" Ben said. "He just, you know... Wanted to make a point. Caught me off guard."

"Yeah, okay. Whatever."

Ben forced a smile but continued anyway. "Second, I didn't get a good look at them. Couldn't actually see him at all, really. I think I might've seen a flash from his gun that second or third shot, but it was all a blur after that. I definitely didn't see anyone's face or body, so I wouldn't be able to say if it was him or not."

"But you *do* think it was him, right?"

Ben thought about this for a moment. It made sense, really. He already knew that this man was hostile; he already knew that this man wanted Ben and his team off the mountain and away from EKG. Could this man be so intent on sending the message that he would actually take shots at them?

"Yeah," Ben said. "It does seem that way, doesn't it? I don't know who else is out there, but I do know this guy, and he definitely seemed angry enough to pull a stunt like that."

"In that case, do you think..." Eliza didn't finish her thought, but she didn't need to. Ben was thinking the same thing.

"I don't think so, Eliza," Ben said. "We would've heard a gunshot last night or this morning. Clive is out here somewhere, but I don't think this guy got to him."

Ben realized as he said the words that they would do little to comfort her. It's not that he didn't believe them, he did. It was just that they both knew there was something out there besides a man with a gun. Something they both knew was actively willing to kill and had in the past.

It had killed three times already, at least in that they had discovered. It was leaving a trail of death and blood behind it, a trail that —

Ben caught himself. He was onto something; he just wasn't quite sure what it was yet. He let the thought percolate in his mind, bouncing around as long as it took to find a home. He had never been someone known for intellectual endeavors, but he was far from stupid. Ben had an uncanny sense of street smarts, an ability to process and analyze a situation from multiple angles at once until they suddenly clicked into place and made sense. He likened it to a puzzle, all of the pieces being jumbled around inside a cement mixer until miraculously being spit out, complete and perfect.

It wasn't an infallible system, but it worked for him. He would add different puzzle pieces and variables and elements to the mix and let them all interact and bounce around together, sometimes for days on end. But at some point, after some number of additional variables or luck or wit or whatever it was that made it all happen, his mind would spit out an answer.

He sensed that he was close to that kind of answer now. He was close to figuring out what it was this place was trying to tell him.

"You're thinking about it again, aren't you?" Eliza asked.

He was sitting on his butt, next to her, and he looked to his left to see her working her right leg back and forth, bending her knee. "What you mean?" He asked. "What am I thinking about?"

She answered. "There's something about all of this that doesn't make sense yet, right? Something that should make sense but doesn't, because we either don't know enough or we aren't thinking of it the right way. I can see you processing it, just like my husband used to do."

"Processing things is what every single living person does," Ben said. He didn't appreciate being psychoanalyzed, and he certainly didn't like the connotations of being constantly compared to her late husband.

"No, it's different from just normal human processing," she said. "It's deeper, something more emotional. You — and him, when he was alive — are able to see things from multiple points of view, driven not just by logic and instinct but also by your emotion. You allow that to help solve problems."

Ben was no psychologist, so he couldn't comment on the veracity of her claims, but it certainly struck him as true. He shrugged. "Yeah, I guess. Julie always told me that I am actually a really emotional guy; it's all just bundled up inside, underneath all these unemotional layers."

"That's pretty much what I told my husband, as well," Eliza said. "He always seemed so... tough. Nothing could get to him, you know? Nothing seemed to bother him, until it did."

Eliza was looking straight ahead.

"He would just keep it all bottled up inside, like some sort of human cliché, but if you knew what questions to ask, or rather, how to ask them, he would let it all out into this beautiful mess of chaotic truth. Like, he could be chewing on a problem for weeks or months and then all of a sudden burst out with some multifaceted, complex solution to whatever problem it was he had been working on."

Ben nodded slowly. *So it seems we did have a lot in common, after all,* he thought. *It's a shame this guy is no longer with us.*

"That does sound like me," he said.

They sat there for a few more minutes, both watching the woods for any movement, anything that might alert them to the hunter trying to sneak up on them. Ben didn't like being motionless, but he knew Eliza needed to rest, to let her knee's swelling go down. Besides that, he didn't mind a bit of a rest himself.

"I read about you, you know," Eliza said. "Before I reached out to the CSO. I did my homework, like I always do."

CHAPTER 37
BEN

"OH?" Ben asked. "What did you find? You know, all that journalistic bullshit is just that — BS with a handful of truth in it. The CSO isn't some mercenary-for-hire organization or some group of superheroes that runs around shooting bad guys."

"No, not that," she said. "I went back further, back to before you guys were CSO."

Ben knew what she was getting at. He knew there was nothing in any newspaper articles or journalist reportings about him prior to his involvement and semi-celebrity status with the CSO.

Except for one thing...

"It's heroic what you did," Eliza said. "But it didn't *feel* heroic, did it? At the time, you probably weren't even thinking or feeling much at all. You just wanted to save your family."

Ben looked at her again, seeing her in a new light. This was the first time anyone had said anything to him like that. "Yeah," he said. "That's exactly what happened. I'm no hero or anything like what all those articles said. I just didn't want my dad or my brother to die. *I* didn't want to die."

"So, you did what you had to do."

"Yeah, I did. I don't know if it was right or wrong or somewhere in between, but I definitely didn't care at the time. I wasn't even *thinking* about it at the time. I knew where the rifle was, and I heard screams. So I ran there and I did what I had to do."

He paused for a second, taking another sip of water. "People got to say what they thought it was, what they thought *I* was. But they never asked me, you know? They just put their spin on it and just sent it out, like they were some sort of expert on me and what I did."

"People love to tell me what I'm thinking," Eliza said. "Maybe it's because I'm a woman, because I have breasts, because I'm attractive and somehow intimidating, I don't know. I don't care. People always like to tell me what I 'meant' when I give a speech or publish a paper. There's always commentary on it, but at the end of the day, there is absolutely no question in *my* mind what I'm all about."

Ben nodded along, enjoying listening to this woman talk. She was intensely smart, and he got the sense that she was wise beyond her years as well.

"The thing is, if enough time goes by when you don't recommit to yourself, recommit to what you know, you start to believe these people. You start to think they might be onto something, that they keep bringing up the same things about you over and over and over again, and eventually you wonder if they might be right."

"How do you 'recommit' to yourself?" Ben asked. "What do you mean by that?"

She shrugged. "I'm not really sure, not yet. That's just my working theory, anyway. But I think it has something to do with this —" she waived an outstretched arm over the land around them. "I think it starts with committing to what you know is right; what you know is true, and then just... Doing it. Forget what they all say about you or what they want you to do or to be. You just have to commit and then do it."

She squeezed her eyes shut, and Ben could see some moisture around the edges. He knew she was thinking of her husband, missing him. Wishing he were here right now in place of Ben.

Then he understood.

She wasn't *flirting* with him; she didn't like him in that way. It wasn't about that; it had never been about that.

Eliza was dealing with the loss of her husband, dealing with a death she thought had been murder. The man had been taken from this world while at the prime of his life, doing something he believed in and something he wanted to accomplish. It was supremely unfair, and Ben had known all too many people who had found similar fates.

He didn't fault Eliza for being reminded of all of this; how could he? She had hired him because she knew his qualifications, because she knew what he stood for and what the CSO had done in the past. But she had also brought him on because she knew something deeper about him that he himself was only just beginning to understand. She knew who he was inside, in his core, and it was *that* man she had wanted to partner with. He shared those qualities, those characteristics, with her late husband, and neither of them could do anything about that.

Of *course* he would remind her of her husband. Of *course* he would act in a similar way.

He reached over and took Eliza's hand in his. He placed his other hand on top, for a moment forgetting about their predicament and setting the rifle by his side. "I'm going to help you figure this out," Ben said. "I don't fault you for getting me involved in this; this is exactly the sort of thing we are trying to fight against. I know you know that, but I want you to hear me say it. I'm going to do everything in my power to end this, to make things right. It won't bring him back, but I sure as hell want to make them pay for it."

When he finished, she began sobbing, the tears falling freely over her cheeks and down her face. They splashed onto her jeans, forming tiny dark spots on her legs.

Ben took a deep, long breath, held it for ten seconds, then let it out.

It was time to act, time to press on and overcome and solve the mystery. It was time to reach down for that reserve of inner strength he knew he had, to tap into that resilient core he had summoned on occasion. He released Eliza's hand and reached down for his assault rifle once again.

They needed to find Clive, and they needed to find whoever it was that was out here with them.

CHAPTER 38
BEN

THEY FOUND Clive in a small gulch, about three-hundred yards north of the cave and downhill a bit. After deciding that they were safe from the shooter, Ben had helped Eliza to her feet, and together they slowly began marching downhill and to the north, pushing toward EKG headquarters.

They had been walking for about twenty minutes, looking for any sign of their third teammate, when they had heard the voice yelling in the distance.

By that time, Eliza had felt comfortable putting some weight on her knee, and Ben had found a blunt, smooth stick for her to use as a sort of makeshift crutch, and they picked up their pace and worked downhill in the direction of Clive's calling.

His backpack was on the ground near a tree, but when they got closer, they saw that Clive himself had fallen into a steep, shallow valley. It was an old, dry riverbed that had long ago cut through the side of the ridge toward lower elevation, about six feet across and between four and eight feet deep.

Ben carefully climbed down the side and knelt by Clive, whose face was a bloody mess. Ben quickly checked the younger man's vitals, finding nothing out of place and nothing terribly urgent. He had a bloody nose, a bunch of smaller cuts and scrapes on his face and neck, and a huge welting bruise on his right shoulder. It was this bruise, hiding a dislocated shoulder that had made it impossible for Clive to crawl out of the ravine. His body, after falling, had been twisted around so that his top half was downhill a bit, making it impossible to move without seriously hurting his arm.

"I'm glad to see you're alive," Ben said.

"Me too, though this thing hurts so bad, I might as well be dead."

"I think I can pop it back into place," Ben said. "But — and I can't stress this enough — I'm *definitely* not a doctor." Ben smiled, trying to lighten the mood a bit.

Clive smiled back. "Yeah, I know. And I get it. This is not the first time one of my limbs has gone awry. Do your best, Doc." He winked at Ben.

Ben pressed on his shoulder, just above the joint, while tightly grabbing the man's upper arm and bicep with his other hand. He waited until Clive relaxed and looked the other direction, then he pulled forward on the arm while slightly twisting at the same time. Clive wailed in pain, but then sucked in a quick breath and went silent.

Ben waited, watching the younger man.

Clive gritted his teeth, then slowly, carefully, put a bit of pressure on his elbow. "Well, looks like you may have a career in the medical field before you know it," he said. "Good as new, I presume."

"Definitely *not* as good as new," Ben said, helping the man to his feet. "But it's certainly not as bad as it was before."

Together, they climbed out of the gulch and reunited with Eliza. Eliza shared her own injury story with Clive before asking, "What happened to you? Why did you leave the cave this morning?"

"I heard it," he said. "Or, I thought I did. It was like a scratching sound, like something out of a movie. Big, intense. It was just outside the cave, I swear."

"And you didn't just decide to shoot it?"

He shook his head. "No, I couldn't see it. It was already beginning to be morning, so there was a bit of daylight. I thought I saw a shadow, but I couldn't actually see it. I didn't want to wake either of you up, so I snuck out with my rifle and sidearm and a few of the magazines. I followed it, or, at least I thought I did, down to the edge of the woods."

"You followed the shadow? Or you found tracks?"

"I did, I saw this shadowy thing moving, like it could go completely silent for long periods of time without moving or making any noise, and then suddenly I would see a small flicker of a shadow. No tracks, though. Almost like..."

"Almost like what?" Ben asked.

"Well, almost like it was... in the trees. But it wasn't. I mean, not when I saw it."

Ben and Eliza were shocked, and it registered on their faces. Ben looked at her, then back at Clive.

Is he messing with us? "What do you mean, you saw it?"

Is he not in his right mind?

"No, I swear," Clive continued. "It was... it was right in front of me." He shuddered. "I *swear* to you guys, I followed it — or at least its shadow — until I was right here. I stopped, waiting for a minute because I thought I lost it, and then I..."

"What?"

"And then I turned around. And then it was *right in front of me.* There was nothing, and then it was *there.* Standing over me. Had to be... It had to be twenty feet tall."

Twenty feet tall?

Ben knew something had gotten into this guy's mind, and it was now playing tricks on him and the rest of them. But still, this was a professional, trained hunter—someone who traveled all over the world to hunt big game. Clive might be going insane, but Ben knew there had to be at least a kernel of truth to his story.

"What was it?" Eliza asked. "The creature that did all of this — the one that killed all these people. What was it?"

Clive nodded slowly, contemplating his answer before speaking. "I — I want to say... I mean, it was a *gorilla*. But, it also wasn't."

"A *gorilla*?" Ben asked. "Like, a jungle gorilla? Black, beating on its chest, King Kong-sort of a gorilla?"

"A silverback, just like what you would see in a zoo. But this one, it was, different..."

"Like, twenty-feet-tall different?" Ben asked. He didn't intend to sound diminishing, but he didn't believe for a moment that an actual twenty foot-tall silverback gorilla was running around the hillsides of Switzerland.

He flashed a glance at Eliza, only to find her giving him the same look.

We're going to have to rein him in a bit, Ben thought. *Whatever got to him, whatever this creature is, it sounds like it does more psychological damage than physical.*

Then he remembered the men they had stumbled upon, back at the campsite and in the cave, and the one Clive had seen yesterday. *No,* he thought, changing his initial assessment. *This thing* definitely *causes more physical harm.*

"I don't really know yet," Clive said. "I've been thinking about it ever since, well, ever since I was pushed into the hole. What it could be and all that. I mean, it was absolutely a gorilla. Older male, I would guess — but the way it looked at me. It was like it was actually *seeing* me."

"Okay, okay," Ben said. "Hold on, go back. It pushed you into that hole? Is that how you got injured?"

Clive shook his head rapidly as if trying to push away the cobwebs inside his brain. "No, sorry. That's not — that's not what happened. This thing was *there*, just like I said, but then... It wasn't. I mean, I'm sure it ran away or climbed a tree or something, but I didn't see it. Or at least, I don't remember seeing it."

"Maybe you should sit down, Clive," Eliza said. "Maybe take a drink of water and —"

"I know what I saw!" Clive snapped, his eyes suddenly flaring open and firing toward Eliza.

CHAPTER 39
BEN

"WHOA, BUDDY," Ben said. "We're just trying to help. We found you; now we need to figure out what this thing was. You have to help us figure it out. You say it was a gorilla, twenty feet tall, that can appear at will anywhere in the forest, and it got away from you: a trained hunter and experienced tracker. So you have to understand, it sounds a bit far-fetched."

"I know what I saw," Clive said again. His voice had calmed, however, and he looked at Ben and Eliza with a pained expression on his face. "I swear to you both, again, I'm telling the truth. But no, it wasn't that thing that did this. He — or it — disappeared, like I said when the gunshot —"

"There was a gunshot?"

Clive nodded. "Yeah, at least one, maybe more. We both heard the gunshot, me and that... thing, and then it just disappeared when I looked away. I wasn't sure where the gunshot had come from at first. I grabbed my own and got it ready, and then... And then some guy rushed me."

"He *rushed* you?" Ben asked.

Clive nodded vigorously. "Yes, he came from my left side, from behind a tree. It was probably too close for him to get a shot lined up before I saw him, so he just charged me, knowing that I also couldn't get a shot off. He tackled me, and we fought for a minute before he punched me and cut my face and then kicked me into the gulch."

Ben was absolutely shocked to hear this. Not only had Clive snuck out and tracked their mysterious apelike apparition, but he had come into contact with the man who was after him and Eliza earlier, and even fought him off.

Ben looked at his watch, trying to determine how much time had passed. "Did he go away? Why didn't he try to kill you?"

"I don't know," Clive said. "He had me — I mean, he kicked me into this gulch, and he had me. He could have easily taken the shot. I must have blacked out or something, but when I woke up, he was gone."

Ben felt Eliza's hand on his arm. "Ben," she said, "he must have heard us shooting back."

"Maybe," Ben said. But the timing didn't line up. Someone had clearly fired at them while they were in the cave, and Ben was sure he had seen their muzzle flash behind the trees. There was no way that same man had been attacking Clive moments earlier.

It meant that there had to be more than one attacker.

"What did this guy look like?" Ben asked. "Big, small, somewhere in between? Did he say anything?"

Clive shook his head. "He didn't say anything, and I didn't even hear him grunt or seem like he was exerting any effort while we fought. But he was big, huge. Kind of hairy, with a beard and mustache. Light brown hair, I think."

Ben looked at Eliza. "That's him, that's the man who attacked me two nights ago." He filled Clive in on his own story of being ambushed by the hairy man.

But that left out another piece of the puzzle, the one Ben had been chewing on before: if the giant bear of a man had attacked Clive out here, then who had been firing at them at the cave?

Ben was about to pose this question to the group when another gunshot rang out from somewhere behind them. Ben ducked and rolled forward, trying to figure out where he had placed his rifle before helping Clive out of the ditch. *Dammit,* he thought. *I'm getting really sick of being shot at by people I can't see.*

He crawled over to the tree his rifle was leaning against and saw Clive huddling next to it as well.

No. Clive wasn't huddling; he was crouching. *Trying to cover —*

"They got me," Clive said softly, under his breath.

He looked up at Ben, and Ben saw the glistening of moisture beneath Clive's hand, which was covering his chest. He glanced up and saw Clive's mouth still moving, but no words came out. Clive fell back, his back against the tree.

"Eliza!" Ben shouted.

"I saw it," she said. She was right behind Ben, but her voice was bouncing off a tree farther away. Ben knew she was looking in the other direction. Trying to find their attacker.

A sprinkle of blood fell over the corner of Clive's lip and caught on his chin. More filled his mouth, and his eyes flickered, widening and narrowing over and over again.

Ben knew there was nothing in the world he could do for the young man. He felt tears coming to his eyes, felt himself steeling against the rage that would be building inside him shortly after. He didn't want to deal with this — didn't want to have to decipher and parse it all and figure out how to tell Clive's father Olaf that his son had been shot and killed out here.

It was a selfish, unfair reaction, but it was the only one Ben allowed himself to feel. Anything more and he would begin to empathize with this young man; he would understand and feel what the kid was going through right now. He didn't want to do that; he couldn't bring himself to do that. Later, holed up inside the small hotel room back in Grindelwald, sure.

But out here, where there was no safety and plenty of things that wanted to kill them, Ben wouldn't allow himself that emotion.

He remembered what Eliza had told him about her husband, what she had told him about himself. He would wear this emotion on his sleeve, eventually, but before that, it would be added to the tumultuous mix of feelings and thoughts and reasons, and they would all be turning around in his mind until they collected together into a cohesive, useful solution.

He knew this, and he didn't like it. He didn't want it.

He watched the young man in front of him die, gasping for his last breath before slumping against the tree, his eyes still open.

CHAPTER 40
BEN

"CAN YOU RUN?" Ben asked.

Eliza shook her head, slowly at first and then more confidently. "It's pretty bad, but I guess I'll have to try, won't I?"

"Whoever is shooting at us is still out there somewhere," Ben said. "And he's not going to rest, now that he knows where we are. We need to get moving, keep working toward EKG and try to cut him off somewhere near the headquarters."

Eliza fidgeted with the crutch she was using, working it around in her hand to find a more comfortable way of holding it. After a few seconds, she placed the end of the stick on the ground and tried putting a bit of pressure on her right leg.

She winced in pain, but she was able to move a few steps without falling.

"It will get better the more I keep moving," she said. Then she laughed. "Actually, I'll just be making it worse, but it will *feel* like it's getting better. By the time we stop, I'll need to have an icepack."

"Well, there's plenty of ice around. Let's start moving. You stay in front to set the pace, and I'll follow behind and make sure there's no one tracking us."

"Okay," she said. She tested her crutch and right leg once more, and Ben was pleased to see that it seemed as though she was able to walk without needing help from him. Hopefully she was right, and her leg would at least feel good enough to move quickly. "Which way?" she asked.

"We need to move east, but if we follow this ridge southeast, we can hide up in the rocks, like we did earlier. That will help us if you need to rest more."

"I'll be fine, I promise. We just need to move, and the more I wait around and think about it, the harder it's going to be."

Ben knew she was right, that by moving toward an objective and having a goal, she could keep her mind off the pain.

Clive was dead. Ben also knew that they were both trying to ignore the psychological impact of their teammate's having been shot and killed, murdered right in front of them. Dying in Ben's arms. He knew they would both have to debrief slowly and methodically over the next few days just to prevent the shock of it all from paralyzing them.

And based on what he knew of Eliza now, he wasn't sure she would be able to handle his death without some professional help.

Ben himself had needed it before, and it never hurt to seek guidance and wisdom and have someone to talk to about it all. He remembered back a few years ago, before the CSO. When he was working at Yellowstone National Park.

He had needed that professional help quite a bit after seeing one of his coworkers fall into a crevasse and die in front of his eyes.

That had been the first time, he thought. *And it was far from the last.*

Ben had seen enough death in his nearly forty years to last multiple lifetimes. It had started young, in his twenties, when his mind hadn't even finished fully developing. Since then, he had seen murder, sickness, accidents, and none of the deaths were easy to swallow. It never got easier — he had never gotten to the point where he wanted to welcome death with open arms — but it did get a bit easier to process. His mind had learned to compartmentalize and cope with it slowly over time rather than all at once.

Clive was far from just a number, far from just one of the people he had seen die on his watch, but Ben knew that his mind would treat it that way. It was the only way through something like this.

Eliza wouldn't have that experience; she didn't have the years of fighting and shooting and death and destruction. She had been through the pain of loss when her husband had passed away, but that didn't mean she was prepared for all the death they had seen in just the two days they'd been out here.

He made another note to himself to check in with her — if and when they got to a point where they could actually rest. They needed to push on now, to stay away from this hunter that was following them. Ben still wasn't sure who was hunting them; he hadn't gotten a good look at the shooter's face, but the silhouette seemed male, but not necessarily large enough to be the hairy, broad-shouldered guy who'd punched him two nights ago.

If that was the case, he thought, *we might need to worry about* three *parties tracking us out here.*

They knew about Clive's apelike monster — the purportedly twenty-foot-tall gorilla — and they knew about this person trying to shoot at them. And Ben, of course, knew about the aggressive man from his pub encounter, and that man's willingness to use physical force to 'convince them not to be out here.'

Three different parties, all willing to kill, all dangerous.

Still, why had Clive's monster not attacked and then killed them? He had been attacked by the man hunting them, and yet Clive had said that he had seen this silverback gorilla and lived to tell about it.

Ben had been struggling with this thought for some time, and he was still working it over in his mind. The germ of an idea had begun back at the rocks where he and Eliza had stopped to catch their breath. Clive's death was only one more puzzle piece in the long chain of pieces they had been collecting. He wondered now if the young man's death would be the final piece or at least a step in the right direction. For Clive's sake, he hoped it would at least help them push forward. He hoped it would help them figure this out.

Ben crouched a bit as he walked behind Eliza, watching her steadily and carefully work through the forest toward the rocky ridge up and to their right. He needed to be alert now more than ever — Clive had already been killed, and Eliza was injured. He had Clive's pack slung over his shoulder as well as his own, but Eliza wouldn't allow him to carry hers for her. He would have to shift the gear around and leave one of the packs behind as soon as they found somewhere safe to stay, but he didn't want to do that here.

He heard nothing out of the ordinary as they crunched through the old, dry snow, the sticks and the leaves breaking free from their wintry enclosures as he walked. He thought he heard a few squirrels chattering with one another far away, but even the birds had seemed to sense their presence and were cautiously quiet.

He kept his eyes forward, on Eliza, hoping she wasn't lying to him and that her knee would hold up for this leg of their journey. She seemed to be okay, but he knew he wouldn't be able to carry her and all of their gear. He focused on her hobbled walk, unable to ignore her tight, fit figure as it swung back-and-forth. Almost graceful, considering the pain she was probably in.

He shook his head, trying to push away those undesirable emotions. He had misread her intentions earlier in the cave, and he felt bad for both of them for it. She hadn't been trying to trick him into flirting with her, nor was she trying to replace her dead husband. He understood a bit of what she was going through, and that didn't excuse any reciprocal actions on his part.

More importantly, he needed to stay focused and vigilant to keep them alive. Eliza was strong and smart, and she didn't need his protection aside for the fact that she was now far more vulnerable than they both would have hoped. He wished she was able to hold a weapon, but he knew their best chance of survival was now getting somewhere where he could defend them both from an attack on only one side rather than a thousand.

With that in mind, he cinched up the backpack straps on both packs and rechecked the magazine installed in his assault rifle. The pistols — his and Clive's — were still in their packs, and Ben decided he would have to start wearing his as a backup since he was now the only fighter they had left. As Reggie had always told him, it was faster to switch weapons than it was to reload in the middle of a fight.

He hoped it wouldn't come to that.

They marched forward, moving slowly, but thankfully faster than Ben had thought they might, and Eliza set their course, heading directly toward the edge of the forest.

He knew it would be about an hour before they could stop again, but that would put them in range of EKG's headquarters if all went well. From there they could regroup and make a plan for getting onto the inner grounds of the company.

He let his mind start to wander but then decided to turn inward once again, to focus on the task at hand and try to put it all together before they got there. Any information they had that hadn't been parsed yet needed to be considered, as any solutions they could bring to one another before they got to EKG would help them immensely in their cause.

CHAPTER 41
BEN

BEN AND ELIZA were able to reach the rocks 45 minutes later — about 15 minutes faster than Ben had expected. Eliza had begun to move much more quickly once the blood in her leg began moving, especially once they were out of the thicker part of the forest and moving over nothing but snow and grass instead.

He found a spot for them behind a line of large boulders; all tucked up against the edge of the ridge. The ridge itself curled northeast, and they were now on the very tip of it. The whole area overlooked a valley to the left of their position, where they had been previously. To the right was another wooded area, and though he couldn't see it from here, Ben's best guess was that EKG headquarters was somewhere just beyond that stand of trees.

He helped Eliza shunt her pack and get situated on the ground, where she guzzled down the last of her water and closed her eyes for a moment.

"How is it treating you?"

She opened one eye and gave Ben a look that told him everything he needed to know. "It's terrible," she said, "but it's not as bad as it was before. It is numb now, and it doesn't really hurt much, but it just won't loosen up. I feel like I can't walk right, and that I never will again."

Ben nodded along as she explained, knowing exactly how she was feeling. "You definitely will be better in a few weeks to a month," he said, "but it's going to take a bit of babying it once we're off this mountain."

"I'm just sorry it happened," Eliza said. "I should be helping more."

"Nonsense," Ben said. "You're doing just fine. Once we get into EKG and start looking around, I will be *way* out of my element. I'll need you more than ever, once we're in there."

She looked off in the distance for a moment, and then back at Ben. "Yeah," she said, "if we ever get there."

"We will. I promise. I'm pretty sure EKG is just down there, past that line of trees. They wanted a remote facility, but they still need it to be accessible for their staff and scientists. I think I remember from the maps that the whole area opens up into a sort of small valley, right? Just like the one we came from. If I were them, that's where I would put the company. A natural border around it to keep away prying eyes, but it's also one that's not inaccessible enough that they couldn't have paved a road to it for access."

"Makes sense to me," Eliza said. "When can we get moving again?"

Ben admired her for her effort and determination, but he also knew that to move too fast now could be devastating to the success of the mission. "Let's take our time. We finally are in a defensible position again, so I can hold off anyone trying to snipe at us. No one's that good a shot with just a hunting rifle, from that distance, so they'd have to get closer. If anyone pops their head up and tries to rush us, I know I *am* a good enough shot to get them while they're out in the open."

"I can help," Eliza said. "If you just give me one of the rifles, I can set it up and use one of these rocks as a —"

Ben laughed. “Before I give you *any* weapon again, you’re going through ‘Ben’s basic shooting class,’” he said. “And judging by what I saw earlier, I think we’re all safer without you having a rifle in your hands.”

She looked at him with a pouty face, but he could see the smile behind her eyes. “Was I that bad?”

“One of the worst I’ve ever seen.”

“Hey!”

“Okay, kidding. Maybe not the *worst* I’ve seen. Everyone needs practice, too. It’s a strange animal, an assault rifle. They’re finicky and don’t really want to be controlled. That first spray shot into the woods probably landed in a circle fifty yards across, but we can get that smaller. Problem is we can’t be wasting ammunition and giving away our location by taking a bunch of practice shots.”

"So, what do you want me to do?"

"I can tell you what I know, just from what I've learned from my friends and some professional shooting instructors. But you can't teach shooting by talking through it, so we'll just have to hope that it will be enough to get us through this week. The best thing you can do from now on is to try as hard as possible not to have to shoot anything at all."

“That sounds like a pretty good strategy to me,” Eliza said.

"It's pretty much the only strategy I follow," Ben answered. "Do whatever you can to not have to shoot anything, not to have to even lift your finger off the trigger guard. If you *do* have to shoot, then by all means wait as long as possible, so it's a can't-miss shot. Let them get right up into the crosshairs, fill them up, so even if you shoot wide or high, you're still hitting something vital, dropping them as quickly as possible."

“Christ,” she said, “you talk about it like it’s easy. Like we didn’t just see Clive get shot and die in front of us.”

Ben sat silent for a moment before answering. "Yeah, it is easy to talk about. Now, anyway. But talking about something and thinking about something — and especially acting on it — are all very different things. Trust me, if I could go back and once again make it hard to talk about this kind of stuff, I would. But I've made my bed; I guess I have to lay in it."

She looked confused. "Is that some American expression or something?"

"I guess," he shrugged. "Something my mom used to say. When my brother Zach and I would mess up our rooms, she would always come in and tell us that. It never really made sense in that context though, because Zach and I were always fine sleeping in a cluttered bed, one filled with toys and books."

"What's he doing now? Your brother?"

Ben shrugged again. "You know, I'm not really sure. He was at my wedding; he showed up there for a little bit but ducked out without saying goodbye. It was like he had some super-secret cool thing to do, but he wanted to see me anyway, if only just for a moment."

"But that was in Alaska, right?" She asked. "Which means he either drove or flew all the way up there just to see you guys. Weird that he would only stay for a little while and then disappear."

"Yeah, it is," Ben said. "But I've stopped asking questions like that of my life, and started just doing my best to do the right thing when confronted with the opportunity."

Eliza frowned. "Very philosophical. But what the hell does that have to do with your brother Zach?"

"I just mean, if Zach is in some sort of trouble or doing something he shouldn't be, that's not my business. I mean I would help him I guess, but I'm not going to insert myself into his life."

"Seems like that's what family is for — to insert themselves into your life."

Ben wasn't sure if she was making a joke or being serious. "Yeah, well, last time I tried inserting myself into my family life it got some of them killed."

Eliza didn't seem to have a response for this. Ben sat there, looking up at the cloud patterns and trying to figure out if the weather would hold. It was warm today, and the snow was even starting to melt when it came in contact with the sunlight. He didn't know if there was snow in the forecast, but either way — he didn't want to be out here when night fell. They needed to keep moving toward EKG and see about getting inside, without being shot by the asshole who had killed Clive.

He didn't want to bet on their odds of getting inside safely, and he didn't want to think about the odds against getting inside and finding nothing in the way of resistance. In his experience, places that engaged in the sorts of things EKG was purportedly doing didn't take kindly to outsiders snooping around in their business.

And yet, the most important part of any defensive strategy was in locating your base of operations in a proper place. EKG had put this division of their company way up here in the Swiss Alps for a reason — they wanted to make it as hard as possible for anyone to find them, and they had succeeded. It wouldn't be overkill to have guards stationed in and around their headquarters, but Ben couldn't imagine anything more than a few armed security forces milling about.

That was another reason they needed to get there as soon as possible: it would give him more time to recon the facility and its protection.

He turned back to Eliza to see her resting her eyes once again. He wanted to wait here long enough for her to let the swelling in her knee recede, but he also wanted to get the company land in his sights. He would give her fifteen minutes, and then he would do his best to explain this crash course in rifle technology and how to line up a shot.

After that, it would be up to her — and they would have to take whatever she had to give.

He rummaged around in Clive's pack, looking for anything that might help them now. The man had been very prepared, and Ben wondered if he would find some sort of painkiller in his first-aid kit.

He dumped everything out in front of him and got to work.

CHAPTER 42
BEN

THEY RESTED at the rocks for half an hour, Ben working on consolidating Clive's equipment with their own while trying to find something that would help Eliza.

He lucked out — in the first aid kit, he saw some bandage wrap material as well as a few pills labeled as generic painkillers. He gave her 800mg of the medication and wrapped her knee, trying to keep it slightly bent so it wouldn't cause her undue stress.

He helped her stand up and supported her as she hopped around in small circles, testing his handiwork. She seemed to be able to move better with it on, and he knew that once the painkillers hit, she would be able to walk almost normally. Running would be out of the question, for the most part, but hopefully, they wouldn't need to run from anything anytime soon.

“Feels good,” she said. She thanked him.

"Well, hopefully, it will at least get us to EKG. After that, you'll either need to get some real medical help or we'll be too dead to care."

She shot him a look of annoyance.

“Sorry,” he said, holding up his hands. “Bad habit. I tend to try to make things funnier so that they're easier to swallow.”

“Emphasis on ‘try to.’”

Ben laughed. “I said sorry.”

“Well, keep it up and I’ll make sure one of us *is* dead before the end of the day,” Eliza said.

Ben smiled again, glad she was still in a good mood considering her injury. “Ready to go?” He asked.

She nodded. “Yeah, ready as I’ll ever be, I guess. We’re heading almost due east now, yeah?”

“Yeah, I think so,” Ben said. “Be on the lookout for anyone trailing behind us or any guards. I’m not sure what EKG is packing, and it doesn’t seem to make sense to be constantly patrolling the woods on the outskirts of their land, but we need to be prepared for anything. Look for anyone walking around, crouched behind trees or rocks, basically anything out of place.”

“Like giant, twenty-foot-tall silverback gorillas?” Eliza asked, one of her eyebrows raised.

“Yeah,” Ben said. “Definitely be on the lookout for those.”

“Do you think he was right? Do you think there’s really something like that out here?” Eliza asked.

He had been thinking about this very thing nonstop for the past hour, but he hadn’t yet formulated his thoughts about it. “I’m not sure,” he said. “Something clearly spooked the guy, and something clearly killed those men. And it wasn’t just murder, either. It was brutal — you saw it. Whatever it was had to be at least twice as strong as a grown man, to be able to pull back the ribs like that and...” He trailed off. It sounded almost too horrific to say out loud.

“Yeah,” Eliza said. “It’s so jarring, so out of place. The fact that there could be something like that out there is insane, but then again this *is* EKG we are dealing with.”

“You showed me pictures of some of their experiments. Those were of a chimpanzee, right?”

"Yes," she said, nodding. "And those chimps — or at least the one in the images — are the most common ape chosen for experimentation, whether it's for drugs or medical research. The reasoning behind it is simple: a chimpanzee's brain structure is most similar to that of humans. The larger apes — gorillas, orangutan, baboon—not only are they too big to deal with, but their brain usually operates at a lower level. It's not as helpful for research purposes, though it's not unheard of.

"Chimps are genetically similar enough that they're actually quite a good fit for neurological testing. And there are other reasons, too: like Hepatitis B vaccination study. Chimps are the only nonhuman organisms that can host the causative vector. But I believe that if done properly, using controlled experiments, it can be above the line, ethically."

"But there are organizations still fighting against using *any* animals in testing, right? Like PETA?"

She nodded. "Yeah, they're braindead, though. To them, it's all about political power and clout and less about animal rights. The rest of us — the ones actually concerned about the *ethical* treatment of animals — are fighting a more challenging battle. One of give and take. It's a fight we've been battling for decades."

They started moving, once again Eliza leading but Ben following behind her more closely this time. They continued to talk as they worked their way downhill toward the valley.

"You think they could be experimenting on gorillas as well?" Ben asked.

"Anything is possible, I guess," she said. "And there *definitely* aren't any gorillas native to Switzerland."

"But why gorillas instead of chimps?"

She shrugged. "Even though chimpanzees are a decent representation of human neurology, in some cases it might make sense that they would use gorillas instead."

"And what cases are those?"

"I don't know; I guess things that require a larger cranial cavity? More mass to work with? It's impossible to tell without knowing what they were working on. That's what I want to find out. If I can get something — anything — that proves they *are* doing this sort of thing, we can bring them down.

"What do we need to find? What would be considered enough proof?"

"Anything and everything that seems to be specific to their research. Documents, medical charts, information on their test subjects. If we can take entire hard drives with us, that would be ideal. There's a good chance they aren't working with paper copies of anything, but if we can find files or folders of hard data, that works, too."

"So, as much as we can carry?" Ben asked.

"Yes, within reason. We can parse through it all later and pull out what we need. But these sorts of battles are fought with information, provable data. If we can get accounts of test trials, experimentation journals, that sort of thing is perfect. But any meeting notes, recordings of conversations, anything like that might be useful as well. We can put things together and read between the lines, but it will have to be a case that's strong enough to make in court, which is why we are targeting hard data here."

"I see," Ben said. He thought back to the time they had infiltrated a research station in Antarctica, fighting against both a few squadrons of professional soldiers that had been hired by the research company as well as a small army of Chinese forces, hoping to extract the same information the CSO had come to find.

They had barely escaped with their lives, but they had been — ultimately — successful. They had brought the place down around them, decimating the facility and destroying any evidence that remained. Eliza would probably disagree with his assessment, but if they weren't able to escape alive or with useful information, there was always the possibility they could just burn it all to the ground around them.

It wasn't ideal, but Ben was starting to get the feeling that it was important enough of a mission to keep all possibilities — even the drastic ones — in mind. The question he had to answer now was whether or not he could do what it would take to bring it all crashing down. Could he sacrifice everything, including his own life, to get the job done? Was it worth it to him?

He and Eliza talked about EKG and their research for another few minutes; then the conversation turned back to Ben. She asked him questions about his past, about his parents and brother, and Ben got the sense that she was trying to repair some of the damage done in his previous life. At first he resented the thought of her meddling in his personal affairs, but then he warmed up to her questioning.

She wasn't hostile, nor was she trying to lead him into some sort of psychological trap.

The conversation was jovial, lighthearted. It was completely different from the sorts of things they had been talking about for the past two days, and Ben welcomed the diversion. There would be plenty of time to get serious again, so he took to joking around with her while they walked slowly and leaned into the opportunity to take his mind off of all the death surrounding them.

CHAPTER 43
ELIZA

THEY CONTINUED for another forty minutes before reaching the edge of a long, flat meadow. Eliza had seen nothing out of the ordinary, and while she appreciated having Ben behind her as she hobbled along, her growing frustration with her knee injury made her want to tell him to stop babying her, to stop trying to take care of her.

He was a good man, and he did remind her of her late husband. Attractive, strong and confident, in many ways like all of the men she had dated in the past. She knew he was married, and she wasn't remotely interested in trying to pursue him in a romantic way, but she still felt the swaying of girlish butterflies when she caught him looking at her. He had only done it a few times, but each time been in a moment of high stress and when there had been no time to stop and discuss it, but it made her wonder what he was really thinking.

He didn't strike her as the type of man who would engage in romantic interludes while his wife was not around, but then again Eliza ultimately didn't know him very well. She wasn't out here trying to land a second husband, nor was she interested in entertaining the thought, but she had to admit it did feel good to be pursued, if that was what he was doing.

He had cared for her well over the past two days, gently working the bandage around her knee and helping her along as it healed, and he had been kind and encouraging with her when explaining to her his thoughts on weapons. Still, none of that meant anything — he would have been the same man when explaining that stuff to Clive or anyone else, and he would have treated anyone on his team with respect. He needed her in good health, so he wanted to do whatever he could to keep her knee safe and secure.

She pushed the thoughts away as Ben yammered on about his younger days at Yellowstone National Park and Rocky Mountain National Park. He didn't strike her as someone who enjoyed talking much, but he had apparently found a subject he enjoyed: the outdoors and nature.

She smiled as he told her a story about cleaning privies at Rocky Mountain when he had just gotten started as a junior ranger. It reminded her of some of the drudgeries she had done at the start of her own career as well, and she was about to bring it up when he changed the subject.

"Hey, I forgot to ask," he said. "Do you know anyone in Grindelwald named Alina?"

"I don't think so," she answered. "Who is she?"

"Well, she's college-aged and was visiting her parents when she disappeared."

"Disappeared? From Grindelwald?"

"Yeah, apparently a few nights before we started out here," Ben said. "I didn't think much of it until we started walking around out here and finding these dead bodies. I mean, of course I hope nothing like that happened to her, but I still can't help but think it's all related."

"Yeah, I've stopped believing in coincidences," Eliza said. "Lately, it seems like everything that's been going on points back to EKG somehow. How did you hear about her?"

"Like you said earlier, the city talks. My first night in town, I was at a bar and the bartender asked me to go check in with her father, who owns a bed and breakfast. He said the town was up in arms about her disappearance, and that while I was in town and looking around, I should keep my eyes open."

"What did her father say?"

"Same thing, really," Ben said. "He told me she was a good kid, that she wouldn't do something like run away, especially not after she'd gotten to town. That sort of thing. Anyway, like I said, I didn't even really consider that it might be related until we started seeing the bodies in the woods."

"You think our giant gorilla thing took her?"

"Who's to say, but that sounds pretty ridiculous to me. If this thing *was* going to kill her, why not just do it in town, where she was? Unless she was walking into the woods and stumbled onto it, the thing that killed these people doesn't seem like the same sort of thing that would walk into town and snatch some college kid."

"And yet none of this makes much sense," Eliza said.

"True. We need to consider every option. And you're right — we need to get to EKG as soon as possible to see what's really going on."

Eliza was about to respond when her eyes darted to the side, something in her subconscious pulling her attention. She stopped. Ben nearly ran into her.

"What's up?" He said.

"Over there," she pointed. "It's — it's..."

"It's another body, isn't it?" Ben asked.

She nodded, then took a step in that direction.

Like the first body they had found, this one was lying against a tree. But that was where the similarities ended. This body had clearly been out here for far longer than the first had. Most of its skin and flesh had been picked off by forest wildlife, and the skeleton was all that remained. It had sunken in on itself, as if it had fallen asleep and simply not woken up. Some of the ribs, however, were lying to the sides of the spinal cord, implying that it, too, had been ripped open and the insides of the carcass pulled out.

The skull, its eyeless sockets boring into Eliza's eyes as she walked closer to it, was sitting right next to the tree. The lower half of the skeleton's body was covered up by a drift of snow and leaves as if the forest had pulled a blanket over the body and tucked it in to keep it warm.

“Hard to tell how old it is,” Ben said. “You can see some bits of flesh, where the animals haven’t picked it clean yet.”

“Still, it has to be much older than the others, right?”

“I would have to guess three to four weeks? But it could be a week or two or a month or two. Really hard to tell.”

"Let's see if there's anything else around," Eliza said, thinking of the piece of clothing she had found and the identification badge Ben had found on the other body. She pulled out her camera and began fastening the flash attachment. The pictures wouldn't be perfect, but they would be helpful.

If there was anything of use here, she wanted to find it. All of these men or women that had died would be useful assets in her case against EKG. There was a minuscule chance these deaths were unrelated to the company, but she was willing to put a lot of money on the idea that they were directly related. The *Grayson* man, especially, had EKG’s fingerprints all over it: somebody at the company had hired that man to do some work out here, and for whatever reason, he had been killed for it.

"Not seeing anything right away," Ben said as she began snapping pictures. "But that doesn't mean there isn't something hidden under the snow. His clothes should be around here somewhere, you would think," Ben said. "Maybe under the snow or something."

Eliza began digging around in the leaves with the toe of her boot, but there was something else nagging at her, pulling her focus away from the dirt in front of her. She let her mind direct her attention back toward the skeleton, letting the image of it flicker around in her head until her attention was pulled toward the bones of its arms.

"Look at the arms, Ben," she said. "They've moved around and shifted, especially after the animals worked on them, but don't you think there — "

"They look like the others," Ben said. "They're pointing, making a line diagonally."

That's what Eliza had noticed as well: the bones of the arms and hands didn't form a perfect line, but they seemed as though they had been dropped onto the ground diagonally, half of them on one side of the body and half on the other. It reminded her of the other bodies, as if the people had died sprawled out on their backs.

"What do you think it means?"

She had some ideas, but it all seemed too unbelievable — too crazy — for her to voice them aloud. If Ben were thinking the same thing, she wanted to hear it from him first.

Ben looked at her, then back at the bones, then back at her. Finally, his mouth opened to speak. "Eliza, I don't know how it's possible, but it sure seems like this is telling us where to go."

She nodded, very slowly. It was uncanny. She had never seen or heard of anything like this before, so she had no idea how to make it all make sense. But she had to admit that what Ben said was true. It was what she had noticed as well, when they'd found the third body in the cave.

Whatever was happening here — whoever or whatever was killing these people — seemed to be doing it in a methodical, purposeful way. And they weren't just *killing* them, either. They were staging the bodies in such a way that whoever stumbled upon them afterward would notice a pattern, would see the arms pointing them along the path.

He thought back to the other bodies that they had seen. Besides the one that Clive had found, she had seen with her own eyes that the bodies all had similar diagonally staged pairs of arms. And she tried to position herself in the cave and in the woods in front of each body, trying to remember where they had pointed.

It took a bit of calculating, but she was able to place the image of the skeletons on the ground and then trace a line from each one.

She looked up at Ben. He was looking back at her, and she saw on his face that he believed it, as well.

These bodies hadn't just been murdered. They had been placed here and set up as *signposts*.

They were urging them along, pointing them directly toward some destination.

And Ben and Eliza had been following that same line.

CHAPTER 44
BEN

BEN WAS ABOUT to respond to Eliza when he heard a rustling in the distance. He immediately dropped to the ground, resting on one knee as he raised his rifle up and examined the forest around him.

Eliza groaned in pain as she stressed her right leg, but she eventually sat on the forest floor next to Ben. “What happened?” she asked. “Did you hear something?”

“I think so,” Ben said. He didn’t want to speak too loudly, for fear that it was the same hunter who had been behind them. “It came from over there.” He pointed that direction with his trigger hand, keeping the rifle aimed that way as well.

They waited there for a full minute, and then Ben saw movement again. This time he was looking directly at the noise when it happened. Another rustling sound, and then the unmistakable look of a man, striding through the trees, perpendicular to their position.

“I see it,” Eliza whispered. “It’s... it’s the hunter.”

"It has to be," Ben said. "But, hold on —" he looked through his scope and focused the center of his sights on the man who was roaming through the woods, moving north. "I don't think he's alone," Ben whispered. "I think there is another — wait, two more guys — behind him."

Eliza looked for a moment and then nodded. "I see them," she said. "What do we do?"

Ben thought through the possibilities. What he wanted to do — what he probably *should* do — was fire a few shots and try to take one of them down. Whoever these men were, they were almost without a doubt the men who had killed Clive. They were the ones who had been hunting them, and they had nearly won.

But he couldn't be sure. There was still a small trickle of doubt in his mind about who these men were. One of them could be the man who had punched him outside the bar, and while he certainly wanted to get him back for his shenanigans, Ben didn't think he deserved a bullet to the head.

Besides that, Ben couldn't see any recognizable characteristics about any of the men; they were too far away and moving farther diagonally. They hadn't seen Ben and Eliza, so Ben needed to make a decision: do they chase after them, or do they stay here and stay out of the way?

"Are we going to shoot at them?" Eliza asked.

"*You* are *definitely* not going to shoot at them," Ben said with a half-grin on his face. "If these are the guys who killed Clive, we are going to get some answers first, before we get our revenge. Life can't die for nothing, so we can't go shooting wild shots in their direction, telling them exactly where we are."

"But they're getting away," Eliza said.

"Don't worry," Ben said in reply. "They are looking for us, remember? No matter what we do, no matter where we go, as long as we are on this ridge with them, they are going to bump into us again. It's just not that big of an area."

"Okay," Eliza said. "But, I want to kill the bastard who killed Clive."

"I know how you feel," Ben said. "Trust me, though, the best thing we can do for ourselves right now is stay low and stay out of the way. I'm pretty sure we are within a few hundred yards of EKG, or at least where we thought it was. Let's see if we can find it, and find a way to get inside. Worst case, if we stir up some shit inside the headquarters, then we won't have to deal with these guys out here."

Eliza nodded, but Ben kept his eyes forward, watching the legs of the men as they marched on. They were getting farther away and keeping their trajectory. When the last in line had disappeared from view, Ben waited until the sounds of his crunching boots over the snow and sticks died away.

Well, he thought, *they certainly aren't trying to be quiet about it.*

"It's strange," he said. "If they were hunting us — if they were looking for us, I mean — they're not being very subtle about it. They didn't even seem to be fully aware; it's like they were just walking through the woods."

"But we know one of them shot Clive," Eliza said.

"We do know that," Ben said, "but we aren't sure that they're hunting for us. There still is something out here that's bigger than all of this, something that EKG most likely wants to keep quiet, if they had anything to do with it."

"So you think they're hunting for this gorilla thing?"

Ben nodded. "That guy that roughed me up back at the bar told me they were going to be hunting out here. He told me not to be anywhere near this area, *or else*. As Clive said, there isn't any big game out here, especially not stuff as terrifying as what killed those men and spooked Clive. They're out here because they are looking for whatever *that* thing is, not because of us. The fact that we're continuing to cross paths means we're on the right track, and that they're getting pissed about it."

"I see," Eliza said. "But I don't like it."

Ben waited another moment to make sure the men didn't circle back around their direction; then he stood up. "Okay," he said. "Let's get moving."

As he spoke, he looked over Eliza's head. Through the trees and away in the distance, he thought he saw a human-made structure. All he could make out was a section of what looked like a roof, the right angle of its bottom half looking strange against the curves and natural bends of the forest.

"Are they back?" Eliza asked as she stood up and stretched her leg.

"No, it's something else. I think I see a building." He pointed and let her look for a moment before taking a few steps toward the edge of the forest.

"Let's get a little farther and see what it is. The edge of the woods will let us know if we are on the right track. There's an open field about a hundred yards across, so we'll have to be careful we don't run into those men again. They're heading slightly farther north than we are, so we might be able to get across before they reach the edge of the clearing."

Eliza nodded and hobbled along next to Ben, who was still holding his assault rifle forward.

They reached the edge of the clearing in five minutes and Ben stopped by a large bush and looked through his scope. "Yep," he said. "It's a building. Two stories, like an office or small manufacturing headquarters. And there's a fence around it."

"Looks like the fence goes all the way around the property," Eliza said. "It's razor wire as well, so we definitely aren't going over it."

"Clive was prepared for that," Ben said. "When I was going through his stuff yesterday, I found the pair of wire clippers I told him to bring along when I was talking to him and his father at their shop. As long as that fence isn't electrified — and I can't imagine the energy cost it would take to do that, or that they would bother with it — we should be able to cut our way through pretty quickly."

"But it's still out in the open," Eliza said. "We're going to need to hurry."

Ben thought for a moment, then turned to look at Eliza. "Best case, it's going to take me five minutes to get across the field walking quickly, and then another 20 minutes to chop a hole in the fence."

"What are you saying?"

"Well, it's not my favorite choice, but I think it'll be safer splitting up for just a minute. You can cover me while I get across the field and start working on the fence, and then once I'm through, I can set up and offer you cover while you run across."

"You mean hobble across slowly like an injured antelope waiting to be eaten?"

"Hey, *your* words, not *mine.*" Ben smiled at her. It wasn't ideal, but having injured her knee wasn't ideal, either.

"Okay," she said. "I can do that. As long as you think I'm good enough to offer cover fire for you."

At that he laughed. "No, I know for a *fact* you're not good enough to lay down proper cover fire for me. But I'm hoping that whatever you're shooting at will be in a completely different direction than me, and it should be enough to at least hold them back for a minute or two."

She didn't look convinced.

"Besides," he said, "I'll still have my weapon with me, and Clive's extra ammo. If you start shooting, I'll know to drop everything and start taking shots as well."

She nodded and checked her rifle. She turned off the safety and set down her crutch, leaning it against a tree. Ben watched her work, and when he was satisfied, he checked his own weapon and gear and retrieved the wire cutters from his pack, placing them in his front pocket. He looked around to the left and right, examining the meadow for any sign of human intervention.

He then stepped into the open field.

CHAPTER 45
BEN

BEN JOGGED ACROSS THE FIELD, opting for speed over stealth. He'd rather make himself a harder target to hit than try not to be a target in the first place. He made it across the hundred-yard expanse in less than a minute, far shorter than he had anticipated. The distance had been deceiving, and he was now at the razor wire-topped fence.

There was nothing about the fence that told him there would be a current running through it. He had a brief flash in his mind of the scene in *Jurassic Park* when Dr. Grant approaches an electric fence and isn't sure how to test it, so he throws a stick at it. Ben knew that the scene hadn't been written to describe an effective way to check for voltage, so finding a stick would provide no more information to him than it had for Dr. Grant. So he took a breath...

...And then he touched the fence.

Nothing happened.

Relieved, he immediately started to work putting a hole in the fence. He hadn't seen any overt surveillance cameras on the shed just beyond the fence, or anywhere else on the fence posts, but that didn't mean there weren't any. Still, there was no need for being discreet —

he didn't want to have to strain to get through the fence, so he made the hole large enough to walk through at a crouch.

He was halfway around the top arch of the hole in the fence, clipping the wires in front of him at chest level when he heard Eliza scream.

"Ben!"

He whirled around, dropping the wire cutters as he fumbled for the rifle he had set against the fence to his left. His pack, forgetting it was still on, swung around and smacked into the chain-link, which pulled him off-balance. He adjusted quickly, then dropped to a knee to make him a smaller target while grabbing his rifle.

By the time he had the rifle up and over his right eye, Eliza screamed again.

He saw her, running as fast as she could. Directly toward him.

She wasn't moving quickly, and he could tell she was in a lot of pain as she stumbled through the meadow. *What are you doing?* Ben thought. *Why are you running toward —*

Then he saw it.

At first it was just a blur. Just a streak of white and dark gray.

Then it disappeared back into the woods, and Ben lost sight of it for a moment until it swung around a tree trunk and then back out into the meadow.

Ben's jaw dropped. He couldn't believe what he was seeing.

As Eliza was working her way toward *him*, the largest gorilla he had ever seen was working its way toward *her*.

It was still fifty yards off of her right side, but it was clearly aiming for Eliza.

"Eliza!" he shouted. "Get down!"

Either Eliza couldn't hear him, or she ignored the order. He wanted to get a shot off, and the longer he waited the closer the gorilla would get to Eliza. At this distance, he knew he was mildly accurate, but there was no way in hell he was going to accept the risk of shooting Eliza as well. With the rifle's rounds, any shot from any distance would be devastating and likely lethal to a human.

Guess it's one-on-one, then.

He stood up, preparing to run toward the animal and Eliza. He threw his rifle over his shoulder, his eyes directed toward the scene unfolding in the middle of the meadow. Then, out of the corner of his vision, he noticed more movement.

This time it was from his right side, from the north.

Three men.

All staring at Ben.

What the hell is happening?

He wasn't ready for this — they hadn't been prepared for this. Both attacking parties — the animal and the men — had caught them both off-guard, at the same time. *Dammit*, Ben said to himself.

The men were all armed, and all were pointing their weapons directly at him. He wasn't going to last long in a firefight out here, three to one, with no protection. He had seen enough westerns and he didn't have a horse to hide behind.

That meant his decision had been made for him. He needed to get closer to Eliza to give her a fighting chance. Hopefully, the men would not be able to hit him as he ran, but they were certainly within range of getting close to him.

He ran anyway, aiming directly for Eliza, not bothering to run in a serpentine way to throw off the men's aim. He was halfway to Eliza in ten seconds; in three more, he had almost completely closed the distance.

He wasn't going to make it. The gorilla, a massive, muscular specimen of silverback gorilla, was bearing down on Eliza.

And then it stopped. For just a moment, the massive male gorilla sat back on its haunches and stared at Ben. Ben made eye contact with it, breathing heavily, wondering if he could get his rifle unslung and aimed before the gorilla moved in to attack.

He knew he couldn't — that if the gorilla wanted to, it could be on Eliza and him in an instant — before Ben could even lift a finger.

And that still left the men to his right.

He heard a popping sound — the men were now firing. He ducked but kept his eyes on the gorilla. The gorilla seemed utterly unfazed by the men's fire as he examined Ben.

Ben looked into his eyes, seeing the intelligence there, watching it examine him as much as he was examining it. For what seemed like an entire minute, man and beast stared at each other, assessing one another.

Come on, big guy, Ben thought. *Don't make me shoot you.*

Eliza was sobbing, and he noticed she was hunched over her right leg, leaning heavily on her crutch. Her rifle and pack were laying in the field nearby, but not close enough that either would be any help to them.

Ben tried to take a step forward.

The gorilla bolted. "No!" Ben shouted, but it was too late.

The gorilla barreled toward Eliza, closing the distance in half a second.

Ben winced, involuntarily closing his eyes.

When he opened them a moment later, the gorilla was gone.

Then he saw it, still moving, picking up speed as it hurled itself toward the men on the other side of the clearing.

Ben didn't hesitate. He ran toward Eliza, closing the last five yards and coming to her side, wrapping her up in his arms and lifting her off the ground. She yelped in surprise, but Ben didn't stop.

She dropped her crutch as Ben spun around quickly and aimed back toward the fence. He threw her over his shoulder, holding her by the back of her legs, and he felt her shaking and heard her groaning in pain as he squeezed on her right knee.

It's okay, he thought. *It's going to be okay*.

"Hold on," he said through gritted teeth. She felt as though she weighed nothing, and Ben tried to run as though he wasn't being weighed down by a full-grown human being. Everything happened in slow motion, but Ben pounded forward with powerful legs, not willing to turn around to see what was happening.

He heard the weapons of the men, firing more rapidly now, but he didn't dare stop to see what they were firing at. He hoped — he assumed — they were firing at the gorilla, but he couldn't be sure they weren't trying to hit him and Eliza instead.

He reached the fence at about the time the firing stopped. All three men were reloading now.

Or the beast had reached them...

"Did you cut through the fence yet?" He heard Eliza ask.

"Almost all the way," Ben said. "But I've cut through enough that we can bend it back and get through. There's no time left to open it more."

He set her on the ground but kept an arm under her shoulder to support her. He once again set the rifle down against the fence to the left of the hole, then reached in and pulled the chain-link back, bending it toward him and Eliza. It moved easily, pliable enough for him to open a triangular hole in the half-arch he had cut earlier.

"We'll have to go one at a time," Ben said. "And you don't have a crutch. Let me go first, and I'll hold your hand on the other side."

"I'm fine," Eliza said, venom in her voice. "Those bastards are shooting at that gorilla. If we can't stop it, we need to get inside."

Eliza was surprisingly lucid, and he wondered if the pain medication was helping her to stay focused. He nodded, letting her catch her balance before releasing her and stepping through the hole in the fence.

He wondered if this was a suicide mission, a guaranteed failure. Eliza wasn't naive, but he understood her more now. The woman was driven, guided by the singular solution she had landed upon. There were no alternatives, no other ways out. Her life's work had been wrapped up in this, and her entire life had been taken from her *because* of this.

And yet Ben knew she wasn't prepared for the death they'd already seen. He could see it on her face, behind her eyes, an adrenaline-fueled determination that he knew would shatter horrifically when things got more intense. It wasn't a question of if — it was *when*. She would go down, and he only hoped he would be in a position to help her back up.

It's too late to back out now, he thought.

Once on the other side he reached through and grabbed his rifle, then held it up as Eliza slowly worked her way through the open hole in the fence. It took a few seconds, but she made it to the other side and used the fence for support.

Before they moved on, Ben reached through the hole and pulled the chain-link back into place. He tried to flatten it out, to make it appear as though it had not been cut. From a distance, he hoped it would look as though they had simply found another way in. It might slow them down, it might not. But at this point, Ben would take any opportunity he could to get another lead.

As he finished the last section of chain-link, he dared a glance upward and across the meadow.

The three men and the gorilla were gone.

CHAPTER 46
BEN

THE WARRIORS RETURNED a few seconds later, as Ben watched on. The men were running, chased by the gorilla, out of the cover of the trees and into the clearing once again. Ben saw the gorilla run toward the other group. The three men stopped near the edge of the clearing, a few feet into the meadow. The grass in that area was tall, and he watched one of the men drop to his knee and nearly disappear behind the wall of thick meadow grass.

That man pulled his rifle out and aimed it toward the gorilla. He fired two shots in quick succession, but neither hit the gorilla.

Or, Ben realized, *neither shot was strong enough to wound the gorilla.*

The gorilla kept running, now only ten feet away from the men. It reached the first man, the one who had fired at it, and it smacked him aside as if he hadn't even been there.

Ben recognized the man as he flew through the grass. It was the large man from outside the pub, the one who had pulled Ben aside and told him not to come out here, underlining his point with *physical* touch. Ben couldn't believe the strength of the gorilla, how the man had just flopped through the air as if he were nothing but a rag doll.

And the gorilla was still moving. It bowled over the next two men, and they both fell, scrambling to get out of the way as the gorilla simply cruised over them. It didn't continue after that, however. The gorilla stopped, whirled around, and looked down at the two men. It was as if it were deciding which of them to kill first.

Ben couldn't see the two men lying in the grass. The large man that had been hit first was now working on standing up, obviously shaken and without his weapon, but he seemed to be intact.

Suddenly the other man jumped up and lurched aside, preparing for a breakaway.

Ben remembered the old joke: *you don't have to outrun the bear, you just have to outrun the other person in your party.*

But this was no bear. Apparently, the gorilla had an eye for this man specifically, for whatever reason. It followed the man and ignored the other two, taking a few huge strides before grabbing the smaller man around his thigh. It snapped him back with almost no effort whatsoever, and the man screamed and flopped to the ground. The gorilla held on, yanking the man's leg and pulling him back toward him.

Ben heard the man's screams from across the meadow.

The gorilla used its other hand now, grasping the man's shoulder and twisting his body around. Ben saw man and beast stare silently at each other for a moment. The gorilla seemed to be examining this man, trying to identify him.

And then, as if it were a twig, the gorilla twisted the body apart, snapping the man's neck.

Ben winced. Never in his life had he seen such a thing. So simple, easy. It was horrifying and brutal.

And yet...

There was something calm, something graceful, about the magnificent creature. The way it looked at the man in its hands, as if it had been *ashamed* of what it had done.

The gorilla held the man, now limp and lifeless, in his hands for another few seconds. It was too far away for Ben to hear, but it looked as though the gorilla chuffed or grunted as he tossed the man to the ground and turned his attention elsewhere.

Eliza was sitting on the ground next to Ben, and he knew she couldn't see what was going on. He didn't want to tell her, but he had a feeling she could imagine exactly what was happening out in the meadow.

The gorilla leaned down, and with a quick snap of its finger ripped the man's shirt from his chest, tearing it into two pieces.

Oh my God, Ben thought. *It's going to eviscerate him, just like the other bodies we found.*

The gorilla raised a hand high above his head, but before it could descend down and begin tearing into the man, Ben heard a gunshot.

The gorilla roared and stumbled to the side.

Ben started walking in their direction.

"What are you doing?" Eliza asked. "You'll get yourself killed."

"I have to go help," Ben said. "That thing is going to kill all of them."

"They've been trying to kill *us*," Eliza said. "Let them get killed."

Ben looked down at Eliza and found that she wasn't even looking in the men's direction. Her eyes were turned toward the entrance to the building behind them. She was riled up, shaking visibly, and Ben knew she wasn't thinking clearly.

"You don't mean that," Ben said. "I've been shot at before, and I'm a pretty good shot myself. If they try to turn the gun on me..."

His voice trailed off. Was he really going to march into a battle between three men and a giant gorilla and hope to come out of it unscathed? He knew it was a recipe for suicide.

Still, he felt he had to do something to help out.

He had always felt an affinity toward animals, how they were driven by pure instinct rather than some bastardized form of logic and emotion that humans had tried to develop. But he had also seen firsthand a deadly animal attack, and the memory had been haunting him for ten years. He wanted to prevent another similar memory if he could.

If there was anything he could do, he would do it.

He crouched down and looked into Eliza's eyes. "Stay here; get some rest. I'll be able to see you from over there, so I'll be able to run back if you need help."

Eliza opened her mouth to protest. "But —"

"No," Ben said, cutting her off. "There's been enough death already. I'm going to stop it if I can. For Clive. Eliza — " Ben looked down at her and waited until she returned his gaze. "— we made it. *You* made it. This is it. EKG. If something happens to me, you can still find a way inside. You can still figure out what they're doing. Your camera is still intact, and we have our phones, with a little bit of battery power. Go in there and record what's going on and get back out."

He thought he saw Eliza nod.

With that, Ben turned again and set off toward the three men.

As he neared the scene, he could see that the gorilla was gone. It hadn't been killed — there was nothing on the ground next to the dead man and his two coworkers — and Ben couldn't see any large, white lumps on the ground nearby. It must have disappeared shortly after getting shot.

Still, Ben ran on. He wanted to have a word with this goon who had attacked him.

CHAPTER 47
BEN

BEN HUSTLED over to the man who was sprawled out on the ground — the one who had been flung through the air. As he drew closer to him, the man shifted, trying to pull himself up onto an elbow. He failed, gasping for air as he sank back to the meadow grass.

Ben slowed, then sank to one knee near the man's feet. He clutched his rifle tightly, knowing that it would be difficult to get a shot off this close to the enemy, but not wanting to be completely unarmed. This was the same man who had taken him by surprise three nights ago outside the pub, and he wasn't about to let this guy get a jump on him again.

For all he knew, this man was just faking his injury and waiting for Ben to get close. Ben squeezed the stock of his rifle, knowing that he could easily smack the man across the face with the butt of the gun if it came to that.

The man grunted, looking down at his chest. Ben followed his eyes, flicking them down quickly to see if there were any open wounds. He saw nothing but knew that the man's clothing could easily be hiding a large bruise or signs of a ruptured organ. The gorilla had lifted this man — easily 250 pounds — completely off the ground and thrown him as if he were nothing but a crumpled paper sack. Surely he had to be feeling it.

"Are you okay?" Ben asked. He wasn't sure he was going to help this man yet, but if he could play nice for a minute to extract some information, he would take the opportunity.

The man stared at Ben for a long moment and then shook his head. "I told you to stay away from here," the man said, his voice a growling whisper.

"I've never been so good at taking orders," Ben said, shrugging. "Probably would have been best for me to join the military to learn how, but I didn't like the sound of getting barked at all day."

The man on the ground took this in for another long pause, and Ben wasn't sure if he was considering his response or if he was trying to parse Ben's words into his native tongue. It was clear from the man's accent that he wasn't a native English-speaker, but outside the pub, they hadn't seemed to have any trouble communicating.

"This wasn't your fight."

"Well, I think it is now," Ben said. "That... thing. That *gorilla* — is that what you were afraid of?"

The man let out a gurgling laugh and then tried to speak again. He coughed, and Ben thought he saw a bit of blood on his closed fist as he pulled it away from his mouth. "I'm not afraid of *it*," the man said. "The men who hired me — one of them is lying dead right over there — *they're* the ones you needed to be worried about."

Ben hadn't expected this response. Sure, he assumed this macho soldier guy would be above admitting personal fears, but he hadn't expected to sell out his compatriots so quickly. "You could have just said as much back at the pub," Ben said.

"You know I couldn't."

"They hired you?"

The man nodded. "The company behind it, they —"

"EKG?" Ben asked again, cutting him off.

"You know about them?" The man asked.

“I know enough. The redheaded woman I’m with; she used to work there.”

Ben thought he saw a flicker of surprise in the man's eyes, a quick widening and narrowing. But a second passed, and the man's face was once again a mask, hidden behind an expressionless pair of eyes and a full, thick brown beard.

“Did the company — EKG — *torture* that thing?” Ben asked.

“No idea,” the man replied. “I wasn’t hired to study it. I was hired to kill it.”

"And us?" Ben asked. "Were you hired to kill us as well? Clive, that kid we were with? You shot him in the chest, and I watched him bleed out."

The man shook his head again. “Not me,” he said. “The other man I was with. The Frenchman. Waste of air, that one.”

Ben looked over. “He did this? Why?”

“Wish I knew,” the man grunted. “Best guess, they don’t want anyone else screwing with their operation here. They hired me to find that thing two weeks ago. Well, I couldn’t do it. No sign of it, either. I was running around like a city-dweller on a camping trip. So they called me in and told me they were going to help me out. That they were going to ‘come with me.’”

"That doesn't explain why he killed a member of our team and took potshots at us," Ben said.

"As I said, I wish I knew *why* they wanted you out of the picture,” the man continued. “But I just know they wanted you dead. Wanted everybody dead. I had a feeling they’d even make a go at me after this was over, just to make sure I’d stay quiet.”

“And so they wouldn’t have to pay you,” Ben said.

“I’ve had enough of this hell to worry about money anymore. I’m old now, tired of this.”

“What else can you tell me?”

"Well, not much. They were sly if anything. One of them kept sneaking off, taking secret phone calls in the morning before he thought the rest of us were awake. I heard the gunshots too, but he always said it was just 'target practice' or 'hunting.' Asshole never brought down any game, though. Worst hunter I've ever seen."

"Who are you? How did you end up all the way out here, working for them?" Ben asked.

The man studied Ben for a long moment, clearly having difficulty breathing. After a long sigh, or what Ben assumed was supposed to be a sigh, he turned his eyes up to the clouds above. "It is beautiful out here, isn't it?"

Ben sat back and waited for the man to go on. It was a strange thing to say, especially in the moment, and coming from a man such as this, but then again, Ben had no idea who he was or what he was indeed like.

"My name is Elias Ziegler. I am a trained hunter, much like that kid you had. He was young though, inexperienced."

"You mean he wasn't used to hunting other humans?" Ben asked.

The man arched an eyebrow. "Yeah, that's about what I mean. Anyway, this is what I do for a living. Or what I *did*. Not sure there's going to be much *living* after this."

Ben had the urge to help the man sit up. He pulled on his shoulders and the man slowly rose to a sitting position, his hands now holding his side.

"Spleen, I imagine," the man said. "I've been shot before, more than once, but I've never been tossed around by a damn ape."

"There's a small hospital back in Grindelwald," Ben said. "No reason they shouldn't be able to fix you up and —"

"I've got a job to do, son. I may be bleeding internally, but that thing is still out there, running around and killing anyone it recognizes. If I'm able to sit up and talk about it, I'm able to kill it, too."

He was about to go on, but Ben held up a hand and stopped him.

It was something the man had said—something Ben and Eliza had been considering.

"Wait. What? What are you talking about? It's killing anyone it *recognizes*?"

"Well, no shit, son. Why do you think it jumped over your lady friend and your dead buddy? Why do you think it just tossed me aside? I was in the *way*, but I wasn't its *target*. Same with you two."

Ben chewed his lip. "Why not? You had a gun, you shot at it, even."

The man chuckled and then coughed more blood. "They hired me, but I wasn't part of their security team. I wasn't in *there*." He lifted a finger and pointed it, shaking, at the building where Ben had left Eliza waiting outside.

"Are you saying this gorilla actually *recognizes* people, and is making decisions to kill based on that?"

The man looked confused. "Are you dense? You saw the bodies it left behind, right? Those were staged — set up to point you in the right direction. But it was staged by *that thing*. To point you here. It didn't just kill those men because it knew they worked there, because it had interacted with them before. It killed those men because it wanted to leave a *trail* for us to follow. A trail for *you* to follow, apparently."

Ben rocked on his heels. *Could this be true?* It seemed so... unbelievable. Ben knew gorillas — like all apes — were on the intelligent side of the spectrum for mammals, but he had no idea they were capable of such a thing. He had no idea that recognition — and selective murder — were parts of a gorilla's neurological potential.

"Okay, then," Ben said. "So it wants everyone who it interacted with at this company dead. That tells me there's something *seriously* screwed up about this EKG place. That's what that woman back there needs to find. We can take pictures, video even, bring it back to —"

"You're insane, son. If you go in there — start poking around and taking pictures — they'll kill you."

"Who's they? There aren't even any guards?"

The man coughed. "There are. They're inside. It's a company called *Grayson*, but most of them have been furloughed while EKG tries to figure its shit out. They needed the guards more when the *humans* were a problem — theft, illegal snooping and pictures, that sort of thing. Now, when it's just animals to worry about, there wasn't much *Grayson* guards could do. They sent most of them home, but a few of them are still out here, hunting."

Ben nodded. *They're not hunting anymore,* he thought.

"They don't have an army in there, but whatever security they have in that place isn't going to take too kindly to a couple people like you breaking in and trying to leave with some propaganda.

"They're not just going to sue you or ask you nicely to leave. If they made that thing that's running around, that means they've got more where it came from. They *did* something to it — I guarantee it. And if you think they're above doing something like that to *you*, you got another thing coming."

CHAPTER 48
BEN

BEN LEFT THE HUNTER, Elias Ziegler, in the field. The guy was far too large to carry, and it seemed as though he wouldn't have accepted help anyway. They talked for another minute, but the man's eyes began to drift, to wander.

Ben didn't think the man was going to make it — his internal wounds prevented him from even staying in a seated position. Ben felt for the guy, but there was a bigger problem to tackle now.

If Ziegler had been right about the gorilla — that it was only attacking people it recognized and worked for EKG directly — it had simply thrown Ziegler out of the way in order to get to the *real* threats: the two other men, one of whom was now dead on the ground near Ziegler.

Ben had returned to Eliza at the building and examined the exterior. It was a nondescript structure, not ugly but certainly not hoping to win any architecture awards, and there were no windows along the walls of at least this side.

About a hundred feet to their right was a small parking lot that backed up to the building and around the other side of it where it met with a tall garage door, a loading dock. The size of the lot suggested that there wouldn't ever be more than a small staff of doctors and professionals working at any given time; the lot itself had only three cars in it that Ben could see.

There was a chance everyone had parked on the far side of the lot and their vehicles were hidden from view, but Ben had a feeling this wasn't the case. This place had the feel of a secretive, tucked-away office.

"How do we get in?" he asked.

He was standing at the doorway, looking inside. The building itself was concrete, the doors some amalgam of metal, thick and impenetrable. All of it added to his suspicion that there were some serious ethical situations going on inside.

"There's a keycard reader over here," Eliza said, pointing to a flat gray rectangle that had been recessed into the wall next to the door.

Ben hadn't seen it before she brought his attention to it, but he knelt down to examine it. Besides the fact that it was flush against the wall, it didn't seem to be any different from the card readers most corporate buildings used. "Yeah," he said. "Problem is that we don't have a key."

"We don't?" Eliza asked with a certain suspicion on her face. "What about that ID badge you nabbed from that dead security guard out in the woods?"

Of course.

Ben had forgotten about that. He quickly withdrew the card from his back pocket and held it up to the door. Before he moved his hand to the left to hover the card directly over the reader, he looked at Eliza. "There's no going back once we do this," he said. "There weren't any security guards outside, but that doesn't mean there aren't any inside."

"I know."

"If we get in there, and someone sees us, there's a chance they could start shooting at us."

"I know," Eliza said again. "But there's no chance in *hell* I'm getting this close to proving my theory without actually going inside and seeing it for myself. We both know what they're doing in there, Ben, and I'm going to get proof of it once and for all. If I get shot while I'm in there, you need to take my camera or at least the card in it, and get whatever information we find out of here."

Ben wasn't so much worried about finding and retrieving proof as he was of his own safety. Ben had no intention or interest in getting shot — no matter how reckless it seemed his partner was going to be.

Nevertheless, he swiped the card over the reader and heard the locking mechanism from within the concrete wall disengage, and the door in front of him popped open an inch. He stepped to the side, mirroring Eliza's position on the opposite side of the doorframe, waiting for some reaction from within.

None came.

He checked his magazine, then ensured the safety on the rifle was off, and finally, he poked the tip of it out and pushed the door open farther.

Still, no shots were fired from inside the building.

He did notice that some light reflected off the ground in front of the door, bouncing out from inside the facility, mixing with the shadows beginning to form in the dusk light outside.

"Seems like someone's home," he said.

"We used to work staggered shifts," Eliza said. "No matter what day, or what time, someone was *always* home."

"Like I said, keep your eyes up and your gun pointed straight. And don't fire unless you are absolutely sure it's going to hit the thing you want it to hit."

It wasn't much of a speech — nor was it much of a training lesson in weapons use — but it was all Ben could muster at the moment.

"Should I go first?" Eliza asked.

"No, stay behind me, and keep your gun pointed to the sides. Never at my back."

She nodded, but Ben was already pushing the door open wider and beginning to rush inside.

The heavy metal door swung on its hinges silently, allowing Ben to enter the brightly lit room without being heard. He immediately ducked to his left, his back against the wall, his rifle forward. Eliza followed behind him, ending up on the same wall just to his right.

CHAPTER 49
BEN

HE COULDN'T SEE anything out of the ordinary — at least nothing that he wanted to shoot at immediately. This room was some sort of antechamber, a large chamber that had been constructed to serve as a makeshift front desk location. That desk was over to Ben's right, and it was a standard office desk, complete with a shiny, green fake plant, potted and situated on the top corner of the two-level table.

No one was sitting behind it.

Ben flicked his eyes around, taking in the rest of the scene. A few generic landscapes hung on the walls, the fluorescent lights doing little to make them look any more attractive, and a simple rectangular trashcan set against the opposite wall to his right. Directly in front of him was a right-angled archway, the size of a set of double doors, but there were no doors blocking entrance to the next section of this facility. He could see straight down the hallway, and he could see where each of the unnaturally bright fluorescent lights sprayed their illuminating wash over the tiled floor below them. The hallway was empty all the way down to the opposite side of the building, about 200 yards directly in front of him.

"I don't see anybody," Eliza said.

"Me either," Ben said. He didn't elaborate. Just because they couldn't see anyone *now* didn't mean there wasn't someone waiting behind a doorway or behind one of these archways, hoping for an opportunity to take them off-guard. He held his weapon at the ready, once again more than aware of the diminishing number of rounds he had available to shoot, and well aware of Eliza's near-incompetence with her own weapon.

"Our goal is to get in, take pictures and files, and get out. No firing that weapon. Best if you keep the safety on as long as possible, and only take it off if you think I'm not going to be able to get a shot off." The last thing he wanted was for her to get spooked by something and fire off a burst of shots into the ceiling, alerting everyone working on either of the two floors to their presence.

She nodded next to him, and he took a few steps forward, aiming for the archway in front of him. He stayed to the left, behind the arch and out of view from the hallway. He hadn't seen any cameras mounted in this room, but that didn't necessarily mean there weren't any. Julie had shown him plenty of incredible security options when she was working with Mrs. E on the security of their own home and headquarters back in Alaska — some modern-day HD and 4K cameras were completely invisible to the naked eye when painted and hidden in a room. One option he had seen was about the size of his own fingernail.

He waited at the arch for Eliza to copy his movement and end up at the arch across from him, and then he quickly and silently slid around the beam to end up in the hallway. He counted ten doors between his position and the end of the hallway, but only eight doors on the right side. It looked as though there was a gap wide enough for a set of stairs or an elevator on the right side of the hall just before the end wall. If they couldn't find what they needed down here, they would have to go upstairs.

He wasn't sure if the place had a basement, but worst case they could search that as well.

"No talking," he whispered. "From now on, it's complete silence unless you absolutely need to say something."

He saw in his peripheral vision Eliza nodding back at him.

Ben stepped forward and walked toward the first of the doors on his left. There was an identical doorway across the hallway to his right, and he saw Eliza emulating his motions and moving toward that door. He hadn't had time to show her how to properly clear a room, but the truth was he hadn't been thoroughly trained on the tactic, either. The best he could hope for was that both of them would open the doors simultaneously, poke their heads in and see what awaited them inside, and then move onto the next doors.

Speed was an issue, so he wasn't concerned about having Eliza's rifle next to his as they inspected each room. By splitting up, they could tackle two rooms every five seconds or so.

He reached out with his left hand and felt the handle in his fingers. He pulled it down, feeling it click and give easily. *Unlocked.* He pulled it open an inch, and then another few inches. Finally, he threw the door open far enough for him to walk inside.

He led with the tip of his rifle, careful to ensure that his head and the bulk of his body stayed inside the hallway, relatively safe from anyone who might try to attack him from inside the room. He reached inside and flicked on a lightswitch.

But the room was empty. There were a few boxes against the wall on his left, and a folding table in the center of the room with one of the same style of boxes sitting atop it, its lid removed and placed upside-down on the table. He could see papers and folders inside the box.

Nothing else in the room caught his attention.

He turned to Eliza. "See anything?" She had just opened her own door on the right side of the hallway and had ducked her head inside.

She pulled back out of the room and turned to face Ben. "Nothing but some boxes; stacks of them. Some sort of storage room, I guess."

"Yeah, that's what I've got, too." He didn't want to keep discussing things out loud, so he motioned with his head to the next room, and together they walked on either side of the hallway toward the next door in line.

He felt the handle again, felt it give again, and opened it a crack once again.

So far, everything had been exactly the same as the first door, but when he opened it, hit the lights, and saw what was inside, he stopped before entering.

This room could not have been more different from the first. It was a full-on medical suite — surgical by the looks of it — with a solid metal table and paper-thin mattress on top, huge bulbs hanging from the ceiling directly above it, and a few stools scattered around it. Against each wall were more tables and shelves full of equipment, all sparkling and silver. He saw an intravenous drip stand with a few empty infusion bags hanging from it, waiting to be filled and put to use.

He turned back to the hallway and waited for Eliza to come out of her room. "Looks like a hospital room," Ben said. She nodded in reply, and Ben walked back into his room to start examining the room in more detail.

There were no computers or servers in sight within the surgical suite, so he knew they wouldn't be able to extract any useful data from the room, but he also wanted to make sure that he'd checked every corner of the space for anything that might be useful before moving on. He couldn't see anything that seemed to be out of place — he hadn't spent much time in a hospital room, but this place seemed to check all of the boxes for him.

Besides having no windows, no glass on the doors, and no viewing chamber along one wall, the rooms appeared to be just office spaces, converted into normal surgical operating rooms.

He even saw a drain on the floor near the table.

He pulled back out of the room and met with Eliza in the hallway. "So far, nothing seems to be out of place, and there's nothing I can think of to grab that would prove what they're doing here."

"Right," Eliza said. "If the other rooms are like this one, I don't think there's going to be anything incriminating on this first floor, at least not in plain sight."

"But Eliza, there's *nothing* here. You said it yourself — there are 24/7 shifts at this company, right? Where is everybody?"

She shrugged, her voice still low. "Honestly, I don't know. I was never with this division after Dr. Canavero was placed in charge. They moved out here, built this place to do God-knows-what, but they could have *completely* different procedures now than what I was used to. Nothing looks familiar. It's all been reconfigured."

Ben considered this. It was possible that they were wrong — that EKG wasn't doing anything at all suspicious.

Possible, but not likely. If this truly was EKG Corporation, there would be something here that suggested it.

They just had to find it.

"Okay, let's keep moving. There's got to be something around we can use. Something that proves what you —"

His words were cut off by the sound of a heavy door opening from farther down the hall.

CHAPTER 50
ELIZA

ELIZA PULLED Ben into her room. "Quiet," she whispered. She could tell that Ben had heard the sound, but she still wasn't going to take any chances.

"Came from down the hall, I think," Ben said. "Footsteps."

Ben tapped her on the shoulder, then pointed to his eyes, then to the hallway. *Watch out*. He turned into the room and started silently pacing around. After a few seconds, he grabbed something off the table and returned to Eliza.

Ben returned to where Eliza was waiting and shrugged. "I was looking for something to use as a mirror, but I don't think it makes sense anyway. If they see something sticking out of the doorway, we're hosed."

Eliza nodded in response. "We'll be able to hear them coming and know when they're close," she said. "What's the plan?"

"I can hear them. Doesn't sound like they're stopping to check every room, which means they're on patrol if they're security, and they don't know we're here yet. Or just some workers walking to another room."

They waited another few seconds, listening to the sounds of the footsteps in the hallway. "We can't take any chances, though. Let's let them pass, and when they're right next to the door, we'll both run out and try to intercept them."

"And if they're armed?" Eliza asked.

"We need to keep the element of surprise on our side," Ben said. "Let me go first and try to knock both of them off balance. But be right behind me — if they are security guards, chances are they'll be trained, and I won't be able to take both of them out."

"You want me to *shoot* one of them?" Eliza asked.

"I'd rather we try to knock them unconscious, but that might be tricky to do. Like I told you before, if you absolutely have to shoot your weapon, make sure they're filling up the crosshairs and it's a can't-miss shot."

Eliza swallowed, trying to physically gulp down her fear. She had never shot at another human before this week, and now she was actually considering — contemplating, premeditating — how to shoot one and kill one. She didn't want to let Ben down, but she was more worried she would let herself down.

She wasn't sure she could handle the stress of a situation like that, if it came to it. "I'll do my best," she whispered.

Ben nodded, then crouched behind the half-open door. She was next to him on his right, and she copied his movements, kneeling down on the floor and gripping the weapon in her hands as tightly as she could.

"Five seconds," Ben whispered. "I should be able to get at least one of them to the ground, but you can't hesitate or I'm dead."

He wasn't helping her to feel any better, but the logical portion of her brain told her that he was just trying to be clear. She knew it was the right call. She had no intention of leaving him high and dry, fighting off two armed security guards alone in the hallway, but she also had no idea how her body would respond.

But it was too late to consider it any further.

The footsteps grew louder, and Ben sprang into action.

Without making a sound, Ben swiveled and turned around the

open door and faced the hallway, all while standing and holding his rifle forward. Eliza moved to a standing position as well, and she caught the action through the crack of the open door.

Ben reached the person closest to them first — a woman holding a small subcompact machine gun— and smacked the butt of his rifle hard across her face. She went down with a quiet yelp of confusion, her weapon bouncing away from her. The other person, a man holding a similar-looking gun, turned and started to lift his weapon before Ben could get to him.

Eliza was now at the open door, and her hands were shaking. Ben jabbed his rifle out again, knocking the man's gun up but not out of his hands. He fired, sending a quick smattering of rounds directly overhead into the drop ceiling.

Dust and chunks of ceiling tile fell around the two men. The sound was deafening and echoed in Eliza's ears. She placed her hand over the stock, her finger over the trigger guard, then lifted it and put it on the trigger.

She squeezed slowly, feeling the pressure and resistance of the trigger beneath her finger. *It hadn't been this difficult yesterday in the cave. Was it only yesterday?* She couldn't even remember when she had last slept.

She pushed the question out of her mind. *Bad time to be trying to figure out things like that*, she thought.

Ben and the second guard were grappling in the hallway, Ben trying to get his hands around the man's throat but having no luck. The guard kneed Ben in the crotch, and Ben doubled over.

The man followed up with his other knee, this time catching Ben in the face. Eliza saw blood smack to the floor.

Now, Eliza, she willed herself. *Fire the gun.*

And yet her finger didn't move. It couldn't.

This isn't what I want, she realized. *I don't want to kill anyone. We are doing this so no more life is lost.*

In the time leading up to this moment, Eliza had wrestled with the possibility that she might have to fire this weapon directly into someone else's face or chest. Up until this moment, she believed herself capable of doing just that.

And yet...

The guard continued pummeling Ben, the larger man having trouble keeping his hands over his face. The guard punched Ben in the gut and then shifted to his side, trying to both get away from the attack and simultaneously gain purchase around the man's legs.

Finally, Ben was able to grab the guard's leg and he wrapped his arms around it. He pulled, and the guard lifted up off the ground.

Ben fell with the man in his hands, and both men crashed against the doorframe of the room opposite Eliza's. Taking advantage of the momentary victory, Ben released the man and let him fall to the ground, then fell on top of his chest and began punching his face.

Still Eliza watched on, unable to react.

"Eliza, now!" Ben shouted.

She couldn't budge.

Ben finally delivered a huge blow to the man's eye, and she watched his head bounce back against the tile floor, and then he stopped moving. Ben waited a few seconds to see if the man was done.

Suddenly Eliza caught motion from her right side.

The woman.

The other guard had gotten to her feet and had nearly reached her weapon. Eliza watched as the woman pulled the submachine gun up and held it out in front of her as she ran toward Ben.

"No!" Eliza screamed.

The woman lifted the rifle to her eye and lined up the shot.

Crack!

The sound of the shot caused Eliza to jump. She watched in horror as Ben rolled to the side, then fell to the ground.

No, it's not...

But the woman in front of Eliza also fell.

Eliza noticed the end of her own rifle smoking a bit, and she felt her hands trembling. She realized then what had happened.

The woman was lying on the floor, motionless.

Ben rolled onto his stomach and then pushed himself up off the floor. "You did it," Ben said. "You took the shot."

Eliza felt tears welling in her eyes. Her hands began to shake even more, and she let the rifle fall to her side, holding it with one hand.

"It's okay," Ben said. "You took the shot, and you saved my life. Thank you."

She nodded, then sniffed, trying to fight back the tears she knew were coming. "I... I did that. I *killed* her."

Ben rushed over and grabbed her shoulder. He gave it a gentle squeeze. "You did what you had to do. What we *came* here to do."

We didn't come here to kill —"

"We came here to stop this," Ben said. "And that's what we're doing. Anyone tries to stop us; we need to stop them first. Got it?"

His words were harsh but accurate. She knew it, and she believed them.

Ben spoke again. "We need to keep moving," he said. "There are going to be more guards, and now they know we're here. Someone will have heard the gunshots."

As if on cue, Eliza saw two doors open farther down the hall. She assumed they were doctors or staff members, poking their heads out to see what had happened, but if they *were* guards it meant they needed to get away from this area.

"Time to move," Ben said. "Let's get to the end of the hallway. We can keep an eye on everything behind us while we move toward the stairs. We need to make sure no one else will shoot at us or take us by surprise, but I have a feeling what we're really looking for isn't going to be on this floor."

Without waiting for her, Ben turned and started down the hallway toward the set of double doors.

CHAPTER 51
ELIZA

THEY TOOK the stairs up to the second floor, but even before they exited the stairwell, Eliza could see that this level was completely unlike the one they had just come from. While the ground floor had been filled with offices — all empty — and a few small surgical suites, this top floor had clearly been designed for a singular purpose.

Storage.

Specifically, the storage of live animals. Ben and Eliza walked a few steps onto this floor, and Eliza could see wall to wall cages, stacked three-high, floor to ceiling. Every pen had a glass front door, with steel reinforcement bars behind them and four small circular holes cut out of each of the corners.

She heard the noises, slight and timid, as soon as she was in the room.

Calling to her. Beckoning.

Asking for help.

"Chimps," Eliza said, her voice barely a whisper. She heard it falter as well, and she knew it wasn't because of the adrenaline that was still coursing through her veins. "This is where they keep them."

Ben hadn't heard her, but she knew he was examining the room as well. Looking for threats, potential dangers.

The cages were stacked along each of the two walls to her left and right, and they ran the entire length down to the opposite side of the gigantic space. She saw a set of double doors on the other side that appeared to be the first set of doors of an airlock. Some sort of containment and clean examination chamber would be just inside the doors.

Between her and those doors, in the central open space in between, she saw two rows of tables, each with three or four stools around them. Some of the tables looked like they were meant for surgery, much like the ones they found downstairs. Steel and rigid, standing sentinel beneath dead hospital-grade lights, awaiting a patient — or prisoner — to experiment upon.

Other tables, however, had computer equipment set up on top and beneath them. She saw four tables in the right-side row that boasted two connected desktop monitors each, with CPUs stored on the floor underneath.

"That's our target," she said. She pointed toward the center of the room toward the tables. "Those computers and hard drives. All of them, or whatever we can carry."

“They look like standard workstations to me,” Ben said. “I guess I was expecting like a server room, or at least a rack or two full of blinking computer thingies. You think all the information we need is on those?”

She shook her head. “No, you’re right. They’ve no doubt got some sort of cloud backup system somewhere. But I highly doubt they would keep it on-site. That said, they’ll have at least something on those machines. If we can just get the hard drives out of them and throw them in our packs, that should be enough.”

Her voice trailed off. Up to this point, she hadn’t let her eyes divert from the center of the room, from her target. But she knew that there was a reason EKG had built storage enclosures on the sides of the room. They were never meant to be empty...

She'd heard them, calling out to her, clicking and shuffling about inside the enclosures, but still, she couldn't bear to know the truth.

She hadn't wanted to see the truth with her own eyes.

Ben saw it for her. "Eliza, the cages. Some of them are full. You can hear them, right?"

She nodded, then slowly moved her face to the left and stared at the wall of cages there. Sure enough, behind every third glass door was a chimpanzee.

Pan troglodyte. Of the tribe *Hominini.* The closest genetic living relative to *Homo sapiens.* The *Pan* name was derived from the Greek god of the wilds, the *troglodyte* name taken from a mythical race of cave-dwellers that the historian Herodotus mentioned 'were the swiftest runners of all humans known' and that they 'ate snakes, lizards, and other reptiles.'

Of the four main lines of chimpanzee, it was impossible from here to tell which Eliza was looking at. Some were sleeping, their faces facing the back wall of their prison cells, nothing but dark shadows against the lighter cage walls.

But some others were facing inward, toward the room.

Facing her.

She locked eyes with one of the chimps, squatting in its enclosure, in one of the cubicles in the middle row. She stared back, seeing its intelligence, its understanding.

What have they done here? What are they planning *to do here?*

She took a deep, slow breath. She sensed Ben next to her, drawing closer, but she stared back at the chimp.

Focus on the mission, she told herself. *Focus on the task at hand.*

Ben started walking toward the computers in the middle of the room. He held his assault rifle low, at his side, but he still gripped it with both hands, pointing it toward the double doors. They hadn't seen anyone in this room, and the entire place seemed suspiciously empty. If there was still anyone inside, they could be hiding out in the airlock or in the room beyond.

And they had encountered the security team already — if there were more guards around, she hoped they'd be able to get the jump on them.

And she knew what she was capable of now. If it came to that once again.

The image of the woman she'd shot, bleeding out while face-down on the floor, flooded into her mind. She shook her head to push it away, but the image she was seeing now — her reality — was not any better.

Seeing these chimpanzees with her own eyes — locked up and awaiting their sentencing — she knew she wouldn't hesitate the next time she needed to protect herself, or Ben, or them. If someone came into the room now, she'd be able to pull the trigger again.

Still...

They needed to adapt, to change their plan. Getting data now was no longer enough.

"Ben," she said. Her voice cracked.

Ben stopped, turned around slowly, and met Eliza's face. He arched an eyebrow, a silent question that she heard all too well.

"Ben, I'm sorry," she continued. "We *have* to help them. We have to free them."

Ben's eyes widened. "Eliza, no. They're... They're wild animals, and they're dangerous. They might —"

"They were most likely born here," she said. They were at least reared here, from a very young age. They're used to captivity, but there's no way they prefer those enclosures."

"Still," Ben argued. "We can't just —"

"We can and we *will*." She felt the confidence pouring back into her. "If there's a way to get them out, a way to prevent whatever sort of experimentation and study is going on here, we're going to do it."

"How?" Ben asked. "It would be utter confusion and chaos. And besides, you can't expect there to just be a big red button that will open all of the doors at once. And besides, what then? Then we've freed a bunch of *apes* into the foothills of Switzerland? There is *no way* that can be a good plan, Eliza. For us, for them, for anyone."

She paused, nodding. He was right, of course. It was a terrible plan, one that could potentially cause more harm than it would in just leaving them here. But to leave them here, locked away, was to solidify their fate.

It was certain death.

There was little chance that these animals would survive if they stayed in this hell.

But there was little chance they would survive if they were allowed to roam free in Switzerland. They weren't adapted to that environment at all, and there would be nothing they could do to protect them if the government decided to euthanize them.

"What do we do, then?" She asked Ben. "We can't just let this continue. We can't let them do this."

Ben walked back over to her and grabbed her shoulder. "We are *not* letting them do this," he said. "We're stopping it. Right now. We don't have to free them today, but if we can get the information and get back to town, we can have it uploaded by tomorrow. Whoever needs to know about it will, and then —"

"No," she said, her voice rising. "No, Ben, you know that won't work. If we steal the data and try to get the word out, EKG will take matters into their own hands long before anyone can get here to rescue them. They have ways of euthanizing these animals that won't even leave a trace. Cremation is just the beginning. They'll have plausible deniability, and —"

"They won't," Ben said. "We'll have the information out there. Everyone will know because we gave them the proof. We just need to get it first."

Ben turned around and began once again toward the computer workstations. She looked once more to the chimp to her left, the one who had met her eyes when they'd entered the room.

It was still staring back at her.

Still pleading with her, silently.

She let her eyes fall as she followed Ben to the center of the room.

Ben began fumbling with the computer mouse when he reached the station, but the moment Eliza approached the table, the doors at the back of the room opened.

A voice called to them, the voice heavily accented but in English.

"And *who* exactly might you be?"

CHAPTER 52
BEN

THE VOICE CAUSED Ben to jump, but he came around the rifle pointed, his finger ready, an ounce of pressure all it would take to send a piece of hot lead into the newcomer.

"Wait!" Eliza yelled, rushing to Ben's side with a slight limp before he could take the shot.

The man in front of Ben was unarmed, his hands raised above his head.

"Yes," he said, still walking forward, "please wait. I — I didn't want to cause any trouble."

Ben frowned, but he kept the weapon pointed. "Stop moving. Now."

The man did as he was told.

"You know him?" Ben asked Eliza. He saw her out of the corner of his eye. She was nodding.

"It's Dr. Canavero," Eliza said. "Lead scientist and surgeon here."

The man raised an eyebrow and tilted his head back as if completely ignoring the fact that there was an assault rifle pointed directly at his chest. "Lucio Canavero," he said. "Nice — I guess — to meet you."

Ben wasn't amused by this man's lack of concern. "It's really not," Ben said. "What the hell kind of twisted scheme are you guys running here?"

"Twisted... nonsense. This is a premier *research* facility. Dedicated to advancing the biological sciences and bridging the gap between —"

"Save the marketing speak," Ben snapped. "We ain't investors."

"Oh," Dr. Canavero said. "I am well aware. We are not in need of any more investment — just time. And the return of our assets. I assume you are *not* here for that, either?"

"You talking about that giant silverback running loose out there?"

At this, Dr. Canavero seemed visibly perplexed. "Ah, yes. Of course. That's all it would seem to be to the casual observer."

He turned to look at the rows of cages along the wall. Ben looked at Eliza, and she shook her head slowly. *Don't kill him,* perhaps. *Yet.*

He didn't want to have to kill *anyone* if he didn't absolutely have to, but they still needed the information from the hard drives. He glanced down at the computer screen. It was booted to the desktop, no login credentials required.

"May I show you what we are working on?" Dr. Canavero asked, his voice falling to a lower register, almost soothing. "It truly is remarkable."

"It's *disgusting*," Eliza said. "That's why I quit."

Canavero studied her for a moment, then nodded quickly. "Yes, yes. Eliza — Lindberg?"

"Earnhardt."

"Right. I knew it was one of those dead pilots or the other. Well — welcome back, regardless of your feelings toward this place. I'm afraid the tour will have to be short; we are severely understaffed at the moment."

Ben waited for Eliza to decide. They needed information — that was their mission. If there was something this scientist could provide, he might just lead them directly to it. And he appeared to be harmless. Certainly unarmed.

Ben weighed the options. There were possibly more guards in the building, and Canavero had said they were currently operating with fewer staff than usual, which meant someone could return at any moment and catch them off-guard.

"You have ten minutes," Eliza said. "One second longer, you're dead. One strange glance or you press any sort of alarm button, you're —"

"Dead, yes, I got the message, darling."

She sneered at him.

"Please, just allow me to explain what it is we're working on here. It may not change your mind, but you will at least know that we are taking strides to ensure our working facilities are the most humane in the world."

"Doesn't change the fact that I saw you cut a chimp's head off," Ben said. "Then sew it onto another one."

Canavero appeared to be confused for a moment. "Right, yes. Subject 19. Apollo. And how, may I ask, did you gain access to Apollo's experiment?"

Neither of them responded.

"Fine. Well, in any case, we are well past that study. The trials were — shortly after Subject 19 was euthanized, we were able to perform a successful operation, and then three more. Suffice to say, we will be waiting on clinical trials and peer review for some time, but I believe strongly that we've cracked it."

He turned and began walking toward Ben and Eliza. Ben tightened his grip on the rifle. But as he drew near, Ben saw the man veer off to his left, closer to the cages.

As he did, the chimps closest to him scurried back in their enclosures and pressed themselves tightly against the back wall.

"Back here," the doctor said. "The airlock. Behind that is the main surgical suite. You will be impressed. There are no surgical suites like it anywhere in the world."

Ben stared at him. "I look like a surgeon to you?"

"No, of course not. Forget it. I can see you will not be warming to our acquaintanceship anytime soon."

Ben followed the man back toward the airlock, Eliza close at his side. He noticed she was now holding her weapon close to her body as well, keeping the tip pointed down. He smiled, happy to see she'd listened to something he'd taught her.

When Canavero reached the airlock, he pressed a button near the wall, and a small rectangular door slid open to reveal a small keypad. He pulled his shoulders down and covered the keypad from view, then a few seconds later the doors hissed and began to slide open.

Ben and Eliza stood, silently waiting as Canavero entered and waved them in.

He repeated the process for the interior door, and it fell open as well, revealing a huge sparkling white, brightly lit room, about half the size of the one they'd just exited.

"This," Dr. Canavero said, obviously proud of this place, "is my pride and joy. A state-of-the-art surgical *ward*, all tables open-air and space-sharing to provide the fastest, most efficient operating conditions for my team.

Ben looked around. There were four tables with lights hanging above them in the center of the room, but many more spaced out around the edges of the room, filled with equipment and surgical instruments. Three sinks and drying stations were spread out, one each against the left, right, and center walls, and cabinets with clear glass doors hung from the walls.

Canavero walked down to the second table, and Ben could see that there was a body on the table. It took a moment for his eyes to adjust to the light, as well as the bright-white sheet covering the body. Tubes and instruments were hooked to the form on the table, all making the underlying shape.

He felt Eliza's hand digging into his arm.

Canavero stopped by the table, his hands slowly reaching down and resting on either side of the body's head.

"And this, my friends, is going to be the pinnacle of my career. What all of this has been for. The world will pay us back with their respect and gratitude."

"What — what the hell is it?" Ben asked, not wanting to know the truth.

Canavero looked up at him, a flash of menace in his eyes. Pure evil, boiling just beneath the surface. "Oh, *this* — this is just the *vehicle* for our success. Nothing at all out of the ordinary. I will explain everything. Trust me."

He peeled back the white sheet as Ben and Eliza walked toward the table, unable to stop themselves. Ben saw a small shape, a human. Revealed from the breasts up. A female. Her face was pale white, blank and unmoving. Her lips seemed blood-red against the cold, pale flesh around them.

Her eyes were closed.

"This, my friends," Canavero continued, the fingers of both his hands now stroking her cheeks. "Is Subject 117. Her name is Alina."

CHAPTER 53
BEN

VERY FEW TIMES in Ben's life had he premeditated the killing of another human. Few times had he gone through with the deadly act, choosing to forgo any possibility of justification and instead of acting on his gut instinct.

Very few times had he stared evil in the face and recognized it.

Very few times had Ben looked another man in the eye and decided, without further engagement, that they were going to die by his hand.

And yet, that was exactly what Ben had decided.

Alina, the young college-aged woman from nearby Grindelwald, was lying on the operating table in front of them, the sick doctor caressing her face and neck as he spoke. Ben was shaking, his rage only half-hidden behind his relatively calm exterior.

He couldn't bear to look at Eliza. This was how she'd felt when seeing the chimps in the other room for the first time. This was how she'd felt *before* that, before she'd ever engaged the CSO's services. She'd known all along.

This was the type of company she had left, and the type of company she'd tried to bring down. Her husband had even died for it.

The type of company that would kidnap an innocent woman off the streets of a sleepy tourist town, then perform twisted experiments on her.

For nothing more than the pursuit of this man's desire for fame.

Ben was going to kill him. One way or another — he would hold himself together for as long as it took to extract the information they needed from him, but then...

"She's healthy," Dr. Canavero said. "Quite healthy. We made sure of it. She may not look like it, but that is only because of the solution we have running through her."

"Saline," Eliza whispered.

"Indeed," Canavero said. "At low temperatures, the solution we are using renders the spinal column fully inert, and combining it with polyethylene glycol allows us to bring the subject back to life, if you will."

"After cutting their head off?" Ben asked.

Canavero seemed shocked. "Oh, my friend, of course not. *Cutting* the head off? How barbaric. The experiments with the early subjects were of a reattachment sort, sure. But *this* — this is the ultimate result. The final test of all my work here."

Ben wasn't sure if he felt relieved or not.

"The first transference — TR-1, as we called it — was a sort of phase one. A true hominid hybrid, mammal to mammal. TR-2, same thing, albeit the other direction, if you will. You already know about that trial, of course."

Ben wasn't sure what he was talking about exactly, but it was good information. Perhaps he and Eliza could parse through it together after all of this.

After they released Alina and got the hell out of here.

"Finally," Dr. Canavero continued, "we were ready for TR-3. The ultimate goal. The purpose of Mr. Tennyson's entire division."

"Tennyson's behind this?" Eliza asked. "I thought he was in his eighties? Ready for retirement?"

"Indeed," Canavero said. "I'm referring to his *grandson*. Lars Tennyson."

Eliza nodded. If she knew something, she wasn't letting on. He noticed that she'd dropped the rifle to her side, holding it with one hand again. His own was still ready, his grip tight, but he kept it pointed below the bed and to the side.

Canavero stepped back from Alina's head and started back toward the airlock door.

Ben was about to call out to him when Eliza grabbed his arm. "Ben," she whispered. "We *have* to get her out of here."

He nodded. "I agree. But we can't, right? The saline?"

She didn't answer at first. "I don't know. Maybe. I need to think about it."

Canavero was almost at the door. "Where are you going?" Ben asked, calling after him. He brought his rifle up and aimed it at the man's back.

Canavero didn't respond. Instead, he hit a large red button near the airlock, and the door began to *whoosh* closed.

Ben fired. The three rounds danced outward, wild, one smacking against the wall and another sparking as it collided with a metal table leg. The third hit the glass just next to where Dr. Canavero had entered. It made a small pockmark in the glass, but otherwise didn't do any damage.

The door was still closing, and Ben fired again as he ran toward the airlock. All three rounds hit the glass, but none punched through.

Shit.

Canavero smiled at Ben from inside the airlock. He reached over to the wall and pressed a tiny button on an intercom device. Ben heard his words through an overhead speaker system in the room.

"We did not have much time to get to know one another, my friend. But as I am sure you know by now, Ms. Earnhardt is not the kind of person you will want to be around if you hope to stay out of trouble."

His smile grew, and his eyes narrowed.

"Just ask her husband."

Ben launched forward, smashing into the glass with his right fist. The entire airlock shuddered, but the only damage done was to his hand. He felt as though he'd punched a concrete wall, but he didn't think there were any broken bones.

Ben roared, half from pain and the rest pure rage. He stepped to the side and smashed the red button, but nothing happened.

Canavero stared back at him from inside the airlock. He'd somehow locked them inside this room.

"I'm going to *kill* you, asshole. Open the door."

"Our skillsets are not identical, friend," the doctor said. "That is the main thing that has kept me so successful over the years. It wouldn't be a fair fight, would it? Why would I stoop to the level of physical harm if I knew you would win? I would rather win my way."

Ben sniffed, rubbing his hand while keeping his eyes directly on Canavero. "And what way is that?"

Canavero didn't answer. Instead, he turned to the wall inside the airlock and twisted a knob. He typed a command into a terminal below it, then pressed a key.

Ben heard the sound of massive air ducts opening somewhere above, felt the cool sensation of air conditioning over the back of his neck.

"What are you doing?"

"Alina has had saline running through her body for a few days, in preparation for the surgery. I had hoped to include both of you in the experiment for TR-3, as it would be a perfect human-to-human transplant. But I'm afraid we've run out of time. I must report back to Tennyson — he should be returning to the office any moment now."

Ben watched in horror as Canavero then opened the rear airlock door that led out of the surgical suite and stepped through the door. He repeated the process of typing a code into the keypad and then stepped back in front of the glass.

Ben saw his darkened shape on the other side of the airlock, standing in the larger room.

Canavero waved, then turned around and walked away.

CHAPTER 54
BEN

BEN STOOD next to the door. Silent. Waiting. Knowing Canavero would not return.

This had been the doctor's plan all along.

He realized Eliza was there now. Standing next to him, also silent.

The ducts were still dumping chilled air into the room, the faraway fans humming loudly. The temperature had already fallen by a few degrees, and Ben knew it wasn't stopping soon.

"It's going to get colder in here, isn't it?" Ben asked.

Eliza nodded.

"Like, *really* cold."

She nodded again. "Most likely just above freezing. That temperature will be perfect for whatever sick experiment Dr. Canavero's got planned with that girl, but it'll also be cold enough to kill us. It'll take some time, but..."

"But time's all he's got now," Ben said, finishing her thought. "He's successfully solved the problem of having us snoop around here, *and* hasn't had to even lift a finger to do it."

Ben recalled some of Canavero's last words to him. *Why would I stoop to the level of physical harm if I knew you would win? I would rather win my way.*

And it appeared as though Canavero had won his way.

No.

"There has to be a way out," Ben thought. "There's always a way."

Eliza was nearly in tears, but she was holding herself together. "No, Ben. This is an airlock. Emphasis on *lock*. This facility isn't a hospital. It's not *just* meant to be a medical and surgical suite. It's also meant to keep patients inside."

"It's a jail."

"Look at the cages out there. Of course it is. The entire place can probably be locked down with the flip of a switch. A press of a button and there might even be electrical currents that run through everything and freeze anyone inside in place."

"That's possible?" Ben asked.

"Who knows? How else would they keep live chimpanzees here, unrestrained? Sure, the enclosures keep them in, and they probably have handlers and plenty of sedatives and drugs, but there's *always* a backup plan with EKG. They have all the money in the world, so they'll have a way to shut it all down on a whim."

Ben chewed on this information for a moment. While he didn't truly believe that there was absolutely *no way* out of this situation

CHAPTER 55
ELIZA

ELIZA CALLED Ben's attention to an unassuming, small door against one wall. "Ben, look," she said. "See if that door is unlocked."

Ben strode over to the door, moving quickly. She felt the air continuing to drop into the room, the temperature now bordering on actually cold. She had been chilly for the last ten minutes as they looked around, and she had the horrible feeling that it was only going to get worse.

Ben approached the door and placed his hand on the handle. He pressed down, and the door snapped open a crack. He looked back at her, then pushed it open farther. He was still holding his assault rifle in his right hand, and now he brought it up and poked it through the crack in the door, waiting for any attackers that might have been hiding within.

Eliza knew it was highly unlikely someone had been waiting inside this room the entire time and that Canavero had locked them inside this surgical suite along with the two intruders. Still, in the past few days, she had seen plenty of things she had thought were impossible become possible.

"Weird," Ben said. "Looks like someone's bedroom in here."

Eliza walked over and peered inside. Sure enough, she saw

pictures on the wall, one with cartoon hyenas laughing hysterically and another that looked like a painting of clouds. There was even carpet on the floor and a rug that had been laid out in front of a small bed.

She looked around the walls, confirming Ben's words, when her eyes landed on the bed in the center of the room.

"Oh my God," Eliza said. She pulled her hand to her mouth. "Someone's in the bed, Ben."

Ben walked over to the bed and looked down. It was a woman — a girl, perhaps — no older than twenty and possibly still in her teens. She was small and seemed frail, as if she hadn't had a hearty meal her entire life, and barely rations besides that. Her skin was pale. Getting closer, Eliza could see bluish veins just beneath the surface of her skin.

"What the hell is this all about?" Ben asked. "Why is she here? And why is this room —"

"It's Lars Tennyson," Eliza said. "This has something to do with him — I'm positive. Some personal connection, like a family member or..." her voice trailed off.

"What is it?" Ben asked.

Eliza began to feel something off-putting inside her. A feeling she couldn't shake, a sense of dread that went beyond anything they had learned in the past fifteen minutes.

Something beyond the physical sense of deep cold settling in around her.

She shivered. "It's his *sister*."

"Lars' sister? *She* is?" Ben asked. He looked down at the bed.

"Yes. I remember reading about an accident relating to the granddaughter of Baden Tennyson, the founder and owner of EKG. I don't remember the details, except that the young woman was stuck in a coma or something."

Ben nodded. "Yeah, I can see how this could be that same girl, but... how long ago was that?"

"I don't know," Liza said. She shivered again, this time not because of the cold. "Years, probably."

"And Alina, out in the main room..." Ben didn't finish the sentence.

Eliza picked up where he'd left off. "*That's* what this is all about, Ben. This 'transference' that Dr. Canavero was telling us about. 'Mammal to mammal,' he said, right? After 'the other direction' was successful? This one — TR-3 — was what he was talking about. The *third* style of transference."

Ben looked at her, a solemn look on his face. "Back when we first met, you told me you were afraid EKG was getting involved with something *way* beyond head transplants on monkeys. You said..."

"Yes, Ben. That's what I think is happening here. What I think Lars Tennyson and everyone else in this division has been working on. It's not just *head* transplants. It's full, procedural *brain* transplants. Between two mammals —"

"Between *that* mammal out there and *this* one right here," Ben finished. "A brain transplant between *two humans.* The 'third transference.'"

CHAPTER 56
ELIZA

SHE NODDED, the full realization of the moment hitting her hard. She walked over to an armchair in the corner of the room and sat down on the edge of it, holding her chin with her elbows on her knees. "Ben, Lars Tennyson is trying to transplant the brain of his young sister into that woman out there. Alina."

Ben continued along with the brainstorm. "And that silverback gorilla we saw running around out there — the reason it seems to recognize some people — the reason it *killed* them — is that it wasn't really a gorilla at all, was it? Or at least not *just* a gorilla."

She shook her head. "No, I don't think it was. I didn't know it was possible, but then again this work, the stuff Canavero's been doing — I knew what he was capable of. And he's been working on this very thing for *years*.

"I think that silverback represented the *second* phase, or transference, or whatever Canavero called it. The TR-2 of these trials. It was a successful test. To see if a human brain could exist in the body of another mammal." She paused. "And it seems like it can. I mean, can you imagine? It's effectively another creature altogether."

"My God," Ben said. "The ethical and moral questions alone are incredible. *Insurmountable*, probably. Which is why this whole operation was moved here and kept out of sight. They couldn't let *anyone* outside of EKG — hell, outside of this specific division probably — know about what they were doing here. Even Lars' grandfather probably has little idea of what's actually going on behind the scenes."

Eliza stood up again, now pacing. The chill in the air was about to cause her breath to condense and form smoky air, and she wanted to keep her blood pumping. The temperature seemed to be dropping faster now, since they had opened the door. She wondered if by shutting themselves inside this room, they could postpone the inevitable temperature drop a bit longer, but she knew it was probably pointless. The cold would seep in, eventually reaching them.

Alina lay on the table next to her, and she knew now that the thing terrorizing the countryside near Grindelwald hadn't been an *ape*, nor had it been some brutal half-ape, half-human experiment.

The terrorists had been human all along — the girl, Alina, had been nabbed by guards, likely wearing the *Grayson* logo but existing on EKG's payroll. They had taken her to be a pawn in Dr. Canavero's game, to play host to his last, sickening experiment.

Eliza saw the IV drip in the girl's arm and wondered if she was on the same sort of saline solution that Alina had been placed on. Something that would allow her blood to cool enough for the impending operation.

The doctors and scientists here had to have been close when the gorilla had escaped. Canavero hadn't lowered the temperature in here *just* to kill Eliza and Ben — he had done it because he was almost ready to perform the operation. He probably wanted to find Lars Tennyson and the rest of his team, to get them back on board before he started, but Eliza had a feeling that they were *very* close to being able to successfully pull it off.

Having the gorilla escape had been a stroke of luck for Alina, but the situation also could make the whole disaster worse — it would be a PR nightmare if the public found out, and it would likely spell death for the entire company, but that meant Lars and Canavero would want to begin work in here sooner rather than later.

If there was any way the doctor could pull this off with a skeleton crew, while the guards brought the gorilla down outside, Eliza had a feeling he would.

"Ben, we need to get her out of here. Both of them. We need to —"

"Eliza, there's no way. They're on some sort of medical IV drip thing, just like Canavero said. We can't just pull out all the stuff that's keeping this girl alive. She'll die within minutes."

"But *Alina* isn't in a coma. We might be able to get her awake if I can figure out how to undo Canavero's weird saline mixture."

"Can you do that? What do you need to pull it off — and how much time?"

"As long as they're cycling it through her bloodstream, we might be able to get lucky and just take her off the feed. It will take some time for her blood to warm up and begin pumping regular cells through it again, but I can't perform a full transfusion even if I had a few pints of fresh blood of her type. If that's what it requires, there isn't really anything I can do for her. And as far as time goes, I have a feeling we'll need more of it than what we've got left."

Ben nodded, no doubt understanding the dire situation they were in. He took one huge stride over to the bedside and yanked the girl's blanket off of her. She didn't stir.

He tossed it to Eliza.

"What are you doing? She's —"

"Wrap it around you. If she's in a coma and she's got that stuff running through her blood, she won't be needing this anyway. We'll need warmth far more than her, trust me."

He then flew over to the small closet and pulled on the doors, sliding one of them to the right. Inside were stacks of blankets and bedsheets, likely there for the nursing staff for replenishment. He removed three blankets from the top of a stack and threw a second one to Eliza. The remaining two he wrapped around himself.

"I was in Antarctica," he said. "It's remarkable how cold the human body can get and still live. But that doesn't mean it's any fun."

"Got it," Eliza said.

"Besides, as you said, he doesn't need it to be ice-cold in here. Just cold enough to ensure the damage he'll do through the surgery is repairable. Maybe high thirties. Nothing we can't survive with a bit of help."

"Okay," she said, throwing the blankets around her shoulders and shivering into them. She was already starting to feel warmer. Her body heat would circulate inside the wrapping she now donned, but it wouldn't protect them forever. They still needed a plan. "What do we do now?"

Ben motioned toward the door. "Time to see if you can get that girl out there to wake up and move on her own. If there's any way we can at least get her functioning, there's a chance we can get her to the hospital back in Grindelwald."

"Right," Eliza said, making her way toward the door. "What are you going to do?"

Ben looked past her, at the banks of computers. "I'm going to see if I can call for help."

CHAPTER 57
BEN

IN THIS DAY AND AGE, where there was a computer, there was an internet connection.

At least that's what Ben hoped. He was far from a computer expert, but he could navigate his way around one when he needed to. And he desperately needed to now. Their phones had died hours ago, and while he could spend this time searching through the surgical suite for a phone charger, he had a feeling EKG would have something in place to block incoming and outgoing cellular signals.

Ben sidled up to one of the workstations at a table near Eliza and the young woman on the table in front of her. He wrapped the blankets tighter around his body, knowing that his ears would start to feel coldest in a few minutes, but also knowing that there was still a large stack of blankets and comforters in the closet in the other room if they needed them.

He shook the mouse, waking up the computer just as he'd done earlier. So far, no password prompts. He was used to his Mac at home in Alaska, but Julie was a PC user, so she'd given him a brief crash course on where things were on a Windows-based machine a year ago, which had actually been a poorly hidden attempt to make fun of him.

He almost smiled at the thought of it. He'd always seen himself like somewhat of an ape when it came to computers. Now, after seeing what they'd seen here at EKG, he'd have to adapt that analogy. Some of these apes were probably *already* better than he was with a computer.

His eyes darted around the desktop. If need be, he could open the Start menu and find a browser, but there were usually links on the desktop for that sort of thing as well. He didn't see anything at first, but there was one icon in particular that jumped out at him.

He examined it for a moment, trying to understand what it meant. After a few seconds, he turned his attention back to finding the browser. He did after a few more seconds, then double-clicked the icon to open a web client.

Come on. Connect, please, he thought. He watched the multicolored globe spin as the page queued.

Finally, a search box appeared onscreen.

"Yes," he mumbled. He clicked in the URL bar at the top of the screen and began typing in an address. He hoped to use a web-based messaging client to reach Julie, or, worst case, email. He hoped she was at a computer now.

He pressed the Return key on the keyboard and waited.

Almost immediately, a dialog window appeared. *ERROR 403: Forbidden. You do not have access to external websites.*

"Dammit," he whispered.

"How's it going over there?" Eliza asked.

Ben shook his head. "Not good. They've got the network locked down. Unless you know how to do fancy router stuff, we're hosed."

"Sorry," she said. "Definitely out of my wheelhouse."

"Yeah, I figured." He knew Julie would have been able to bypass the security in about a minute or two, and it was ironic that she was the very person he had been trying to hail. *I'm never going anywhere without you again, Jules.* He sighed, then looked up at Eliza, hunched over the girl on the table. "What about you?"

She made a face of concern. “Hard to tell without some monitoring instruments. I’m almost positive she’s fine to move — there aren’t any drips going into her that seem to be critical, and she’s not on any respirator or any sort of maintenance machinery. But I could be wrong.”

“What’s your gut feeling?” Ben asked.

“My gut says to pull her off this IV line and see what happens. If it causes any sort of massive failure, I should be able to reattach it with enough time to keep her alive.”

Ben was about to give his blessing when Eliza popped off the tube from the back of the inserted needle. A bit of clear liquid splashed over her hand and the table, but she let it fall to the side.

They waited for twenty seconds. Nothing happened.

“That’s... good news?”

“I believe so,” Eliza said. “Could be the cold in here keeping her in stasis, but I think we’d be safe to move her if she doesn’t come to on her own. Still, we need to get her medical attention right away.”

“Well, I’m not sure we’ve got any of that available. How long can we wait?”

“If we move now, we can get to the local hospital. But we’ll have to find a vehicle. There’s no way we can carry her all the —“

“Then that’s the mission.”

“Ben, we —“

“We have to save her life, Eliza,” Ben said. His voice was calm, but he heard his words beginning to clip. He was stressed, ready to be done. *Keep it together, man. You’re almost out of the weeds.* “We have to get her professional help. If there’s anything we can salvage from this, it’s her.”

“There’s *a lot* we can salvage, Ben,” she snapped back. “All of this — the experiments, Canavero, that *comatose girl* in there, the chimps — *everything* here should be part of our case.”

Ben shook his head. "It's triage now. We have to decide what to take and what to leave behind. We can still pack a few of the hard drives with our gear, but this girl will die without our help. That girl in the other room — Tennyson's sister — *she's* going to be fine without us. Hell, she's been fine without us for *years*. And we know Tennyson won't let anything happen to her."

Even as he said the words, they struck him as odd. *Tennyson won't let anything happen to her.* It was the man's younger sister, a woman he'd kept alive far longer than most people would.

He knew with just a single glance around this place that Tennyson had to be deranged, but he hadn't understood the extent of it until now. Ben considered the angles, the options, that Tennyson was probably facing. He had shut the division down to protect his own reputation, but more importantly, because it was the only way to keep his sister alive.

The man *had* to keep moving forward. He *had* to keep his sister here, attended to by Canavero and a skeleton crew of staffers. He *had* to rid the area of the escaped experiment, or it would all come crashing down.

"Ben," Eliza said. "What are you thinking about? Whatever our decision is, we need to act *now*, before —"

Before she could finish the sentence, the airlock's outer door slid open. The sound was muted in the inner chamber, but Ben and Eliza had both heard it.

Ben gripped his rifle and brought it up to his face. He peered through the scope and aimed it in the direction of the still-closed inner door. *If it opened...*

He was prepared to take the shot, to protect themselves.

Ben squinted and tried to get a better view of the figures that had entered the airlock.

Canavero. Two formless shapes. Likely more guards. Each was holding a weapon shaped like the small subcompacts they'd seen downstairs.

And next to Canavero, leaning on a cane for support, was a man Ben almost didn't recognize.

Bloodied, bent, and watching him with one eye, the other bruised shut. He wore a look of pure menace, the rage and contempt surging through him with an energy Ben could feel through the glass.

It was the man who had been with Elias, out in the meadow. One of the three men whom the gorilla had smashed aside like nothing. This man had been lying in the field, facedown, when Ben had spoken with Elias Ziegler.

Ben knew immediately who it was, but it was Eliza who spoke his name first.

"Lars Tennyson," she said, softly.

CHAPTER 58
LARS

LARS TENNYSON FELT his nostrils flare as he looked through the glass at the two figures standing in the lab. In *his* lab. He clenched and unclenched his free fist, careful to keep the other planted firmly on the smooth, rounded section of the cane.

He'd needed a cane to help him walk, his right leg having been bruised and nearly broken by the beast outside. As it turned out, his replica office had a cane that his grandfather had used long ago after a surgery. The old man didn't need it anymore, and Lars had asked for it as a gift many years ago, before he'd even considered building an exact copy of the man's office.

After returning to the building and gaining access, he'd marched toward his back-corner office, through what appeared to be the remnants of a brief scuffle and firefight. Ceiling tile chunks had fallen around a lump on the floor, which had ended up being one of Lars' security team, a woman whose name he'd never bothered to remember and who he barely recognized.

He examined the area quickly, looking for more threats, but instead finding a second guard leaning up against a wall, a hand holding the back of his head. This man — Darren, or Darrel, he wasn't sure which — he did recognize as one of the men who patrolled during the night shift when Lars did most of his work. The guard had filled him in on the fight, telling him that a man and woman — the same man and woman who Lars had seen out on EKG's property trying to gain entry — had overtaken them and killed the woman.

Lars didn't care about death, or this man's health, only that these two intruders were still in his building. The guard seemed to think they'd gone upstairs, but he hadn't been sure. Without asking more questions, Lars headed upstairs.

He met Canavero in the stairwell.

The kind doctor had offered to help Lars up the stairs and into the hallway, where they'd stopped for a moment so Canavero could fill him in on the details of what had transpired.

Canavero had, apparently, locked the intruders inside the surgical lab at the back of the containment room.

With his sister still inside.

Lars was fuming, but he hadn't yet decided where his wrath would be directed. Toward Canavero, the brilliant scientist who had idiotically left Lars' prized possession in the hands of these two intruders? Or the intruders themselves, who were on some half-baked mission to bring everything he'd ever worked on to a crashing halt?

He wasn't sure.

But there was time to dole out punishment. First, he needed to regain *control*.

After Dietrich's bloody death in the field, after Lars had run away from the massive silverback — Jonas, they'd called him in the lab, before the transference surgery — Lars had waited in the woods, out of sight.

He'd watched as the gorilla had ripped apart the only person on earth who seemed to care for Lars. It hurt to watch, but Lars had summoned all his remaining strength and courage to watch until the gruesome end without calling attention to himself. He knew he could grieve later — there was still work to be done.

Dietrich was dead. The hunter was dead — the newcomer, one of the intruders, had run up to him and had a chat before the man perished — and now Lars was alone. The gorilla, Jonas, was still barely alive, having suffered numerous critical wounds, but he'd pulled himself toward the fence line surrounding EKG's building.

Lars had put three bullets through the gorilla's head, then checked for his pulse to make sure the job was finally done.

The cost had been high, but Lars had never been worried about the cost.

Now, standing in his airlock, looking into his laboratory, watching the intruders stare back at him, he was beginning to feel the need to let out some of his anger in a productive way.

"Open the door," he said quietly.

One of his guards nearest the door seemed shocked. "But sir, that man in there is armed. Assault rifle, aimed directly toward —"

'*Open the door!*" Lars screamed. He felt the spittle at the corner of his mouth fly away and toward the floor. He sneered at the guard, and saw Canavero's eyes on him, full of surprise.

"Mr. Tennyson, it would probably be best to engage them in conversation first. We can get a feel for what we are dealing with here, and how best to —"

Lars was at Canavero's side in an instant. He raised his open palm and brought it around as hard as he could, swinging it directly at Canavero's head.

The smack reverberated through the small airlock, but the gasp from Dr. Canavero was almost as loud.

"I. Will not. Be repeating myself. Any longer." Lars spoke in breathy bursts, his words stifled and stilted by the anger. The other three men in the room nodded along, the man nearest the door pressing the button inside.

The door began to slide open, and immediately gunfire erupted into the tiny space. The guard fell to the floor, dead on impact.

Canavero fell as well, covering his head. The second guard leaned over and began pulling the doctor out of the way of the widening gap in the open door.

"No, you idiot!" Lars yelled. "With me!" He yanked the guard's arm back and the man stood again, stumbling toward Lars.

Lars waited until the armed guard was steady, then he pushed him forward. "Go! Shoot him!"

The guard complied instantly, leaving Canavero ducking in the airlock as he rushed by. Lars followed behind the man, careful to keep his bulk in front and protecting him.

There was a brief exchange of gunfire, and Lars, while covering his head, saw that the intruder fell back, now out of view behind one of the tables that he'd pulled over to use as protection. The red-haired woman he was with was to his side, her hands high above her head, still standing.

"Stop, stop," Lars said. "Enough. Okay, enough."

He was frantic, and he didn't like the feeling of it. He forced himself to calm down. He breathed, slowly, creeping forward, his free hand now on the guard's back, nudging him forward. The guard was stuttering his steps as he approached the downed intruder, but Lars was flicking his eyes back and forth between the man and the woman.

The red-haired woman was standing close to an operating table, and on it Lars could see the young woman they'd kidnapped from the nearby town of Grindelwald. His team had reported back that the tiny village was up in arms about her disappearance. Apparently, the place had nothing better to do than worry about a college student's welfare.

They don't know yet, but they will discover how wrong they are. He knew that what he was doing here could *save* them one day. What they were about to accomplish was something the world would thank them for.

The guard stopped, about fifteen feet from the table behind which the man hid, and the woman stood.

"On your knees," Lars snapped. The woman complied. "You — next to her — hands above your head."

There was no reaction.

"I said *put your hands on your head.*" Lars was improvising now, doing what he assumed was right. The guard didn't seem to want to contradict him, which gave him the confidence to press on. He needed to regain — and maintain — control of this situation.

Which meant that he needed to kill these two intruders if they weren't going to comply.

He looked to the guard, still standing in front of him, and quietly spoke. "Kill them. Now."

CHAPTER 59
BEN

WHEN THE SHOOTING BEGAN, Ben was already in motion. He backpedaled, then half-fell into the stool behind him, and grabbed the edge of the table with his hand, pulling it over. It fell backward, toward Ben, the legs poking out toward the onslaught of bullets flying into the room.

It wasn't going to be strong enough to hold forever against the subcompact machine gun fire, but the small, fast rounds would still have trouble punching through the steel. He ducked behind it just as another volley erupted.

"Eliza, what are you doing?" he asked.

Eliza was standing nearby, still standing, unarmed with her hands above her head.

"Eliza, *come on,*" Ben said. "You're going to get —"

Before he finished, the submachine gun in the guard's hands lanced out again, the rounds working their way through the steel. For now, it was holding.

Eliza jumped at that moment, landing on her belly and skittering across the floor until she was next to Ben. She pulled herself up into a crouching position, hiding behind Ben's table.

Ben knew how this would play out. He'd been in a similar situation in Antarctica, holed up in a room with no exits while an army of soldiers bore down on them and worked their way into the room.

They hadn't all made it out alive.

But this time it was different. There was one armed man, possibly another, shooting at him. Well-trained but not a soldier. Ben was likely less trained but more experienced than this security-for-hire agent shooting at him.

That meant he had an opportunity to get the jump on this kid if he played his cards right.

"Ben, what are we going to do?" Eliza asked, whispering after the gun stopped firing.

"Hold on," he said. "I'm working on it."

He knew the move — the advancing troops would work their way toward him, pinning them in place by firing as often as necessary. They were stuck behind this table until it gave way or until they appeared around the side and flanked them.

That meant he had to act quickly.

"Hold this," he whispered. He handed his rifle to Eliza, knowing she'd set hers down earlier to attend to Alina.

"Me? You want *me* to —"

"Relax," he replied. "Don't have to shoot it, just *hold* it. I'm trying to —"

Another blast from the submachine gun made Ben jump. He gritted his teeth and pulled his head up, just above the long edge of the table. When he'd pulled the table over, he'd also pushed the whole thing *forward*, locking the entire object underneath the still-upright table in front of it. That particular table was the one on which sat the computer Ben had been using.

Eliza's table, in front of that, was the one Alina was on.

His head was sufficiently hidden behind the computer monitor. The gunman was shooting at the sideways table itself, trying to punch a bullet hole through the steel sheet, so the computer was still unharmed. His right hand came up as well, and he placed it on the computer's mouse as he worked.

"What are you doing?" she asked. He realized she had her back to the table, so she couldn't see what was happening on the screen above them.

Ben responded as he moved the mouse around and clicked. "I'm taking your advice from earlier. Using your plan."

"*My* plan?" she responded. "And what plan is that?"

The man who'd been screaming at them began yelling again. His voice was strained and desperate, and Ben knew they were being lied to with every word out of his mouth. "Listen," the man said, his voice much closer now. "I really do not wish you any harm. I believe we can work this out in a diplomatic way."

As he said the word *diplomatic*, the gun flared up again and sent a short burst hurtling into the top of the upturned table.

Ben hovered over the mouse button as he looked at Eliza. "Remember the plan that would be nothing but utter confusion and chaos?"

Her eyes widened. "But how..."

"Remember how I said, 'it's not like there's going to be a giant red button that just opens all the enclosures at once?"

Her eyes grew again, and she nodded. He couldn't tell if it was a look of fear or curiosity on her face. "Yeah, I remember that. But again, how?"

Ben had seen the strange icon on the desktop of the computer when he'd been looking for a web browser, but it was the string of words beneath that icon that had gotten his attention. *EKG Cleaning and Maintenance Control.*

He'd double-clicked on it then before he'd launched the browser, and it had loaded in the background.

As it turned out, it seemed to be precisely what he'd hoped for: a custom program built by the IT department of EKG, intended for the remote control locking and unlocking of each and every enclosure on the floor. There were a few schedules loaded when he'd opened it, one labeled *Weekend: General*, that ostensibly allowed for the caretakers to open certain enclosures along the walls independently, to clean and maintain each of the animals' environments and prison cells.

But now, he wasn't paying attention to the list of schedules and maintenance protocols that scrolled across the screen.

He was looking at something else entirely that had caught his eye earlier.

A blinking, rectangular label at the top-right of the window, with a simple word spelled across it.

Status: Ready.

And directly beneath that, another rectangular icon with rounded corners, with the mouse pointer hovering over it. It also had a label, and it was this button that Ben clicked on.

UNLOCK ALL.

CHAPTER 60
LARS

LARS TAPPED the guard standing in front of him on the shoulder, and the guard fired into the table once more. The pair was working their way around the table, keeping their distance, hoping to flank the two intruders and take them down from the hard angle.

The guard finished his volley and began to reload while Lars waited for his ears to stop ringing. The ambient hum of the room's giant air conditioning system eventually filled his mind, and he forced his active listening toward the upended table.

He heard nothing. Perhaps a whisper or two, but he wasn't sure. Had any of the bullets made their way through the steel tabletop?

If not, it wasn't a big deal. The two were sitting ducks now; their entire strategy shot to hell. They were pinned down, and while the large man was armed, Lars knew that between himself, the guard, and Canavero who was still whimpering back in the airlock, they would make short work of these people and be on with the final phase of the trials.

Lars flicked his eyes toward the table directly to his right. It was fortunate that the young woman lying there was still undisturbed, unharmed from the firefight that had transpired. He needed her more than ever now, especially since their time was running out.

The last phase, the final transference, would need to be completed by the end of the week. His sister's health was fading for some unknown reason, and Lars intended to be working on reviving and rehabilitating her by this time next week. Her skin was beginning to deteriorate, a fact that he had not noticed until Dr. Canavero had pointed it out. It had something to do with the length of time humans could remain in a comatose state, but Lars hadn't been interested in the details.

He needed to finish this project. Now.

He was about to tap on the shoulder of the guard once again, to order the man to fire once again.

Instead, his attention was pulled *behind* him.

Somewhere back there, back where Canavero was still waiting around for the danger to pass, Lars heard something.

At first, he thought it might have been Canavero himself, standing up and grabbing the downed guard's weapon and clicking it into gear, reloading it.

But he glanced over his shoulder and saw that Canavero was *already* standing in the room, against the far wall, *already* waiting. No weapon in his hands.

Another clicking sound, followed by three more in rapid succession.

What the hell?

Lars hadn't spent a lot of time in the main containment lab or in the airlock surgical suite, opting instead to complete his work in his office or in the armchair in his sister's room just next door. Most of his interactions with his team and scientists had been during his walks back and forth through these halls.

So he wasn't sure if what he was hearing was a *normal* sound or one that was out of place. To his untrained ear, it sounded out of place.

He met Canavero's eyes and only then realized that Canavero

seemed to be in distress. The doctor's face was registering shock, confusion. Uncertainty.

That can't be good, Lars thought.

But what is the cause of the —

Another few clicks, and then a second type of sound entered Lars' mind. This sound was different in every way.

It was *organic.* Alive.

No.

It was a gentle squeaking sound, then louder as it transformed into one of questioning hoots. Then it became a more excited, anticipatory hollering.

It's not possible.

Canavero began running toward him. Lars watched as the man jogged, then started to sprint. He wasn't far away, but it seemed as though time had slowed.

And then, over Canavero's shoulder, a shadow. Followed by another.

And another.

The shadows — hominid shaped, with arms and thick legs and wide bodies — danced across the ceiling as the hooting and hollering grew in volume.

He knew then that what he was seeing was no apparition. It was no illusion. The sound and the visual inputs flew into his brain, and he *knew.*

The thirty-four chimpanzees and five gorillas they had nurtured and grown here, inside these walls, had escaped. For years Lars and his team had cultivated the most exquisite mammalian test subjects, choosing the finest stock to breed from. It had taken far more money than Lars had ever imagined, but he had eventually obtained completely off-the-books chimpanzee and gorilla babies, including five chimpanzee breeder males and two gorilla mating pairs.

One of those gorillas, Jonas, after a successful TR-2 trial, had escaped last week due to an unfortunate miscalculation in sedatives.

The beast hadn't even bothered to destroy anything during its sprint through the facility, opting for speed over destruction.

Lars now understood why — the hybrid human-gorilla test had intended to escape and call attention to the laboratory.

Where the hunter they had hired had failed, Lars had succeeded.

But now, with at least thirty apes on the loose, Lars wasn't sure *what* to do.

He knew they were intelligent, but that it was a spectrum. Chimpanzees and gorillas were intelligent *in comparison to humans.* They weren't going to defeat their human cousins in a spelling bee or a debate.

He told himself that they wouldn't harm him or Canavero. These creatures wanted *freedom* — one of the long-standing tenets of the animal kingdom, baked into every living creature from the dawn of time. *Freedom over free thought.* That's the understanding he had been working from for years.

So Lars was especially concerned when at least ten of the chimpanzees seemed to acknowledge their presence inside the surgical suite.

Those chimps looked on at them, then at each other.

Then they began creeping toward the airlock.

CHAPTER 61
BEN

BEN FELT Eliza's hand gripping his arm again. They were still crouched behind the upturned medical table, but the gunfire had stopped. Ben peered over the edge of the table, sliding over to see.

"Ben," Eliza said. "What's that —"

She'd heard it too. The slow, sputtering start of the sounds of chimpanzees whining. Gentle at first, and then louder as more of the animals began to stir.

"Turn around!" Lars Tennyson yelled. Ben saw the man staring back through the airlock, focusing on something while grabbing the arm of the guard next to him. Ben watched as the guard spun, just as Lars reached down and pulled the walkie-talkie off the man's hip. He held it up to his mouth. "Attention — all agents on-site. Please report to the second-floor containment laboratory immediately. I repeat —"

He never finished the second half of the command. The guard sprang into action and began firing at the chimpanzees.

"No!" Eliza stood and rounded the corner of the table. Ben pulled her back down.

"Stop," he said. "You'll get yourself killed."

She glared at him. "We have to *do* something, Ben. That's why we're here. I'm done arguing about this."

She stood again, and before Ben could respond, she was running, full-speed at Lars' back. The guard had moved closer to the airlock, and Ben noticed that there were three chimps approaching the inner doors of the airlock. They were moving steadily, stealthily, keeping their bodies low and sneering at the people inside the room.

Eliza collided with Lars, and both went to the floor. Ben was standing now as well, and he'd moved from the side of the table to the narrow hallway between the rows, where Lars, Eliza, and the guard were.

As the guard was preparing to shoot at the first chimp through the doors, Ben's eyes were drawn to his left side.

Canavero was moving, running quickly toward Eliza and Lars. He had halved the distance, and he'd make it there before Ben could, but Ben still had his assault rifle.

"Stop!" Ben shouted over the noise. The cacophony had grown now to a dull roar, and Ben could see that there were twenty or so apes idling about in the main hall beyond the airlock doors. He also noticed a few more guards collecting in the stairwell, shocked and amazed at what was happening inside the room.

One of the guards looked to be the same one Ben had taken down in the hallway. He wasn't sure if they were going to begin to fire on the apes inside the room, but as it turned out, they never got the chance.

Four or five apes immediately ran at the stairwell, overwhelming the three guards and silencing them before they could begin shooting.

Ben winced at the brutal display, but he felt nothing toward the guards. No pity, no sorrow.

Canavero stopped and stared at Ben. Eliza and Lars were rolling around on the ground, but it was clear to Ben that eventually Lars would get the upper hand. He was a bit larger, stronger, and seemed to know how to fight. Eliza was fending off his attacks, but she wasn't able to get her punches landed.

He needed to stop this. He needed to end it, fast.

But there were three wars being waged here. The chimps, the guards, Lars and Canavero. All against him. All against Eliza.

He wondered if the chimps would be as discerning as the gorilla had been — if they were able to recognize their captors and torturers, and let Ben and Eliza off the hook.

Or if they'd assume they were hostile since they shared the room with Tennyson.

He was about to find out.

"Get down, now! On your knees!" Ben shouted at Dr. Canavero. The man complied. Ben knew he wouldn't stay there, but for the moment, he could at least focus on Eliza's battle.

Two of the chimps made it past the airlock doors just as Ben reached Lars and Eliza. There was a third still inside, but the two that had appeared in the surgical suite were spread out, flanked around the sides of the guard.

This isn't going to end well for him, Ben thought.

The guard stood his ground, slowly raising his weapon up and aiming it toward the chimp on the right.

Ben smashed the butt of his rifle against the back of Lars' head, and the man rolled off of Eliza. He was mildly injured but still awake. He rolled away and came up to a crouching position, unsteady.

The guard near the airlock tried to trick the apes — at the last moment, he swung his gun around to the left side and quickly opened fire. The rounds sang out from his weapon and swept in a wide arc around to where the chimp was.

Or at least, *had been*.

That chimp had anticipated the attack and was running on all fours *behind* the guard. With a smooth, calculated motion, the chimp pushed off the edge of a table and launched itself into the air toward the guard's back.

It latched on, hanging from the man, while the *second* ape lunged.

Directly toward the guard's face.

With an equally swift and smooth motion, this chimp pressed its fingers *into* the man's eye sockets and then pulled, yanking away flesh and bone as if it were paper mâché.

The guard screamed in agony, a bloodcurdling noise that startled everyone in the room — man and ape.

The first ape fell from the man's back as he fell forward, face-down on the floor, his own face bleeding and staring back at him from a few feet away.

Both chimps looked directly at Ben, then Eliza, then at Lars.

And then they began to creep back toward the doorway.

"They're afraid," Eliza whispered.

"Of him?" Ben asked.

Lars was groaning, seated in front of one of the tables, rubbing the back of his head. His brow was covered in sweat, and he was breathing heavily, but otherwise he seemed to be okay.

"Of this room," Dr. Canavero said. "They know what happens here. They refuse to be in here any longer than necessary."

Ben nodded. "Great. You've been torturing the poor guys their entire lives so much that they've got PTSD because of a *room*. You know how screwed up that is? What the hell is wrong with you?"

Eliza stood and brushed herself off. Her hair was falling out of the many ties that had been in it, and a few strands of bright red hung from over her forehead, but she too seemed to be fine. She took an aggressive step toward Lars, and the man winced.

"It's over," Ben said. "Finished. We're done here. All of us."

"And what are you planning to do about *them*?" Lars suddenly asked. His finger was shaking, pointing at the chimps guarding the airlock.

Ben shrugged. "No idea. Seems to me we don't need to do

anything. Those guys know exactly who the enemy is here. And it's not me or her."

Eliza nodded, then moved to the far wall away from Ben. She seemed to be trying to put more distance between herself and the airlock, just in case. "That's right," she added. "They'll let us leave. Not you two."

Canavero seemed to be amused by this statement, and even Ben wondered if it were true. "You believe that, do you?" Canavero asked. "You think they are as intelligent as that gorilla? As Jonas? You are mistaken, my dear friends. These *beasts* are just that — beasts. Operating more from instinct than a desire for revenge."

"Then why did they kill that guard and then back out of the room?"

"They have an *instinctual* fear of this place. It's something that has been ingrained in their beings from birth. They don't care *who's* in here — they'll kill any one of us if we try to leave."

Ben nodded. "Fine," he said. "I'll take my chances."

He started back toward the table that held Alina's body. When he got there, he looked down at the young woman lying on the bed.

Her eyes were open, staring up at him.

CHAPTER 62
BEN

"CAN YOU MOVE?" Ben asked the girl.

She looked up at him, confused, then slowly shook her head. "I — I do not think so," she finally uttered. "My body... it feels as though I am asleep."

Her English was good, but she spoke slowly and deliberately, following Ben with her eyes. She was scared, but she seemed calm.

"Okay," Ben said. "Just rest. We're going to get —"

"You will do *no such thing,*" Lars said, now standing behind Ben. "This... this is not finished. We must —"

"No, Lars," another voice said. Ben looked over. *Canavero.* He was standing closer now, behind one of the tables with a computer on it. "This man is correct. It *is* over."

"But the research..." Lars said. "All the work. And my —"

"The research is all still here, my friend." He threw an arm out and swung it around the room. "Nothing is missing. Every bit of it is here. All of my work, it's —"

"*My* work, you mean," Lars interrupted. "This is all *my* work. *My* dream. I *slaved* over this for years, working to pull it together. I hired you to see it through; to do the mundane work I could not. Everything here is *mine.*"

Ben frowned, still standing next to Alina's bed. He gripped the rifle in his hands. As he'd said before, he didn't want to use it unless it was absolutely necessary — they might need all the ammunition to fight their way out of here.

Canavero smiled. "Of course. You do believe that."

Lars sniffed and then started toward Canavero. "It's the *truth*, Canavero. It would be wise for you to remember that —"

"Your leadership is a joke here, Tennyson," Canavero said. "Your *dream* is nothing but a pipe dream. A hopeless waste of precious resources."

Ben wasn't sure if Tennyson was about to cry or start trying to rip the doctor's head off. It was a twist in the discussion; a turn Ben hadn't seen coming.

But he knew the important thing was to get ready to leave. They needed to be out of here as soon as possible, and they needed to make sure this young woman was able to come with them.

He leaned down again and began slowly moving her leg, bending her knee. "I need to see if you can walk, eventually," he said. "Does this hurt?"

She shook her head. "No, actually it feels better. I believe I can move if you will give me a few minutes."

Ben nodded, then set her leg back down. She grimaced in pain, but she did try to wiggle her feet and legs as well.

He turned back to listen to the conversation between Tennyson and Canavero.

"You think this all for *you*, don't you?" Canavero said, his voice now rising. Tennyson had stopped about ten feet in front of the man. The doctor was still at the workstation, standing behind it as he faced the others in the room. "You believe this is all part of some plan you put in motion? That this is all *your work?*"

"I built this division from the ground up!" Tennyson yelled. "I *made* this happen. All of it. It was —"

"It was your *grandfather* who did it," Canavero said. "After the accident — after your sister, we needed a way to push this forward while still keeping you involved in the process. He hired me years ago to begin research; I was available at the company when you brought me here because *I was told to be*, Tennyson."

Tennyson stopped. The mere mention of his sister had seemed to spook him. "What... what are you saying?"

"Your... whatever he was... Dietrich? He was the real brains behind the operation, Tennyson. What, did you think, that you'd just *happened* to meet him at university all those years ago, and that you just *happened* to have the same interests? That he just *happened* to be of the personality that wanted you to dominate his entire life?"

Tennyson licked his lips, and Ben could see his nostrils flaring and his eyes firing. The man had been riled up, and he still couldn't tell if any of it was true. But something had clearly struck a nerve with Lars.

Canavero continued his barrage. "For *three years*, Lars, I have been putting *everything* into this project. The *real* project. The *actual reason* we are here—the *actual reason* Baden Tennyson built this place. Your idiotic pet project of saving your sister's life was a decent side job, something we would work on if time permitted.

"But that — all of that little dream of yours — is *nothing* compared to what we are *actually* doing here."

"And what is that?" Tennyson asked. He seemed to be in denial, crossing his arms over his chest and dropping his head back a bit. Testing his lead doctor.

"You don't *know*? You can't *see* it?" Canavero was legitimately worked up; now, he seemed as angry as Tennyson had been a moment earlier. "You simply are not capable of understanding. The research, the trials, the *successes* we have had here. Lars, you have *seen* the investment. The men and women who had offered their support of this place. Do you believe they are hoping for an altruistic end to all of this? That they wish to spend their fortunes and their futures on philanthropic endeavors?"

Lars looked perplexed. Ben glanced over at Eliza, who was watching on from her spot alongside the far wall, near the bedroom door of Lars' sister.

The temperature in the room had seemed to level off, and while Ben and Eliza both still wore their blankets, the other men were not wearing extra covering. They must both be cold, but neither seemed to show it. Besides, they hadn't been in the room for very long.

Ben shivered, wishing he hadn't reminded himself of the chill in the air.

"They are supporting this vision because it is also *their* vision, Lars," Canavero said. "They want what *we* want — what your grandfather and I want."

"Again, please," Lars said, "fill me in. You seem to be so much more in the know than I am."

Canavero actually laughed at this. "Are you actually this far removed, Tennyson? You have been working nights, early mornings, purposefully isolating yourself. You have not been around enough, apparently. Yet every signature on every paper is yours — surely you understand what this all about?"

Lars didn't speak.

"You think this is about *you*. Your *sister*. But it's not. It never has been. Dietrich knew it, and it was his main job to keep you working toward your goal, because for a long while *your* goal aligned with *our* goal."

"Dietrich was loyal to me."

"Dietrich was loyal to your *grandfather*, Lars. He may have expressed other feelings toward you, but his main concern was in getting to market with this technology. Getting into the hands of the people who want it most. The people who *paid* for it."

CHAPTER 63
BEN

BEN'S EARS perked up at this. He had been in situations before that involved wealthy, influential people exchanging money for things they believed they needed. But knowing a bit about what EKG was doing here, what they had been working toward, gave Ben an idea as to what Canavero was talking about.

"This place was created by the people, like your grandfather, who were *especially* interested in taking advantage of this technology."

"You mean my sister's life —"

"Your sister was to be the final phase of the transference test, Lars," Canavero answered. "She may have lived, but she was only ever to be an *experiment.* A *proof of concept,* if you will. But with the progress we have been making — progress *you* have been behind, I might add — her successful transference is unnecessary."

Transference. That word again. Ben walked a few steps toward Canavero's workstation. "You've said that to us before. 'Transference.' What does it really mean?"

Canavero seemed glad to have the question, impressed that Ben had asked it. "Have you not wondered why we are not calling these trials simply 'transplants,' my friend?"

Ben nodded. "Yeah, something like that."

"Well, that is what I was just explaining to Lars. The fact that he could not see it — the fact that he has been blinded to Dietrich's betrayal and the rest of his team's focus elsewhere — proves how lost in his sister's life he has become.

"But what our investors are interested in is far more than some organ farm. The research we have done here provides us with the ability to go beyond mere *transplants* — placing one organ inside a new body, a new host. It gives us the ability to *fully transfer* a human life. From one host into another."

Ben saw Eliza's hand go to her mouth, something she clearly did to register the shock she was feeling. Ben didn't have a similar tell, but he was feeling exactly the same way.

"You've got to be kidding me," he said.

"Must I?" Canavero asked. "And why is that? Is it beyond reason that there are people who wish to continue their lives long after their physical bodies have given up? Is it unreasonable to expect that medicine and science simply *halt* after exploring the possibilities of brain transplant and neural function reconditioning? Why? Because of human-created ethics?"

Ben didn't respond.

"The men and women who have built this place want *more*, my friends. They want *true freedom*, forever. To be able to jump from one host to another, at will, whenever their current biological vehicle gets too old? Can you *imagine* the possibilities?"

Ben could, and he didn't like it. Besides the terrifying experimentation that had led them down this path, he couldn't understand how anyone would ever be able to justify the killing of one human so another could take its shape and form.

Transference.

It was a crushing realization, but Canavero had made his point. There were people out there who wanted this, and those people would stop at nothing to make it happen.

"But... but I can't..." Tennyson seemed broken, an android

unable to perform his built-in programming. He stumbled to the side, the shock of it all, not allowing him to react properly. Finally, he placed a hand on the table, favoring his good leg, and looked up at Canavero. "You... *asshole*. This — this was *mine*. Everything here was going to save *her*... and — oh, my God."

He fell forward, almost completely losing his balance, but gripping a stool and hovering precariously for a moment. "You... you are going to *kill* her. You can't —"

He stopped, turned to Eliza and the door she was next to. He started toward her, limping along quickly, ignoring the pain.

Eliza's eyes widened, and she slid to the side. Lars didn't change course.

"Lars," Canavero's voice called out. "Why do you believe *we* are the twisted ones? Why do you think *we* are to blame? Are we not the ones working to advance the science of medicine?"

Lars didn't stop. He reached the doorway, completely ignoring Eliza, and pushed it open.

"What do you think I have been doing over here, my friend?" Canavero asked.

At this, Lars *did* stop. He held the handle of the door in his hand, halfway over the threshold.

He released the handle, turned around slowly, and stared at Canavero. There were tears in his eyes. He seemed completely beaten.

Ben kept the rifle ready, preparing to take out one or both of these men if they decided to hash out their differences physically and get Eliza or him involved.

"Lars, you were always bright, but naive. You believed in something impossible. But you *had* to know it was never going to work this early, right? And yet you kept her alive — or whatever you might call that — for *three years*.

"My friend, that alone seems like torture. What life is that? Lying empty on a bed while your thoughts and dreams and memories race through your mind, unable to wake up or go to sleep or do anything at all that resembles human life?"

Lars shook his head. "No... she... she is —"

"She is *dead*, Tennyson. Just like the day you brought her in here."

Canavero made a point to click a key on the computer's keyboard loudly, with deliberate precision.

"No — what have you —" Lars' voice faltered, and he fell to his knees in the doorway.

"She is dead, Lars."

An alarm sounded, a quiet yet noticeable beeping that emanated from the young woman's private room. Lars turned his head to look, then he stood and raced into the room.

"What did you do?" Ben asked. He began moving toward Canavero. "What the *hell* did you do?"

"Anaphylactic shock," Canavero said, raising his hands in the air as if trying to prove his innocence. "By altering the compound that is running into her body, it was an immediate reaction. Within two minutes, she'll be gone."

"Two minutes?"

"Or sooner," the doctor said. "She was frail, weakened from years of consuming nothing but liquids and existing in a less-than-human state."

Eliza walked over from the doorway. "That was not your call to make," she said. "Her life was not yours to take."

Canavero raised an eyebrow. "Oh? And your decision would have been different? You would have chosen to keep the poor girl alive, even if it meant *years* of living in a hospital bed?"

Ben didn't answer. He couldn't. He felt something tugging at his heart, pulling it side to side as his internal psyche fought with itself. It all seemed wrong, and yet he wasn't sure Canavero *was* wrong.

There was a scream — a deep, throaty yell — from the room, and Ben knew Lars was watching his sister die, completely unable to stop it. The man was broken, completely destroyed, and still this final piece of his life was being ripped away from him, brutally and slowly.

After a few seconds, Ben heard footsteps. Running.

Out of the room came Lars, barreling toward Canavero. Ben stepped to the side. He watched as the two men squared off near the airlock.

The distance closed, and Ben wondered how long he would allow them to fight before stepping in to end it.

And then, just before Lars reached Canavero, the chimpanzees made their move.

CHAPTER 64
ELIZA

THE CHIMP REACHED in and simply *flung* Canavero through the airlock. Lars stood, a look of awe and terror on his face, for precisely one second before he too was yanked by one of the chimps and tossed into the airlock.

Eliza watched it all happen while she was standing by the doorway at the side of the room.

"Eliza!" Ben called. "Help me!"

She ran over, trying to ignore what was happening in the airlock.

But she couldn't block out the sounds. The screams. The noise of ripping — clothing, body parts. It was gruesome.

She reached Ben and immediately started dismantling the IV line and other devices that were still connected to Alina's body. There weren't many, as she was stable on her own, unlike Lars' sister in the other room.

When they finished, they both gently helped Alina up and onto her feet.

"Can you walk?" Ben asked her.

She paused, testing it for a moment. "Yes," she finally said. "I can walk. But I may need your help."

Ben and Eliza kept their position on either side of her, steadying her as the young woman tested her legs.

The noise from near them was impossible to miss, and Eliza knew they would have to walk dangerously close to the chimpanzees to get by them. Even then, they would have to sneak by the remaining chimps in the larger lab outside.

If they *were* going to attack, it would be mere seconds from now. She could see that Lars' broken, bleeding body was now simply being tossed back and forth between the chimps inside the airlock.

She heard the sound of gunfire, the tiny rounds pockmarking the glass of the airlock. She wondered how long Canavero had before the chimps got to him.

"Let's go," she said. "Now, while they're occupied with Lars."

Ben nodded, and together they half-pulled Alina around the three chimps standing nearby. None of them looked up from Lars' body.

Canavero was inside, shaking, cowering in the back corner of the tiny airlock. He was alone, obviously terrified. "Shut the door! Quickly!" he yelled. "They will get in."

The doors slid shut on their own, and Eliza watched the doctor for a moment, hoping he wouldn't try to shoot at them. If the man fully intended to take out the chimps, he'd need as much ammunition as possible. Eliza hated the thought of it, but she knew they were probably safer from his gunfire because of it.

They made it to the inner airlock doors before any of the chimps seemed to pay them any attention. But when Eliza looked out, she noticed two larger males that seemed to be guarding their escape. They were blocking the outer airlock doors, and Eliza caught the eyes of the one on the left from the other side of the glass.

She slowed her breathing, forced herself to relax. She hoped her nonverbal communication was visible through the pane of glass, but even more she hoped the chimps understood the dynamic of what was happening. *We are on your side, friend*, she thought. She wished there was a way to get the message into the small mammal's brain, but she knew their life was most likely going to come down to the animals' desires.

She was torn between two horrible alternatives: stay with the mad doctor and wait until they ran out of air or someone found them, or open the outer doors and hope for the best.

Thankfully she didn't have to make the call.

"Canavero," Ben said, turning to the doctor. "Stay here."

"What?" The doctor responded. "Are you insane? They will *kill* me. They will shred me like paper. You saw what they did to Lars — to the guards! I am not going to participate in your idiotic plan to sneak around them."

Ben sniffed, then handed the young woman to Eliza, who leaned against the airlock's wall for additional support. Ben walked over to Canavero; his weapon pointed directly down at the man.

"Wh — what are you doing?" Canavero asked. He slid sideways in a pitiful attempt to get away from Ben.

Ben sidled up next to the man, then crouched down so his face was directly in front of the doctor's. Eliza watched on with curious intensity.

"You're a man of science. A doctor. The kind of guy who's supposed to understand things like life and death."

Canavero sneered at him but finally nodded. "What is your point?"

"I'm the kind of guy who tries my best to stay out of that sort of thing. It ain't my call who lives or dies. I've always left that up to someone else; someone bigger than me. But the thing is, I also believe that someone gives us all opportunities. Opportunities to prove whether or not we're *worth* that life.

"You — folks like you, anyway — you're the kind of people that make me pause. You make me wonder if it's worth taking the high road. People like you seem to forget that there are *two* sides to every equation. You think you're all about *life* because you understand it, what makes it tick, how to give it to other people by *cutting their brains out and plopping them into someone else's head*. But you know what?"

Canavero didn't respond.

"I think you've totally forgotten to study the *other* side of that life-death equation. You forgot what it feels like *to die.* I know what that feels like, *my friend*, because I've been there a few times. Came out of it okay, but it's no fun to experience. I think you're the kind of person who's never experienced that, and *that's* why you can do the kind of shit you've been doing here. Because you haven't really studied the *other* side of the equation."

"Ben," Eliza said. "We have to go. Now." There were more chimps gathering outside the airlock, watching in on the humans as they conferred.

Ben nodded but kept his gaze on Canavero. "You've made this really difficult for me, Canavero. I'm usually the kind of guy who wants to save as many lives as possible, but lately I've been changing that perspective to saving the *right* lives. Doesn't matter how many it is, as long as it's the right ones.

"And people like you, who ignore the equation and try to forget that this strange, twisted form of 'life' you think you're creating comes at a cost, you forfeit that right. So, no, you're not at all part of my 'idiotic plan to sneak around them.' In fact, that's not my plan at all."

Ben leaned back, then swung the butt of his rifle up and over his head, bringing it down violently onto the doctor's left leg, right at the kneecap. Eliza heard the sound of bone crushing all the way from the other side of the room.

Canavero wailed in agony, dropping the submachine gun and squeezing his hands over his leg. "You — you basta —"

"We're done here, Doc," Ben said, standing up. He returned to the side of the room where Eliza and Alina were waiting, then looked at each of them.

Finally, with his free hand, Ben smashed the red button near the outer airlock door. It slid open slowly.

And twenty chimpanzees glared back at them, no longer separated from them by thick glass.

CHAPTER 65
BEN

BEN CALMED HIMSELF DOWN. The adrenaline was coursing through his veins, the chemicals in his brain secreting and producing all sorts of exotic compounds it thought he might be needing right now.

In truth, he wasn't sure *what* he needed. Everything was confusing; everything was strange. He was standing face-to-face with scores of apes, all watching him, all interested in what he was about to do.

He wasn't sure how he felt about what he'd done to Canavero. He had never signed up for this sort of thing, never intended for his life to take a turn like this. And yet he couldn't argue with his decision. He wanted Canavero dead, for what he'd done to these animals, for what he'd done to *humans* under his control.

But it didn't mean *Ben* was the person responsible for taking the man's life. He'd wanted just to put a bullet through his head, to end it quickly, fairly even. Yet if Canavero deserved *fair*, he deserved a fate far worse than death. He deserved to be judged not by a jury or a panel or by Ben or Eliza.

The man deserved to be judged by his subjects. They all did.

So Ben had opened the airlock door, watching as the twenty-odd animals looked on at the three of them. He didn't understand the expressions on their faces, but he had a feeling he didn't need to be an animal behavioral expert to know the message they were trying to convey.

This ends now.

Ben looked at Eliza once more, to make sure she was ready, and he slid his arm underneath Alina's to help support her once again.

Here goes nothing.

He swung his left leg forward and pressed it into the floor, directly over the sliding door's threshold. Immediately the chimpanzee to his left, closest to him, bared its teeth and frowned.

Ben stopped. He waited, but the chimp didn't change its expression.

Finally, Ben leaned to his side slowly, placing the assault rifle on the floor, just inside the airlock. He released it gingerly and stood up again, feeling the stress of knowing his best chance of defending himself and the others with him was now lying on the floor, out of reach.

The chimp's face relaxed, and it hopped sideways, out of the way.

Ben waited for another second, but the chimp seemed satisfied, so Ben took a step into the larger room. Eliza and Alina were right there with him, but he still tensed his upper body, holding his breath.

All throughout the room, the chimpanzees seemed to follow the cues of the first one, and they stepped or slid out of the way, clearing a path in the center of the room.

Ben sighed a breath of relief, feeling the wave of terror subside. He walked slowly, purposefully, keeping his head up and focused on the doorway at the far end of the room.

The first chimp watched him pass; then, just as Ben stepped forward again, it scampered toward the airlock door.

Ben's rifle was still sitting on the floor halfway between the lab and the airlock, and the chimp pushed at it with his foot. It slid to the edge of the airlock door just as it began to close. As it did, the door caught between the magazine and stock and pressed it tightly up against the doorframe, the rifle keeping the door open about a foot.

Ben was about halfway through the room when he turned to look back. Three chimps were working on the door, using their strength to try to force it open. It slid a few inches, and four more chimps slipped inside the airlock.

Where Canavero waited.

They reached the opposite end of the room safely, and Ben helped Eliza get Alina shifted around to prepare for the descent down the stairs. She was fully lucid and even starting to put weight on her legs.

Ben took a final glance at the doorway across the large laboratory, noticed more and more chimpanzees spilling through the crack, and saw the dark shadows of moving shapes just beyond. He didn't hear anything — no screams, no gunshots, no hollering from the animals inside with the doctor.

He decided not to imagine what might be happening to Lars' renowned doctor and instead focused on the stairs.

As they climbed down over the pieces of the bodies of the guards that had tried to run, he sighed once more, feeling the weight of what they'd just been through beginning to take its toll. He needed to get to Grindelwald, to get Alina back to her father.

And, more than anything, he needed a beer.

The *Downtown Bar* still had his tab open, if he recalled.

CHAPTER 66
BEN

THREE DAYS **Later**

Anchorage, Alaska

Ben rolled over onto the edge of the bed, precariously perched above the floor, trying to slide away without waking Julie. He'd arrived in the middle of the night last night and had been greeted by a zombie-like "*mmmwwwrrrr*" from his wife, so he'd opted for the stealthy approach of sneaking under the sheets.

As he put his feet on the floor and pressed upward to stand, the entire cabin seemed to groan in despair. The wooden floorboards of the old place spoke to the walls, which yelled for the ceilings, and before long, the entire house seemed to be screaming in agony with a high-pitched whine.

Ben sighed. *If that doesn't wake her up, I don't know what will.*

He'd seen the empty bottle of wine Julie had finished off last night as he'd come in, and he knew she'd been excited to see him. But it seemed the wine had worked faster than Ben's drive home, and his wife was now going to be sleeping off a bit of a hangover.

He chuckled as she snored loudly, watching as she yawned and then rolled back over as if the loud deterioration of their home falling down around her was the least of her worries.

She was cute in bed, wearing an old ratty t-shirt, a collar that was so worn the head hole slipped down and revealed almost both of her shoulders. He considered sneaking back into bed to see if she was more awake than she had been letting on.

Instead, he put on his slippers and bathrobe and strode through the door to the living room, and then into the kitchen. It was barely 7 am, and he'd been flying for the better part of two days, but he was home, and his body seemed to know it. It wanted to return to its regularly scheduled programming, including waking up with the sunrise.

He yawned, stretched, and ran a hand through his hair. The past week had been insane — first discovering what EKG *could* be up to, and then finding out that the truth was far worse. Add to that the fact that Ben had had to crawl back to Olaf's outfitter shop and home and explain to the man what had happened to his son Clive.

A search party had retrieved the young man's body and returned it to his father, who was planning a proper funeral and burial.

The chimps had stayed inside the laboratory and building since there was no way for them to unlock the exterior doors. A local nature reserve sent in truckloads of specialists and equipment, including tranquilizers, to rehabilitate and re-home the animals in sanctuaries and zoos across Europe. The chimpanzees were unfortunately unable to be re-released back into their wild habitat, as all of them had grown up in the lab.

Roger Dietrich and Lars Tennyson were — supposedly — going to be under investigation posthumously for a long list of crimes that Ben didn't even begin to understand, and Eliza Earnhardt was already being prepped by animal rights activists and the lawyers of humanitarian organizations as a prime candidate for questioning.

She was excited about the opportunity and had emailed Ben a list of questions she wanted his input on.

He started the coffee pot, opting for the production level of the larger carafe instead of the single-cup pod machine Julie had bought on sale last year that was sitting next to it. It was going to be a three-cup day, for sure.

He rubbed his eyes, wondering if he'd be getting through today without a nap or if he'd need to sneak away sometime after the CSO scheduled debriefing that was supposed to take place. Julie had arranged the time with Mrs. E, and the entire team was planning to videoconference in from wherever in the world they were, excited to hear the details of Ben's story.

As he waited for the pot to heat the water and prepare the elixir he needed most right now, Ben paced over toward the small kitchen table where he and Julie shared most of their meals. Her computer was lying on top of a stack of papers, and Ben opened the laptop.

He wanted to check his email, and so after the screen turned on and the WIFI icon signaled that the machine was connected, he clicked on the icon for Julie's web browser.

The window that opened wasn't a new window, but one that had been minimized.

It filled the laptop's screen and began to load — a news website.

Ben frowned. Julie had been reading up on EKG and related businesses, apparently.

But when the article finally loaded — translated automatically into English by some fancy algorithm — Ben read the headline and swallowed.

It wasn't about EKG, per se — it was about its founder and leader, Baden Tennyson.

And it wasn't *research* Julie had been doing. The article had been published about twelve hours ago, on a regional economic website's blog. It was current news.

The title was in large print and hard to miss, and it gave Ben a sinking feeling in his stomach as he read it.

EKG Owner Outraged at Betrayal; Seeks Recompense

The article detailed some of the legal battle Baden Tennyson was facing for negligence, though the author of the piece suggested that his attorneys and shareholders would simply buy their way out of any serious trouble. The man was incredibly wealthy even outside of his company, and he — like his grandson — was used to throwing whatever resources necessary at his problems to make them go away.

Ben read on, and one particular line made him grip the table tightly as the coffee machine sputtered to life. It was a direct quote from Lars' grandfather.

"This division was extremely important to the future operations at EKG. I am disappointed in my grandson's failure to maintain order there, but I am more concerned with the fact that there are unknown parties seeking to upset and sabotage our existence.

"I plan to make it my personal mission to find, root out, and bring to justice these individuals, using every means necessary."

Ben looked up at the ceiling, not wanting to believe what the article was claiming, but knowing it was the truth.

So it continues.

###

AFTERWORD

If you liked this book (or even if you hated it...) write a review or rate it. You might not think it makes a difference, but it does.

Besides *actual* currency (money), the currency of today's writing world is *reviews*. Reviews, good or bad, tell other people that an author is worth reading.

As an "indie" author, I need all the help I can get. I'm hoping that since you made it this far into my book, you have some sort of opinion on it.

Would you mind sharing that opinion? It only takes a second.

Nick Thacker

BOOKS BY NICK THACKER

Mason Dixon Thrillers

Mark for Blood (Book 1)

Death Mark (Book 2)

Mark My Words (Book 3)

Harvey Bennett Mysteries

The Enigma Strain (Book 1)

The Amazon Code (Book 2)

The Ice Chasm (Book 3)

The Jefferson Legacy (Book 4)

The Paradise Key (Book 5)

The Aryan Agenda (Book 6)

The Book of Bones (Book 7)

The Cain Conspiracy (Book 8)

The Mendel Paradox (Book 9)

The Minoan Manifest (Book 10)

Harvey Bennett Mysteries - Books 1-3

Harvey Bennett Mysteries - Books 4-6

Jo Bennett Mysteries

Temple of the Snake (written with David Berens)

Tomb of the Queen (written with Kristi Belcamino)

Harvey Bennett Prequels

The Icarus Effect (written with MP MacDougall)

The Severed Pines (written with Jim Heskett)

The Lethal Bones (written with Jim Heskett)

Gareth Red Thrillers

Seeing Red

Chasing Red (written with Kevin Ikenberry)

The Lucid

The Lucid: Episode One (written with Kevin Tumlinson)

The Lucid: Episode Two (written with Kevin Tumlinson)

The Lucid: Episode Three (written with Kevin Tumlinson

Standalone Thrillers

The Atlantis Stone

The Depths

Relics: A Post-Apocalyptic Technothriller

Killer Thrillers (3-Book Box Set)

Short Stories

I, Sergeant

Instinct

The Gray Picture of Dorian

Uncanny Divide (written with Kevin Tumlinson and Will Flora)

ABOUT THE AUTHOR

Nick Thacker is a thriller author from Texas who lives in Colorado and Hawaii, because Colorado has mountains, microbreweries, and fantastic weather, and Hawaii also has mountains, microbreweries, and fantastic weather. In his free time, he enjoys reading in a hammock on the beach, skiing, drinking whiskey, and hanging out with his beautiful wife, tortoise, two dogs, and two daughters.

In addition to his fiction work, Nick is the founder and lead of Sonata & Scribe, the only music studio focused on producing "soundtracks" for books and series. Find out more at SonataAndScribe.com.

For more information and a list of Nick's other work, visit Nick online:
www.nickthacker.com